Bantam Books by Lillian O'Donnell
THE BABY MERCHANTS
DIAL 577 R-A-P-E

THE
BABY
MERCHANTS

by
Lillian O'Donnell

*This low-priced Bantam Book
has been completely reset in a type face
designed for easy reading, and was printed
from new plates. It contains the complete
text of the original hard-cover edition.*
NOT ONE WORD HAS BEEN OMITTED.

THE BABY MERCHANTS
*A Bantam Book | published by arrangement with
G. P. Putnam's Sons*

PRINTING HISTORY
Putnam's edition published June 1975
Bantam edition | November 1976

ISBN 0-553-02511-2

Published simultaneously in the United States and Canada

*Bantam Books are published by Bantam Books, Inc. Its trade-
mark, consisting of the words "Bantam Books" and the por-
trayal of a bantam, is registered in the United States Patent
Office and in other countries. Marca Registrada, Bantam
Books, Inc., 666 Fifth Avenue, New York, New York 10019.*

PRINTED IN THE UNITED STATES OF AMERICA

THE
BABY
MERCHANTS

1

A MEAN wind, wet and salty from the Jamaica marshes, swept across the runway. Shivering, Lieutenant Joe Capretto turned his back to it—it had to be at least ten degrees colder out here than in the city! He wished he'd listened to Norah and zipped the pile lining into his raincoat, but he'd hardly expected to be standing around like this. He could have stayed inside in the Port Authority police office, but after an hour and a half of waiting he'd just had to get out, move around, breathe. He sucked in a lungful of the sharp, briny air, held it, then slowly expelled it. As usual, that exercise calmed him. He looked up beyond the ground glare into the black November sky and watched the myriad red and green wing-tip lights as they moved confidently among the frosty stars. The sense of awe was dispelled by another chilling gust of wind.

Where the hell was that plane?

Waiting was part of the game, and Lieutenant Joseph Antony Capretto, presently working out of Narco, Manhattan South Division, was certainly used to it by now. But why tonight of all nights did the damn plane have to be late? He looked at his watch—five after seven. No matter how smoothly everything went once the plane landed, he just was not going to make it in time. Hell! As soon as he'd been informed of the delay, he'd called home and warned Norah that she'd have to go on alone. Policemen's wives, like doctors' wives, had to get used to last-minute disruption of social plans. A police officer herself, detective second grade attached to the Fifth Homicide and Assault Squad (Joe's squad before he was transferred), Norah

1

certainly took it in stride. Just the same, she'd be disappointed. The party tonight wasn't one she was particularly looking forward to anyway, and now to have to go alone. . . .

Joe's dark, strong face with its high brow and long, straight, classically Roman nose softened as he thought of his wife. He didn't realize that he was smiling in the darkness; he always smiled when he thought of Norah, but he wasn't aware of that either. Joe Capretto had married late—at age forty-one; that was two years ago. A man married for two reasons: sex and comfort. As a bachelor living at home with his mother he had certainly been comfortable, cosseted, and indulged. As to sex, Joe, then a sergeant, had had a long list of obliging girlfriends. Why change? For one thing, his mother, torn between the desire to keep her only son out of eight children to herself and the longing for a male grandson (so far the girls had produced only more girls), began to drop hints that he should find himself a nice, compliant wife. But Joe began to hear what she was saying only when he met Norah.

Not that Detective Norah Mulcahaney was what Signora Capretto had had in mind. Nor Joe either, for that matter. Joe liked them flashy and available. Norah had been neither. She didn't flaunt her wares; you had to look twice to appreciate her. And Joe had known right from the start that with Norah it couldn't be another passing affair, none of this "what we do is our own business" and "love is the only valid bond" jazz. With Norah it had to be all or nothing, not because of her strict upbringing—after all, plenty of good Irish Catholic girls managed to overcome their scruples—but because of her fierce sense of dedication. Committed as she was to her job, she would certainly be the same toward her man. To his own surprise, Joe found that instead of being put off, he was attracted.

There had been no premarital sex. Once he decided to marry the girl, Joe became morally old-fashioned. He never regretted it.

Norah was sensitive to his needs, her responses as varied as the mood and yet unchanging. She gave herself joyously and completely, not merely to the act of love but to him as an individual and her husband. And there were dividends, Joe thought, still smiling, the cold forgotten, dividends he hadn't expected from his strong-willed, efficient, impulsive, and often stubborn detective wife. She could cook; she was a good housekeeper; and she was very, very patient with his mother.

"Lieutenant!" A voice called out of the darkness beyond the runway lights.

Startled out of his reverie, Joe turned. The shrill jet whine drowned out whatever the Port Authority man was shouting. Shielding his eyes against the glare, Joe could just make out that he was pointing and looked to see at what. Suddenly, like a ravening mechanical monster, the airplane materialized out of the star-sprinkled sky, seemingly headed straight at him. Instinctively he dived to the side. The rush of air nearly knocked him over. Alitalia flight 426 from Rome was finally down.

Again Lieutenant Joseph Antony Capretto looked at his watch: seven sixteen. Okay. They'd be taking Abruzzi off first thing. He'd be searched; that shouldn't take too long. By now traffic should be relatively light. He ought to be back downtown in, say, another couple of hours at most. If he left the booking and the paperwork to Ryder, he could still make the party. It was, after all, his second wedding anniversary.

The last Norah heard from Joe was that the plane was expected to land at seven. They were due at his mother's at eight, so he couldn't possibly get home to pick her up. Yet she waited till the last possible moment before leaving. She had planned exactly what to wear, but somehow it didn't look right. Norah was tall, five-eight, which was okay, but she was also large-boned, so she had to watch her weight. Her hair was thick, a brown so dark it might be called black, but not being really black, it contrasted less harshly with her pale skin. Her eyes were her best feature, large, gray-blue, as her mother's had been. Tonight, when she wanted to look her best, her skin seemed sallow and her eyes dull. The blue jersey gown that was Joe's particular favorite didn't cling as it should—either a bad cleaning job or she'd lost more weight than she'd realized. Even the new hair style, recently cut to shoulder length and worn loose, couldn't soften the defensive thrust of her square, prominent jaw.

Norah hadn't been happy about the offer by Joe's mother to "make the party" for their second wedding anniversary. Signora Capretto had taken it for granted that her daughter-in-law would be delighted, but Norah didn't see it as a family occasion. Christmas, Thanksgiving, birthdays even, yes, but an anniversary should be private for just the two of them. She hadn't wanted a party at all, no matter who gave it.

"I'm sure your mother will understand," Norah had said to Joe, but they both knew Signora Emilia would not. Though Norah addressed her as Mamma, she always thought of her mother-in-law formally. She knew that Signora Emilia would be hurt, disappointed. If Norah said they didn't want the party, it would bolster the signora's opinion that as a career woman she was not sufficiently family-minded. The signora would not see it as a joint decision but would hold Norah wholly responsible.

In the end they compromised—the party first, their very own, private celebration the night after. Norah wished everything could be so easily resolved.

She gave up fussing about her appearance and spent the last few minutes before she'd have to leave in wandering around, adjusting the angle of a chair, rearranging ornaments—an occupation that gave her great satisfaction. Norah was proud of their home. She and Joe were not cramped for space, as most couples are in their first apartment. They had found a place on East Sixty-eighth Street in a remodeled town house, so that the rooms were large, high-ceilinged, airy.

There was even a window in the kitchen and an extra room that they were temporarily using as a dining room. The unsolicited donations of furniture from both her father and Joe's mother, which they had not had the heart to refuse, turned out to be surprisingly compatible with the modern things they bought. Norah was glad now that they had accepted them, for they were a link to the past, a past from which neither she nor Joe wanted to be dissociated.

At seven thirty Norah accepted that Joe was not going to miraculously appear and, as he had the family car, took the subway to Brooklyn.

Signora Capretto lived on a quiet street in an old building tenanted by quiet old people whose children had long since grown and moved out. Before she even got out of the elevator, Norah could hear the party sounds stirring the silence like memories. It wasn't fair to spoil everybody's pleasure by moping, she told herself, and straightened, lifted her chin, and got ready to smile.

Joe's mother and Norah's father came to the door together—it touched Norah. She kissed Signora Emilia's cheek and embraced her father. As she walked into the old-fashioned parlor, everyone turned toward her expectantly: Obviously they had been told to come early to give her and Joe a tumultuous welcome. With Joe absent, it fell a little flat. It was up to her to pick the party up again.

"Joe's been detained," Norah announced lightly. "He apologizes. He'll get here as soon as he can."

Signora Emilia's eyes flickered for just a moment, but she made no comment. Patrick Mulcahaney reached for his daughter's hand unobtrusively and squeezed it. The awkward moment passed. Everyone converged on Norah. She was kissed, hugged, congratulated, and made much of. The wine was poured; the party moved into high gear.

She had not expected anything so elaborate. It seemed as though everyone who had been at the wedding was present—not outsiders, just family; but Joe's relations—his seven sisters with their respective husbands, uncles, aunts, and cousins—made quite a crowd. On Norah's side there was only her father. Her two brothers, Michael and Pat Junior, lived out West, and it was hardly feasible that they would make the long and expensive trip, but she was sure they had been invited.

Through the open arch she could see the dining table laden with covered dishes—Signora Emilia must have been cooking for a week! Probably the girls had brought platters of their specialties as well. Everyone had certainly brought gifts—there was an impressive stack of packages on the credenza. By unspoken consent, these were left unopened to await Joe's arrival.

But where was he?

After a while not only Norah but the others began to cast surreptitious glances at the small ormolu clock on the mantel, then at the table. What was keeping him?

At nine thirty Signora Emilia decreed they should eat.

At eleven thirty the girls cleared; the men sat down over cigars and, in honor of the occasion, cognac. Norah was ordered out of the kitchen—this was her night, she was told; she should go in with the "boys" and enjoy herself. The phone in the bedroom rang. Signora Capretto went in to answer it. When she came out moments later, her face, smooth for a woman of her age, was creased with disapproval.

"He wants to talk to you," she told Norah.

Norah went in, sat on the bed, and picked up the receiver. "Joe?"

"Honey, I'm sorry."

"That's okay, I understand. Where are you?"

"At Kennedy."

"Still?" She was dismayed. She had expected him to say he was just leaving the precinct and would be with them in at most another half hour. "Kennedy!"

she repeated. That meant he wasn't going to make it after all.

"I'm really sorry, *cara*."

He sounded both disappointed and depressed. Ordinarily Norah would have tried to cheer him, but she was too let down herself. "What happened? I thought you said the plane was due at seven."

"It came in just a few minutes after. The trouble was we didn't find the junk. He didn't have it on him. Abruzzi was clean."

"Oh, Joe. . . ." Now Norah forgot her own pique, and her sympathy was all for him.

He sighed. "Could be he was expecting a welcoming committee. Customs is going through every damn piece of luggage."

"It wouldn't be in the luggage. How could he expect to get it through in anybody's luggage?" Instantly Norah was tackling the problem.

"I know, but we have to look. Unless Koslav gave me a bum steer."

"Why should he?"

"Who knows? The point is, I couldn't dump it into Sid Ryder's lap and just walk away."

"Of course not."

"So . . . apologize again to everybody for me, will you? And . . . *cara*, I love you. I'll make it up to you tomorrow as planned."

"Sooner than that."

Joe's voice lifted. "That's a date."

"If I'm asleep when you get home, wake me," she said, though neither of them ever fell asleep till the other got in.

"You bet."

"Promise?"

"You can count on it."

Norah hung up. She was still smiling when she came out of the bedroom, then Signora Capretto caught her eye and waved to her to come over. Joe's mother was in full festive regalia, dressed in the same beige silk she'd worn as mother of the groom and wearing the pair of tiny but perfect diamond earrings that Norah now knew were the traditional Italian baptismal gift to a baby girl and later formed part of the young woman's dowry, but her manner was grave. Norah suppressed a sigh—she knew she was in for another session of good advice.

"Yes, Mamma?"

"I apologize for my son, Norah."

Norah's eyes opened wide. "Mamma, it isn't necessary. It's not his fault. Joe couldn't help—"

The signora raised her hand. "He could if he wished. He would if he thought it was important to *you*. What a man does or does not consider important is up to his wife."

So it was her fault. . . . Norah stifled a sigh.

"You are too easy with Joe."

That was the last thing Norah had expected to hear.

"Joe must be made to realize that he cannot stay out till all hours as he did when he was a bachelor."

"He's not out with the boys, Mamma; he's working."

Signora Capretto ignored that. "It will do no good for me to speak to him. You are the wife. It is your responsibility. You must demand that he come home when he is supposed to. In the house you are the boss."

"We don't see it like that, Mamma. We see it as a partnership."

"You are wrong. If you ever expect to have children. . . ."

"We do expect to have children."

"I hope so." The old, sharp eyes searched Norah's face. "Meanwhile you must establish your authority. Don't shake your head, child. You listen to me. I have raised eight and I know what I am talking about. Joe's time is not his own anymore. It belongs to you."

"And to the police department. If I had been on duty tonight, I would have stayed till the job was finished."

"Ah . . ." Joe's mother sighed. "And when the babies come?"

"Then it'll be different."

Signora Capretto's stern face softened. She took Norah's hand and patted it. "Don't wait too long, eh? For your own sake, child, don't wait too long." Then she let her go.

Flushing, Norah escaped, but not for long. Her father cornered her next.

"I take it Joe's not going to show after all."

"Don't you start on me, Dad." She was so touchy these days. "I'm sorry, Dad, I'm just a little upset."

"Sweetheart, I know Joe wouldn't willingly miss this party." Then, because Norah was still frowning, Patrick Mulcahaney added, "The old lady means well."

At that Norah had to smile. Her father was exactly the same age as Signora Emilia, but he would have been indignant if anyone had referred to him as "the old man." "Sure, Dad, I know. It's been kind of tough, though, and I don't feel like any more lectures. Okay?"

Mulcahaney hesitated. He was a strong man. His beloved wife, Jenny, died of cancer when Norah was just thirteen. Shortly after that his left leg was mangled in an industrial accident. The doctors had been pessimistic: He might be crippled for life. But Patrick Mulcahaney had not indulged in self-pity. Goaded by responsibility for his motherless girl and the two boys, he had by sheer willpower overcome the threatened disability. He had made himself walk. Now the drag of the left leg was barely noticeable. In spite of forced retirement, he'd kept busy with a regimen of long walks and workouts in O'Flaherty's Gym for his health and afternoon sessions at Houlihan's Bar for sociability. But the will could flog the body for only so long. As the years passed, Patrick Mulcahaney had worried more and more about his daughter. The boys were all right—married and settled out West with families of their own. He had longed to see Norah settled too—and out of police work, work he had never approved, considering it too tough and unwomanly. When she finally decided to marry, he had been overjoyed, though he'd wished she'd chosen anyone but Capretto.

He had to admit that Joe was a good man, very fami-ly-oriented, in this day and age a big consideration. At the same time, Mulcahaney was convinced that if Norah had married anybody but a policeman, she would by now have quit her job and he would be dandling his first grandson on his knee. Still, if he could be sure that she was really happy. . . .

He just couldn't hold back. "Sweetheart, I'm worried about you. You're not yourself. You haven't been for weeks. Your color's bad. You're too thin."

"I'm fine."

Her father shook his head, and almost involuntarily Norah looked into the big mirror over the mantel.

The first thing she saw was that she was frowning. She made a conscious effort to smooth her brow, but the ugly lines remained. Signora Emilia hadn't said it—she hadn't needed to—Norah was thirty-two, and the years were slipping away. Her father was right— she did look gaunt.

"What's the matter, sweetheart?" Mulcahaney asked gently. "Is there something wrong between you and Joe?"

Startled, Norah turned from the mirror. "Oh, no, of course not."

"Then what? Something's eating you, darlin'. Can't you tell me?"

"There isn't anything to tell, Honestly."

"Are you sick?"

"No. No, Dad, I'm fine. I went to the doctor. I'm one hundred percent."

He picked that up instantly. "Why did you have to go to the doctor?"

"Not for the reason you think. I wish it had been."

Now he had it; now he understood. It wasn't the time or the place, but having been given the opening. Patrick Mulcahaney just couldn't let it go. Neverthe-less, he knew his girl, knew she was sensitive on this subject above all others and that he must proceed cautiously. He framed a couple of approaches, dis-

carded them, and as usual ended up just blurting it
out. "Are you sure you want a baby?"

"Dad!"

So he'd said it. All right, if they couldn't be honest
with each other. . . . "I think subconsciously you don't.
You examine your conscience, darlin'; you look into
your own heart."

Norah's blue eyes filled. "I have," she answered. At
that moment she was ready to tell him everything.
She needed to unburden herself, to get his opinion
and advice, but Joe's sister Lena and her husband,
Jake, came up. They had their coats on.

"We're going. Can we give you a lift?"

The party was breaking up.

Norah sat up in bed, the light on, a book on her lap,
but she could no more read than she could sleep.
Lucky that Lena and Jake interrupted when they
did. If she were going to confide in anyone, that person had to be Joe. From the time Norah had met Joe,
long before they were married, she had never held
anything back from him—not anything important.
Why was she holding back now? She closed the book,
set it aside, and slid down on the pillow. Body relaxed, soothed by the late-night street sounds, Norah
at last acknowledged the reason—to talk about it
would be to admit that the problem existed. But it did
exist; it had to be faced—and shared. Closing her
eyes, Norah tried to think of what she would say.

But at a little after two A.M., when she heard his
key in the lock, Norah forgot everything but how glad
she was that Joe was home. Jumping out of bed, she
ran and threw herself into his arms.

"Hey, hey! For this kind of greeting I promise to
miss every party we're ever invited to." He held her
close. "You're shivering, love. Come on, back to bed."

"How'd it go?" she asked as he sat on the edge of
the bed beside her.

"It wasn't a total loss. We found the junk. Looks like

prime stuff; maybe a couple of million in street value."

"That much? You'll get your picture in the paper," she teased.

"I hope not."

"Supersleuth strikes again!"

"It's not funny. All this publicity isn't doing me any good. The brass is cool on folk heroes in the department."

"But you've made some fantastic busts this year. You've had two commendations."

"There'll be no commendation on this one, I can tell you. In fact, I don't think Dietrich is going to be too happy with me." He didn't seem really worried.

But Norah was. "Why?"

"For one thing, we had to let Abruzzi go. We had no choice; as I told you, he was clean. So then we had to go through the whole plane inch by inch, and we had to hold the passengers while we did it. You should have heard them. Not that I blamed them. First the flight was delayed at takeoff, then after finally arriving to be delayed again and searched. . . . They were tired and irritable and they squawked plenty. On top of that, a quarter of the seats were taken up by a group of Italian businessmen and their families on a package tour. You can't believe what it was like—seventy-seven Italians yelling at the same time."

Norah started to laugh.

"The only one who could speak English was the tour director."

"But you speak Italian."

"My family's from the north. Most of those people come from around Rome and Naples. As far as I'm concerned, Neapolitan is a foreign language. Anyhow, the tour director was no help; he got right on the phone to the consulate."

"Oh, boy."

"No, it was for the best. I was just as glad to have the consular representative present to see that we offered no discourtesy in our search."

"You searched the passengers? How could anyone hide that much stuff on his person?"

"Not the stuff, the claim check for it."

"But you'd already gone through the luggage." Norah frowned. "It came in as freight!"

"Right. We'd given Abruzzi a thorough going-over and the claim check wasn't on him, so he had to have planted it."

"On an accomplice."

"Not necessarily."

"It had to be someone traveling with the group so that he could get it back later."

"You want me to tell it?"

"Sorry."

Joe grinned. "Yes, one of the group; they'd all be staying at the same hotel, so it wouldn't be any trouble for Abruzzi to get the claim check back. I didn't like the idea of subjecting all those people to a personal search, so with Donato's help—that's the consular official—we interviewed them instead. We explained the situation and asked each one individually to go through his own pockets. We found it."

"Terrific!"

"Common sense." Joe shrugged, but he was gratified. "Once we had the freight receipt, we rushed over to the cargo depot and had them locate the crate. The bill of lading listed the sender as Confetti Speciali, a candy company in Naples, contents listed as *campioni*, samples, and marked *hold for pickup*. You've never seen so many kinds of goodies in so many fancy wrappings in your life; all cellophane-sealed, naturally. Under ordinary circumstances customs wouldn't have opened the individual vases, jars, tins, baskets, and so on. We did, every one. We cut into chocolates, marzipan, caramels. . . ."

"Don't tell me the stuff was in the individual pieces?" Norah exclaimed.

"At the bottom of the crate there were half a dozen *panettoni*—you know, those fancy round loaves of bread with the fruit? Mamma bakes them for Easter."

"Sure."

"The centers had been hollowed out and the packets of heroin were inside."

"Somebody went to a lot of trouble."

"Right—somebody. We couldn't prove anything against Abruzzi, and as for the poor guy who had the claim check . . . Donato vouched for him. Anyhow, we know where they all are and we can get hold of any one of them if necessary." He shrugged. "So. Enough of that. How about you? How was the party?"

"We missed you."

"Did *you* have a good time? At all?"

"Sure. You know I love your family, and they were all there, everyone. Your mother really went to a lot of trouble." She pointed to the dresser. "Look at the loot."

"Mamma was pretty upset with me, huh?"

"You know your mother. She suggested . . . she *told* me it was my fault. She said I should lay down the law to you."

"Mamma means well."

He sounded so much like her father then that Norah laughed. "I just wish that when we go over there she wouldn't stare at my stomach before saying hello."

They both laughed, a little uncertainly.

Norah licked her lips. "Sweetheart, I was thinking . . . it's a year since I went off the pill."

"So?"

"Well, I thought that by now . . . I expected. . . ."

"Instant pregnancy? *Cara,* you can't schedule a baby like . . . like programming a computer. You have to give nature a little option."

There was an awkward silence.

"Do you think I'm being punished?" Norah asked at last.

"*Cara* . . . come on. It was a mutual decision. We wanted the first year free, without encumbrance, without worry, so we could get to know each other, adapt, have some fun. We as good as told the priest before the ceremony that we were going to do it. He didn't tell us not to. In fact, he as good as admitted that we were one of the few couples who were honest about their intentions."

Norah had already favored those arguments herself.

Joe went on. "Maybe we did do wrong; I don't know. But God will forgive us. He'll give us a child when we're ready for one. Okay?"

So he was worried too and feeling guilty. But the fault was hers; she was the one who had suggested and taken the contraceptive. It wouldn't be fair now to suggest. . . . She went at it another way. "Do you think there's something wrong with me? I mean, maybe I should see a doctor?"

Joe reached for her and took her into his arms. "*Cara,* I don't think there's anything wrong with you. I think you're the most perfect woman in the world. But if it's going to make you feel better to have medical confirmation, then go ahead and see a doctor." He paused for a moment. "I already have."

"Oh, darling, so have I!"

They clung to each other. Joe stroked her hair. After a few moments he drew back, raised her chin, and kissed her gently on the mouth. "You know what I think? We're both trying too hard. I think we should just relax and enjoy ourselves. Like starting now."

2

FOUR days after Lieutenant Capretto and Sergeant Ryder from the Manhattan South Narcotics Squad, in conjunction with the Port Authority police and acting on a tip from "Muscles" Koslav, a paid informer, confiscated eight packages of heroin from the cargo hold of Alitalia flight 426, an anonymous call was received by the New York police. It came at three A.M. over the 911 emergency number. The caller reported having seen a car at the end of a deserted pier on the East River. A man had got out and rolled a suspicious-looking bundle over the side. By the time the radio patrol car reached the scene, there was nobody around and nothing to be seen. A police boat went searching the polluted waters and recovered the body of one Johnny Allegro, a reputed member of the Nerone crime "family." He had been shot and, in accordance with the best gangland tradition, his feet encased in cement. The event attracted little attention. With the over-abundance of crime and corruption stories available to the newspapers, Johnny Allegro rated only a couple of paragraphs on an inside page. He was just a "soldier" in the Nerone family. The public was conversant enough with the vernacular of the subculture to understand immediately how unimportant such a death was, both to his associates and to the police.

Of course, Homicide went through the motions, but aside from the slugs—of a Colt .45—recovered from the body, there were no clues. The pier from which he had been dropped was not only unused, it was condemned and due for demolition to make way for a much-touted housing, commercial, and recreation com-

plex that was to serve as a model for city planning
in the future. Nobody lived in the vicinity. Nobody could be found who had seen anything. The
anonymous informant remained anonymous.

Like the rest of the public, Joe read about it in the
back pages. He'd been acquainted with Allegro, and
the man was even less important than the papers labeled him. His character was in harmony with his
name—he was a happy-go-lucky incompetent whose
only talent was keeping his mouth shut when he got
caught. Years ago, when Joe first joined the force,
Allegro had fronted a couple of nightclubs for the
mob. That had been the high spot of his career. He had
ended up an odd-job man, a "gofer." Well into his
sixties, he should have been retired, yet they found
work for him. Out of loyalty, of course; the mob took
care of its own. Joe wondered what the poor sap had
done, what boner he had pulled big enough for anybody to take the trouble and risk of killing him.

He also wondered idly about the anonymous tip-
ster. Probably an innocent citizen driving along the
East River Drive or maybe a kid prowling where he
knew he didn't belong and whose conscience got the
better of him. Joe was too enmeshed with the after-
math of the events at Kennedy to dwell on it.

The narcotics underworld had been hurting for
some time. Due to the serious shortage of heroin,
caused principally by improved international control,
business had been slow for over a year. The wholesale
problem had reached the street—prices were up,
quality down, demand falling off. The new, strong
drug law sponsored by Governor Rockefeller for the
State of New York had made the dealers cautious.
Since it went into effect on September 1, 1973, action
was almost nil as the big boys waited to see how the
law would work. Narcotics arrests for the months of
September and October had risen two and a half
times. Now there were stirrings; buys were being
made again, but by the middle-echelon dealers. These
men were not as vulnerable as street pushers; dealing

in volume, they were willing to take greater risks for greater profits. They were also careful and wily. Some of the syndicates were switching to cocaine, but it took time to locate new sources and make new contacts. Most stayed in the game they knew.

Therefore, the information regarding the shipment supplied to Joe Capretto by Muscles Koslav had more than the usual importance. It was strategic. It could have put the syndicate for whom it was intended a giant step ahead of the rest of the New York competitors; it could have given them control of the market. Muscles had not known for whom it was intended, only who was bringing it in. As soon as he located it, Joe had called his boss, Inspector Dietrich. The possibility of letting the shipment through and tailing the courier had been discussed and dismissed. The entire planeload of passengers knew he had the heroin. The loss would be a major financial blow, but nobody would be likely and foolhardy enough to try to claim the crate from Confetti Speciali. He was ordered to seize it.

He had not expected to be called off the investigation, though, or as good as. The word came down from the State Department the very next day—no further interference with the tourist group.

The commissioner passed it down to Inspector Dietrich, who in turn informed the lieutenant.

"Nobody's blaming you, Joe. You did what you had to do. But from here on, it's hands off."

"We handled them with kid gloves, I swear, Inspector. You check with Donato at the consulate; he'll tell you. . . ."

"Sure, sure. But those men are all bigshot lawyers, doctors, executives, members of some kind of Italian fraternal group. One of them is a second cousin to the Italian Minister of Labor."

Inspector Otto Dietrich was a pale man, thin, dried out, with a constantly bemused expression that some people took for stupidity. Otto Dietrich was far from stupid. He was cautious. He tested the ground in front of him before stepping forward and trusting the weight of his future on it. The sometimes vacant look of his myopic eyes, magnified by heavy lenses of rimless, pince-nez glasses, actually hid the pain of a nervous stomach. Stress could bring on excruciating cramps, even vomiting; he avoided stress as much as he reasonably could, given the job he was in.

"The Italian authorities will cooperate." He attempted to mollify Joe. "They'll give us any information we need, but you're not to contact the individual tourists."

"How about Abruzzi?"

"So far he's as clean as the others."

"I've got a tail on him."

A knot formed at the pit of the inspector's stomach; he winced. "Take it off. Sorry, Joe. That's the way it is."

"In two days the whole group is leaving for Washington."

"We can't stop them," Dietrich said. He opened his drawer for a couple of Gelusil tablets. "We've got strict orders not to interfere with their itinerary."

Two days after the Italian tourists left New York, Vito Lambroso, an alleged lieutenant in the same crime organization of which Johnny Allegro had been such an insignificant member, was killed. This one was staged à la Dillinger. On that Saturday night, Lambroso came out of Loew's Tower East, a small movie house on Third Avenue near Seventy-second Street. While he stood at the curb waiting for his limousine, a car streaked past and gunned him down. A sizable crowd—patrons coming out of the 8:32 show, a line waiting to get into the 10:05—was terrorized. There were no other fatalities, but two teenagers were injured and had to be rushed to New York Hospital. The city was outraged. If criminals wanted to kill each other off, that was all to the good, but when innocent children became casualties, something had to be done.

The mayor gave interviews to the press and appeared on television looking severe. Criminal elements would not be permitted to turn the city into a battlefield. The citizens of New York would be protected. No effort would be spared to apprehend the culprit. He was putting the mob on notice. He had ordered the police commissioner to take all appropriate action.

The police commissioner gave interviews to the press and appeared on television looking determined. A special squad would be formed to devote full time to the investigation; it would be headed by the most capable and dedicated officer available. A special phone number would be set up for use by the public. Anyone with information could be assured that his identity would be protected. He pleaded for cooperation. Then he sent a memo to the chiefs.

The chiefs and deputy commissioners were busy men with full calendars. Before a time convenient to all could be cleared, for none wanted to be on record as absent from such a meeting, before it could take place, in fact on the night before, Giorgio Nerone, the *capo* himself, was shot. His murder made headlines, not only because of who he was but because of how and where it happened. The much "respected" head of the crime organization was shot while in bed with his mistress. The city was titillated, the gang world appalled. That kind of thing was just not done. The unspoken code marking inviolate the women and children close to a member, not out of sentiment but because of the ease of retaliation, had been violated. True, the woman hadn't been harmed, still. . . . No man wants to be caught in bed. Killed in bed, Giorgio Nerone had been made ridiculous. His wife, Lucia, long privately aware of the affair, was now publicly shamed. The Nerone gang was indignant. A council was called. Caution prevailed: It was decided the murder must be a crime of passion with no connection to business. The word went out—let the police deal with it.

The police would have been only too delighted to concur with the council assessment of the nature of the crime. Unfortunately they couldn't see it as a crime of passion. Mariarosa Martinelli had been Giorgio Nerone's official mistress for going on sixteen years, a little late for any of her relations to avenge her "honor." Besides, it was known she had no relations in this country. If she'd been so foolhardy as to take another lover on the side, the lover would have had to be insane to kill Mariarosa's "patron." What could he hope to gain by it? Unless Nerone had left her money in his will? It was quickly determined he had not. At the time Nerone set up an establishment with Mariarosa he had made a generous settlement on her, endowing her with various properties, one of which was the building in which she lived. The receipts from the properties were well and securely invested. She had nothing additional to gain from his death. If she'd had a lover, it was far more likely that Nerone would have had him killed.

As for the widow, it seemed just as unlikely that after sixteen years Lucia Nerone should develop a thirst for vengeance. If she had ordered the killing, would the mistress have been left unharmed?

Shortly before midnight on the night of the shooting a tall, dark, well-dressed man of middle age entered the building and asked for Miss Martinelli. He gave his name as Smith. While the doorman went to the house telephone to announce Mr. Smith, the man entered the self-service elevator. He was gone before the doorman could stop him.

As the building's owner, Miss Martinelli had a private elevator to her penthouse. There was no other apartment on that floor. When Nerone was visiting, his bodyguard was on duty in the outside vestibule. As Mr. Smith got off the elevator, the guard stepped forward to ask his business and was instantly and competently sapped into unconsciousness. By the simple use of a plastic card—under the kind of protection that Miss Martinelli enjoyed fancy locks were deemed unnecessary—the killer let himself in. He walked straight to the bedroom and fired two shots at Nerone. The first hit the *capo* high, in the shoulder; the second went straight into his heart. Then the killer let himself out the back door, down the stairs to the service elevator on the floor below. While the doorman, not having been able to raise Miss Martinelli, was calling the police, he let himself out of the building. All neatly planned and efficiently carried out.

When the radio patrol officers reached the penthouse vestibule, Nerone's bodyguard, one Bernie Francese, was just recovering consciousness. Inside, Miss Martinelli was screaming. She was too hysterical to hear their calls and knockings and admit them. As the killer had had the foresight to bolt the door behind him, they had to break it down. They found Miss Martinelli standing in the middle of her vast living room. She was wearing a nightgown so sheer she might as well have been naked; her eyes were wild and unfocused; long black hair disheveled; saliva trickling from the corner of her mouth.

The two officers with Francese, still dazed but mobile, went into the bedroom. One look at his boss lying on the blood-soaked sheets was enough to make the bodyguard wish he hadn't regained consciousness. By the time the homicide detectives arrived, the realization of the personal consequences of this disaster had reduced Bernie Francese to a condition not much better than that of the dead man's mistress.

As a witness, Mariarosa Martinelli was just about useless. She couldn't give any kind of description of the killer. Couldn't or wouldn't. She claimed that when he burst into the bedroom and leveled the gun, she thought her own time had come. She was sure she was going to be killed along with Nerone. She'd closed her eyes and waited for the end. She hadn't opened them again till the shooting stopped. Actually, she'd waited till some time after, hardly crediting that she was still alive. Finally, when she did dare to look, the killer was gone. Her next thought was for her lover. As she turned to look at him beside her in the bed, her movement must have caused his body to slump and fall against her. She jumped out of bed and ran screaming into the living room.

Retelling it, she instinctively looked down toward that part of her body that had briefly supported the deadweight and saw a damp patch of blood on her filmy gown. Frantically she began to rend the fabric.

Not till then had anyone thought to find some kind of cover for her nakedness. One of the detectives took off his own raincoat and put it over her. She continued to shiver violently.

Bernard Francese, twenty-two, a wrestler who had found a more profitable use for his muscle, couldn't do any better. Or wouldn't. Livid scar tissue distinguished what would otherwise have been an ordinary face not worth a second look and made it hard to read. However, his overdeveloped chest straining against a too-tight jacket as he breathed in spasms betrayed his anxiety. He had barely got out of his chair, he claimed, hadn't even opened his mouth, when the stranger belted him in the gut and, before he could straighten, sapped him over the head. There was the lump to prove it! He bent his head, offering anybody who wanted to a chance to examine it. Francese continued to insist that he had never laid eyes on the man before. He refused even to commit himself to the vague description offered by the doorman.

So, reluctantly—because it widened the field of inquiry—Homicide discarded the "crime of passion" theory. In view of the two earlier crimes, they labeled it a gangland execution. Nerone had been killed in a struggle for power. Unaware of the Nerone council's decision, they steeled themselves for a spate of retaliatory bloodlettings.

The deputy commissioners and chiefs canceled all appointments and met the very next morning. They tossed it around, but no one had any ideas as to what had triggered the power struggle or who was behind it. Well, the commissioner had announced that a special unit would be formed. The members of that high-level conference were skeptical that such a unit would uncover anything, but not one of them said so. Setting it up would at least show the department's concern, would take off the pressure from the press. They were there to set it up. So—which command should have the responsibility for the unit? Nobody volunteered. They shunted it back and forth across the board table. Homicide and Assault seemed logical. Homicide and Assault thought it belonged under Crime Prevention. Crime Prevention argued for the Organized Crime Squad. Everybody talked at once. The deputy commissioner for Public Relations solved it: Why not take personnel from each command? Instant assent. But who should head the unit?

It should be a man with a good public image. Somebody well enough known and trusted, but who was also a good police officer in the sense that he was content to work within the recognized concept—no innovator or idealist. A good, solid, unimaginative cop.

How about this guy Capretto? He'd made a lot of good busts lately and had had plenty of exposure in the press.

They sent for his folder. Lieutenant Joseph Antony Capretto was presently working out of Narco, so he was familiar with the organized-crime setup. Previously he'd been a member of the Fifth H and A and before that Homicide North. A lieutenant for the past two years, he'd been a detective sergeant for twelve before that. In spite of all his recent publicity he was part of the establishment—no Durk or Serpico; Lieutenant Capretto was not afflicted by any Batman and Robin syndrome; he went by the book. And wasn't he married to a policewoman? Certainly. Actually, his wife was a detective. Eyebrows went up. Mrs. Capretto had made detective after less than two years on the force and had been promoted to second grade the year after that. She was presently working out of the Fifth, using her maiden name to avoid confusion. Detective Norah Mulcahaney. Smiles all around.

And wasn't Lieutenant Capretto the one who had recovered that big heroin shipment last week from the Alitalia jet? Somebody recalled he'd tangled with the Italian consulate and the State Department. Inspector Dietrich was summoned.

Dietrich hesitated. He had long experience in picking his way through the minefield of departmental politics. He was also loyal to his men and considered Capretto competent for the job. Just the same, he had to assess the mood of his superiors. Was it favorable? He decided it was, that they wanted to be told "Cap" was okay. The knot in Dietrich's stomach relaxed.

He defended Joe. "It was a delicate situation. I consider that Lieutenant Capretto handled it well. He didn't throw his weight around. He used tact and persuasion. The Italian representative, Mr. Donato, particularly mentioned that he appreciated Lieutenant Capretto's courtesy and consideration toward the Italian nationals."

More smiles. The chiefs and deputy commissioners sat back and relaxed.

Dietrich relaxed—almost. Being the man he was, out of sheer habit of self-preservation, he had to qualify the praise. "Of course, being of Italian extraction himself was a help."

Everybody nodded—an Italian cop to investigate a predominantly Italian organization. Not bad. The release would make no particular mention of the ethnic link, but the public would catch it. The decision was made. Inspector Dietrich was instructed to inform Lieutenant Capretto that he had been chosen for this important assignment.

"Tell him he's to have a free hand," the first deputy commissioner began expansively, then caught himself. "Within reason, naturally."

"Naturally," Dietrich echoed.

Public Relations was studying Lieutenant Capretto's file in order to draft the release. "About Mrs. Capretto . . . uh, Detective Mulcahaney. . . . I see she worked with her husband on several cases before they were married."

"That's correct," Dietrich replied.

Looks were exchanged, heads shaken slowly.

"He's not to use her on this one," the first deputy decreed. "Too risky for a woman."

Joe received the news of his appointment with outward calm. His dark face remained impassive; only his eyes flashed briefly, then he lowered them till he was sure they no longer betrayed his excitement. In that brief moment the excitement passed and he understood why the job had filtered down to his level. Nobody else wanted it. He also realized that he was not really expected to succeed—there were too many possible suspects and too few direct clues. Failure would tarnish a chief; even an inspector's record would be blemished, but how much could it hurt a lieutenant? And anyway, who cared about a lieutenant? His appointment would be announced with fanfare; the formation of the unit would be publicized; then the whole thing would be allowed to fade quietly while other matters captured the public attention.

Joe Capretto had never started an investigation of any case, no matter how apparently hopeless, without full expectation of solving it. He expected to solve this one. He would surprise them all. His face was set in determination as he looked up at his boss. It was important, however, to know Dietrich's attitude.

"Why me, Inspector?"

Dietrich had already asked himself that question and come to the same conclusion as Joe, but he was startled that Joe, being the man he was or at least the man Dietrich took him to be, should bring it out into the open. He gulped. His Adam's apple traveled in jerks up and down his neck like an overloaded elevator. He started to hedge, then changed his mind. He owed Cap the truth. "You've been getting a lot of publicity lately."

"Yes, sir." Joe paused. Dietrich was being honest; he had to be too. "It's a big opportunity for me, Inspector. I intend to make the most of it."

Their eyes met. "Good."

Joe was satisfied that he would get support. "About an office for the unit, Inspector? What command are we to work out of?"

Dietrich hadn't been instructed on that. He could ask, of course, but he knew he'd only be told to base the unit in his own headquarters. He was stuck. He sighed. "I suppose we can find space here."

"Thank you, sir."

So now Inspector Dietrich had a direct stake in the outcome. "If you need anything, ask for it. I'll see that you get it."

"Yes, sir."

Dietrich's uncertainties applied only to the intrigues within the department; when it came to the job, he was an effective administrator and a staunch officer. "Pick your own men from any command, say, thirty for a start. And keep me informed."

Joe nodded. "About the Abruzzi business, Inspector?"

"Ah, yes. Any leads from Italy or from Interpol?"

"Not yet."

"If there'd been anything, we would have heard by now. Where's the group?"

"Disney World. From there they go to the Coast for a week, then back here for two more days and home."

Dietrich shrugged. "Nothing we can do. Forget it, Joe. If something does turn up, Ryder can handle it. The Nerone case takes precedence."

"Yes, sir." Joe got up to go.

"Ah . . . one more thing. About your . . . ah . . . about Detective Mulcahaney. You're not to put her on the team. It was specifically mentioned."

Joe was surprised the chiefs had given that much attention to his background. He was encouraged. "I wasn't intending to use Norah, Inspector, but it's just as well to have it come from the top." He grinned.

3

NORAH liked to put her feet up while watching television, and Joe had adopted the habit. So they were sitting side by side on the sofa, shoes off and feet on the cocktail table, watching Joe being interviewed on the late news.

"Do you have any hot leads on these crimes, Lieutenant?" the reporter on the screen asked and held the microphone in front of Joe.

"If I had, I wouldn't divulge them here," the image of Joe replied with a good-natured smile.

"Sure, sure." The reporter grinned back. "Can you give us any idea how you're going to conduct the investigation?"

Joe photographed well, Norah thought proudly. His dark face, shown now in profile, was very handsome and serious.

"Glad to," he replied. "We intend to use knuckle power."

"Ah. . . ." The reporter's smile became uncertain. "Could you clarify that, Lieutenant?"

"The term isn't mine. I wish I could give credit to the police officer who coined it, but I don't at the moment remember his name. Knuckle power is knocking on doors and asking questions. It's the basis of police work. It means that every detail of the lives of the three victims will be investigated—their families, friends, enemies, and their families, friends, and enemies as far back as necessary. It means every lead and every scrap of information will be followed up. Nobody that calls our special number is going to get the brush-off. When we ask for help, we mean it."

"Terrific!" Norah swung her feet off the table,

jumped up, and turned the set off. "The commissioner's going to love it."

"What do they expect me to say?"

The phone rang. They looked at each other.

"Are you home?" Norah asked.

He shrugged. "Might as well hear it now as later."

"Hello?" Norah answered, then her shoulders
dropped with relief. "Oh, hello, Mamma. . . . Yes, he's
here." She held out the receiver. "It's your mother."

Joe got up and took the phone from her. "Hi, Mam-
ma. You saw it, eh? How did you—" He listened. "I
see. But—" He listened some more. At length. "Sure,
Mamma, I'll try next time." He hung up. "She thought
I should have behaved 'more dignified,'" he quoted.
"But she's proud of me."

"So am I," Norah said.

The phone rang again.

"You wanna bet who it is this time?" Joe asked, but
Norah shook her head. "Oh, Dad. . . . Oh, really? It's
nice of you to say so, Dad." Joe covered the mouth-
piece. "Your dad thinks I did great." As Mulcahaney
continued, however, Joe's pleasure abated. "Yes, yes,
that's true. . . . Well . . . well, I'm glad you approve.
And thanks for calling, Dad." He hung up. "Your father says it's good for people to realize that policemen
don't have miraculous powers, that they have to work
hard like anybody else. He says I appeared an ordinary person with a job to do."

Norah bit her lip. "He meant well."

Joe laughed. "Oh, hell, I know that. They both did.
. . . They both always do."

Norah became serious. "Are you going to solve it,
Joe?"

"Yes."

No hesitation and no qualification. Norah waited.
If he wanted to tell her more, he would.

"The brass see this as a struggle to control the Nerone organization, either internally or from the outside.
I'm not so sure. Ballistics shows that the three men
were all killed by bullets from the same gun. Okay.

But you can't tell me that a nothing guy like Johnny Allegro stood in the way of anybody's power grab. And the manner of the crimes—the style! Allegro shot, his feet encased in cement, and the body dumped in the river. Who does that anymore? It's been out for years. Why bother? Why not leave the body in an alley or an empty lot? Afterward, why tip the police?"

"The tip could have come from some perfectly innocent—"

"Maybe. But who's wandering around an abandoned dock at three A.M.? I get the feeling somebody was issuing a warning. That's one. Two: Vito Lambroso. Why did that have to be a public spectacle? And three: Nerone shot in bed with his woman. Now that's guaranteed to make headlines. It looks to me as though the killer wanted it advertised."

Again Norah waited, but Joe apparently didn't intend to pursue it. She changed the subject. "Who are you going to get for the team?"

"Sid Ryder, naturally, then I thought David and Roy...."

Sergeant Ryder worked closely with Joe on Narco, but Norah didn't know him as well as the other two men, who were personal friends. David Link was on the Fifth H and A along with Norah. Young and intuitive, he had been steered by Joe through his first big case just as he had helped and advised Norah when she first joined Homicide North. Roy Brennan was on the same squad but an old hand, a veteran, taciturn and meticulous. "Who else?"

"I haven't decided." Joe hesitated. "I'm supposed to take men from various commands, and as I've already got two from Homicide...."

But Norah wasn't thinking of herself when she asked. It didn't occur to her that she might be considered. She not only had plenty of work on hand, but she was still deeply concerned over her failure to conceive. Joe's medical examination and her own proved that there was no biological impediment to their having children, so she kept coming back to what her father had asked her at the party—did she really want a baby?

Though they worked out of separate commands, Norah and Joe's tours of duty usually coincided—with the recent elimination of the night watch for all but a skeleton crew of detectives, this was relatively easy to arrange. Each worked a week of eight to four, then a week of four to midnight. Barring a crisis, of course, when the clock meant nothing, they shared a home and social life just about as normal as that of any other young couple. In addition to which they shared their work. There was no denying that a baby would change things.

To begin with, Norah would have to take maternity leave. A considerable interval would follow after the birth before she could go back to work. Even then they couldn't be as carefree as they were now. It would probably be necessary to work opposing shifts so one or the other could be at home, at least until the child was old enough to be sent to nursery school. They would hardly see each other. They would become strangers, she thought glumly, passing each other in and out the door. The camaraderie that meant so much to both of them would be gone. It would either be that or give up her job for good and all. There was the block. Her father was right.

Having acknowledged it, Norah set about for a way to get around it. Adoption. Adoption offered the least possible disruption of their lives. There would be no maternity leave. The time till the baby could be placed in a day-care center—and Norah had taken the trouble to find out that there were now one or two such places accepting infants of working mothers—would be minimal. There would be no wailings, diaperings, night feedings. Adopting would ease them into parenthood. And then, as they both became accustomed to a new life-style, maybe she'd relax and they'd have a child of their own. It happened that way for lots of couples; it could happen for them. Because Norah did basically want a family, not only for Joe's sake but for her own, and, as Signora Emilia and her father kept hinting, time was running out.

The more she thought about it, the more certain Norah became that adoption was the solution. Her spirits rose. She was cheerful again. Joe noticed the change, was delighted, and figured that her good sense had reasserted itself and she was accepting God's will for them. Norah said nothing, intending to get the whole thing lined up first. Not that she had any doubts that Joe would agree to an adoption, just that actually locating an available baby would be the best way to convince him that she was sincere, that she really wanted to do it and was not making a gesture for his sake.

She knew it wouldn't be easy: Like everything else nowadays, babies were in short supply. There were all kinds of stories around about the lengths to which couples went to get a child, but Norah couldn't believe it was as difficult as everyone said. After all, she and Joe were young, employed, responsible, good church-goers—most desirable parents. They would have no trouble getting approved. Another reason for keeping quiet was Signora Emilia. Joe's mother might be less than enthusiastic, but confronted with an accomplished fact, she would have to accept it. As for her father, he would understand both the need and the hope behind it.

The New York Foundling Hospital run by the Sisters of Charity was right in her neighborhood. It was the logical place to apply. On her next day off Norah went for an interview. The morning was cold and bright. As she walked the short distance from the apartment over to Third Avenue, Norah thought that in spite of violence and poverty, lack of communication and resentment, New York was still a fine place to live—galvanic as no other city she knew and full of opportunity. Before entering, she stopped on the sidewalk to stare up at the ten stories of the foundling hospital. A huge place and full of children who needed homes. Her hopes were high.

Her first surprise came in the person of Sister Agnes herself. Of course nuns hadn't been wearing the traditional, antiquated, and cumbersome habits for some time, but Norah had expected some kind of modified uniform and headdress. If Sister Agnes hadn't introduced herself, Norah would not have known she was a nun. She was about Norah's age, tall, with straight dark hair cut very short, and she wore a plain green dress, flesh-colored hose, and black pumps. She had nothing on her head at all. She was kind, but she was blunt.

"I'm afraid you don't qualify, Mrs. Capretto. We require a couple to have been married at least three years. You've been married only two. It's a matter of the stability of the home situation. We wouldn't want to place a child only to have the couple break up later on."

"I assure you, Sister, that Joe and I intend to stay together. We're Catholics."

Sister Agnes only smiled.

Norah was dismayed. "I understood that even single persons are now eligible to adopt."

"Under certain circumstances, very special circumstances, yes. In any case, the problem is academic, Mrs. Capretto. Last year we placed two hundred and twenty children—of these only ten were white infants. The others were black, Puerto Rican, interracial, handicapped, and between the ages of six and sixteen. I haven't counted recently, but I would estimate that for every available infant there are two to three hundred couples waiting. A man called me just this morning—he and his wife have been approved and have already been waiting three years. I couldn't even tell him how much longer it might be."

Norah shook her head in disbelief.

"I'm really sorry, Mrs. Capretto, but you might as well face the facts. The moral climate is so different now; it has changed so much even in the past five years. Out of the hundred and thirty girls to whom we gave maternity care last year only twenty surrendered their babies. Grievously afflicted children, mentally retarded, deformed, for whom there would have been no hope of finding a home just a short time ago, are now being placed. Would you take such a child?"

Norah flushed. "We're working people, both my husband and I. . . ."

"Of course. Would you take an older child, probably a teenager?" Sister Agnes asked.

"I'm sorry."

"Don't be. There's no need to apologize. You want a baby. I wish I could give you some hope. Frankly, there's almost none."

Norah left the foundling home disappointed, but far from defeated. There were other agencies. She made a list and there were more than she had expected: public and private, religious—of every denomination —some city licensed, some licensed by the state. She visited them one by one. Essentially, the situation was the same. Some took her name but she knew it was a meaningless formality—they were compiling statistics of the number of applicants, no more.

Thank God she hadn't told Joe; at least he was spared the disappointments that were piling up. He was worried enough about the investigation. He didn't talk about it, and that was how Norah knew it wasn't going well.

Meanwhile the more turndowns she got, the more determined Norah became to find a baby. Each agency referred her to another; it was an easy way to get rid of her. She plodded from one impersonal, antiseptic office to the next. She was interviewed by administrators, social representatives, caseworkers, family counselors—the titles differed, but the women were the same. They dealt with deeply emotional situations, but they were long past feeling the emotions themselves. Most were past middle age. They scorned makeup, wore a version of hand-printed madras shifts as suitable for a bedspread as a dress. What had been in the forties a mark of artistic individualism had become in the seventies a uniform, even to the ethnic jewelry—ropes of colored coffee beans, melon seeds, macaroni bits hung around their necks and wrists. They were pleasant women, professionally sympathetic, and Norah knew that they forgot her as soon as she walked out the door.

It was now Thanksgiving week and Norah had long since given up her goal of having the baby home by Christmas. She could hardly believe how naïve she'd been. Now she found herself, like the women who interviewed her, just going through the motions. As she handed over yet another of the useless forms, Norah caught the woman behind the desk, according to the name plaque, Miss Endicott, looking at her with unusual interest. Probably Miss Endicott was going to offer the usual sop—a referral to another agency.

Norah just wasn't interested. She gave up hard, but she was close to accepting the inevitable. Yet the way the woman continued to scrutinize her, the fact that she had not put Norah's application aside, but still held it in her hand. . . . All the tremulous longing was reawakened. All right, once more, one last time. . . .

"Can you suggest any other agency I might try? Frankly, I've run out of places."

"Well, I do occasionally hear of a special situation," Miss Endicott replied carefully. "Sometimes a doctor as a favor to a patient will try to help her place her child . . . quickly, without the usual red tape."

Private adoption! Gray market! Norah caught her breath. It was common enough and not necessarily illegal, but up to now no one had broached such a possibility to her. Maybe it hadn't happened because, though she wasn't advertising that she was herself a police officer, her husband's occupation was plainly shown on every form she filled out. But Miss Endicott was too busy gauging Norah's desire and her ability to pay to even glance at the paper in her hand. Before, Miss Endicott had been just another social worker; now Norah took a good look at her. In her late thirties, discreetly fashionable in a Chanel-style suit, with long gold chains around her neck that could very well be the real thing, hair crisply cut and tipped with gold, she was certainly far above the others in her tastes and evidently also in her ability to satisfy them.

The two women sized each other up.

"Yes?" Norah prompted and she didn't have to simulate eagerness.

"Well, you seem like the kind of woman who should have a child, Mrs. Capretto. I feel that you would give a child a good home and plenty of love—that's what it's all about, isn't it? That's what all the rules and regulations are intended to ensure. So, I'd like to help you." Suddenly Miss Endicott smiled warmly. Whatever the test, Norah seemed to have passed it. "I do know of a gynecologist who occasionally has as a patient some indigent young woman too sensitive to apply for assistance to a public agency for unwed mothers and who wants to be certain her baby will be placed in a good home. If you want to contact him. . . . Of course, I can't promise anything. . . ."

"No, no, of course not. I understand."

Miss Endicott gave Norah another long, hard look. "In that case, we won't be needing this." She tore Norah's application in half, then tore the pieces again and again and let the scraps flutter into the wastebasket.

So now there was no evidence that Norah had ever visited the Chelsea Child Services or ever talked with Charlotte Endicott.

"Call Dr. Janus at 223-4210."

Neither did it escape Norah that Miss Endicott didn't write or type out the number for her. If Norah should ever change her mind or want to bring charges, there could never be any proof of complicity on Miss Endicott's part.

Why should anyone willing to adopt by way of the gray market turn in the person who made it possible?

Norah wondered. By taking part in the transaction, the adoptive parents themselves became accessories to any illegality. Her thoughts were in turmoil as she walked out into the street. Should she contact Dr. Janus? It was possible that he was honest. The reasons for a mother who couldn't keep her baby and wanted to avoid the usual channels could be valid. How could she know if she didn't look into it? Norah went to the nearest phone booth, called, and made a routine appointment through the doctor's secretary. She was asked if she was a new patient, but she was not asked who had referred her.

Dr. Phillip Janus' office was on the ground floor of a modern building just off York Avenue. There were at least five other physicians in the building, which was just across the street from the New York Hospital, Rockefeller University, and a whole complex of medical pavilions and research centers. It certainly gave an aura of respectability. The reception room was clean, bright, and crowded. The women waiting were of all classes, but all young. To Norah they seemed very, very young and very happy. They shared a certain glow. She struggled to pinpoint it and decided that they were all, in an odd way, innocent. Maybe being pregnant did that. The receptionist wore a white nurse's uniform, which didn't mean she was a nurse, though she could be. She filled out a card for Norah with cheerful efficiency, reeling off the medical questions matter-of-factly.

"Any serious illnesses? Operations, miscarriages, abortions?"

The last question had not embarrassed Norah when she'd gone to her own doctor; now she blushed. "No," she replied softly.

"What is it you want to see doctor about?" the girl asked, professionally encouraging.

Norah was ready for that. "I'm having trouble getting pregnant."

The girl nodded and made a note on the card, then she handed Norah over to an older woman, definitely a nurse, who led her to an examining room. She was ready for that too. "I want to speak to the doctor first."

The nurse shrugged and took her from the examining room to a large office, book-lined and chintz-swathed, and left her there. After a few moments Dr. Phillip Janus strode in.

He had one of those homely yet attractive faces that inspire instant confidence, heavily-lined, yet youthful. His eyes were mild; his unruly red hair was fading into blond. He wore a rumpled lab coat over loud plaid slacks. Norah could well imagine that the most nervous patient would feel at ease as soon as she saw him—her own trepidations were allayed, at least temporarily. Janus appeared preoccupied, but then so did most doctors—it was part of the medical image. As soon as he saw Norah, though, he threw it off and gave her an engaging smile and a firm handshake.

At his desk he picked up her card. "Ah . . . Mrs. Capretto. Good to see you. Sit down. So you're having trouble getting pregnant."

"Miss Endicott sent me."

There was a slight pause, but no change in his attitude. "Ah, yes. I see you've already consulted a gynecologist about the problem."

Norah looked straight at him. "I want to adopt."

"I don't run an adoption agency, Mrs. Capretto."

"I know that, Doctor. Miss Endicott said that sometimes. . . ." She let it hang.

"Charlotte is too kindhearted. She wants to help everybody." Janus sighed. "It's a sad thing when a woman who really wants a child can't have one. When such a woman doesn't qualify to adopt through ordinary channels, usually because she and her husband are too old, then I'll admit I do try to help. But surely you don't come into that category." He smiled again, encouragingly. "Are you sure you can't have children? Has your husband been examined? There are so many new drugs, so many new treatments. . . ."

"I want to adopt."

"Ah . . . of course, there are instances when the lack of a child causes severe trauma in a woman. In such instances the long procedures of adoption, the investigation, the waiting and uncertainty add to the tension and anxiety pattern."

"Put me in that category."

Phillip Janus reached for the cigarette box, got up, and coming around to the corner of his desk, offered it to Norah. She shook her head. "Would you be willing to undergo psychiatric testing?"

"That's ridiculous!"

He lit up, tossed the match into an ashtray, and took a long, slow drag. "You seem to be under a misapprehension, Mrs. Capretto," he said, and now his voice became cold and his homely face hard. "I'm not running a black market in babies. I do occasionally place a baby in an adoptive home, but it is principally as a health service to an emotionally disturbed expectant mother. I also have to assure myself that the adoptive parent is not only fit but has a need so urgent that it too warrants bypassing the usual channels. Everything is done in a strictly legal manner."

His anger added to his credibility. Certainly Norah wanted to believe him. "I wouldn't have it any other way."

"As long as that's understood." Janus nodded. "It happens that one of my patients is about to come to term. The father of her child has disclaimed responsibility. She is estranged from her parents. You would have to pay her medical expenses and the legal fees."

"Naturally." The cold excitement was on her again, part eagerness, part dread.

"I must warn you that there are complications in her pregnancy—oh, nothing that could affect the health of the child, but her lying-in could be expensive. There's no telling exactly what the bill will run to, but you should prepare yourself for something in the neighborhood of fifteen hundred dollars. Most of that will go to the hospital, though I have to make a living too."

"Of course."

"You can expect the legal fees to run to about twenty-five hundred. That seems a lot for a couple of hours of paperwork, but. . . ." He shrugged. "It's the going rate."

"Couldn't I use my own attorney?"

"If you wish, but the man I have in mind will expedite matters for you considerably."

"I see. Well, I suppose that would be best then."

Now Janus returned to his earlier, easier manner. "Obviously I can't promise whether it will be a boy or a girl. Does it matter?"

Norah hesitated. "I was thinking of a boy."

"If it's a girl, will you take her?"

Norah took a long, deep breath, then slowly let it out. "I'll take her."

Janus ground out the half-smoked cigarette, got up from the edge of the desk against which he'd been leaning, and put an arm around Norah's shoulders as he escorted her to the door. "You'll be hearing from me, Mrs. Capretto."

4

ONCE she was out of Janus' office, all Norah's doubts returned. By now she'd learned enough about the adoptive process to know that a private adoption was handled basically in the same manner as one through an agency. Once the natural mother relinquished her child and the court accepted the adoptive parents, it was just as legal. The difference lay primarily in the higher fee and a less thorough and demanding examination of the prospective parents. The court seldom turned them down, their ability to pay being their *bona fides*. Janus had indicated that she could expect to pay a total of four thousand dollars. She was prepared to see it go to five, and she knew that even at that it was a bargain.

Phillip Janus, his office, the patients in his waiting room all had contributed to the good impression Norah had received, but she checked him with the AMA anyway. There was nothing against him. She should check the lawyer too. She hadn't asked his name. She could call and get it, of course. She didn't.

By now Norah had reached the stage where if there was anything wrong, she didn't want to find it out. She shied from telling Joe for that very reason: He would insist on checking every person concerned with the proposed adoption. She decided she would tell Joe as soon as the baby was born—not before, but not any later either. Then she waited for the phone to ring. Five days after Thanksgiving it did.

"Mrs. Capretto?"

She recognized his voice instantly. Her throat was dry, tight.

"Yes, Dr. Janus."

"It's a boy."

She swallowed. Sweat broke out all over her body. She could hardly breathe.

"I'll bet you didn't expect to hear from me so soon. The birth was premature, but no need to worry—the boy is absolutely healthy."

"That's good," she replied. It was hardly adequate; it was all she could manage.

"Can you come to my office tomorrow, Mrs. Capretto? At twelve?"

"I'm working till four."

"I see. Well, four thirty, then? Can you make it by four thirty?"

"Yes, all right." She should be happy, ecstatic. Why couldn't she be?

"And I'll require the first installment, Mrs. Capretto. Five thousand."

Norah licked her lips. "But you said . . . you quoted four thousand as the total fee."

"I did warn you that the mother was having a hard time. It develops that she'll require additional surgery. I'm sure that you would also want the mother to have something to see her through her convalescence."

"How much? How much will it all come to?"

"It's hard to say, Mrs. Capretto. I know you want this child, and I think you should have him, so I want to be as helpful as possible. Let's put a ceiling of, say, five thousand more? If it exceeds that, I'll take it out of my own fee. I can't say fairer."

"Well. . . ."

"Of course, if you feel you can't afford to go that high, Mrs. Capretto, I'll understand. You're not to feel obligated. I wouldn't want you to go into debt or anything like that. And don't worry about our finding another home for the baby. I could step into my reception room at any moment—"

"Yes, yes, I know. It's all right. We can afford it."

"Are you sure, Mrs. Capretto? Maybe you want to

talk it over with your husband? Why don't you do that and let me know? But no later than tomorrow morning. Okay?"

"No, no, that's not necessary. We want the baby. I'll be at your office tomorrow with the money."

"In cash, Mrs. Capretto. If you don't mind."

Norah stayed on the phone for several seconds after Janus had hung up. The sick feeling at the pit of her stomach grew into nausea. She was gripping the receiver so tightly that her hand trembled and continued trembling even after she'd put it back into the cradle. She couldn't fool herself anymore. She couldn't continue to rationalize that the adoption was legal. The escalation of the cost and Janus' demand for cash was plain—he was selling and she was buying. What should she do? What should she tell Joe? Oh, blessed Mary! What was she going to tell Joe? She thanked God that he hadn't been at home when the call came; at least she had a little time to think.

From the small entrance hall in which they kept the telephone Norah turned back to the living room and went to stand in front of the window. Madison Avenue was bathed in the flat golden glow of the recently installed vapor lights. The traffic signals changed from green to red; the cars moved and stopped and moved again—the effect was almost hypnotic.

What should she do? Could she morally justify buying the baby? Even if she could justify it to herself, would Joe agree?

She went into the spare room, the one they were using as a dining room but that would become the nursery, and visualized how she would redecorate—where the crib would go, the playpen, a chest for toys. That made her feel worse. She snapped the light out, closed the door firmly, and returned to the living room. But she was too restless to watch television or to read. She might as well go to bed. But first she went to the kitchen, got the sherry out of the liquor cabinet, and poured herself a drink. Maybe it would relax her.

It didn't seem to Norah that she'd been in bed long

when she heard Joe at the door. A glance at the bed-side clock showed her that she'd been lying rigidly awake for over an hour. Panic seized her. She real-ized suddenly that she couldn't talk to Joe about the baby, not yet. She wasn't ready yet. Quickly she reached and turned out the bedside light, drew the covers up, closed her eyes, and lay very still.

Though her face was buried in the pillow, Norah was nevertheless conscious of every movement in the other room. She knew when the light went on, when Joe hung up his coat in the hall closet, and when at last, very quietly and taking care not to disturb her, he came into their bedroom. She could feel him stand-ing over her and looking down at her. Finally he turned away. She listened to the small sounds that in-dicated he was getting his pajamas out of the closet and undressing. She felt the bed sag as he sat down on his side, sensed when the light went out. The bed sagged some more as he lay down beside her. She felt the warmth of his body. If he were to take her in his arms now, if he kissed her, she couldn't go on pretend-ing she was asleep. She'd have to respond, she wouldn't be able to help herself, and then the whole sorry problem would come spilling out. He edged closer. Stirring, as though in restless slumber, Norah turned over so that her back was to him.

Gently Joe kissed her hair, then turned over himself so that they lay back to back.

God forgive me! Norah cried out within herself. She'd repulsed Joe's tenderness. It was the first time. It was the first time they'd gone to sleep in silence. It might be a small thing, but to Norah it was a terrible betrayal of their love. She'd make it up to him, she vowed, but she could never, never tell him. Her silent tears wet the pillow. Maybe it was God's way of an-swering. If merely the problem about the baby had become a wedge between her and Joe, then the baby —any baby illegally acquired—was not for them. Norah made her decision. In the morning she would call Janus and tell him she'd changed her mind. Opening her eyes wide in the dark, she turned to Joe. He was asleep. Norah kissed his bare shoulder and fell asleep too.

In was just under two weeks since Joe had been appointed to form and head the special unit for the investigation of the three gangland murders. Things weren't moving. He had personally interrogated Nerone's mistress, the sole eyewitness. Three days after the crime she was still in bad shape. She received him in the half gloom of drawn venetian blinds, sitting in a corner, her face masked by huge dark glasses. He could hardly ask her to open the blinds and remove the glasses. In any case, it wasn't necessary: Joe could see enough of her—hollow cheeks, slack mouth, hands limp on the chair arms—to know she wasn't faking. He could well understand that she still hadn't recovered; she'd had a traumatic experience, her lover murdered beside her, expecting to die herself. What struck Joe most particularly, though, was her attitude. Nerone's mistress wore deep mourning and bore herself with the dignity of a wife. Joe found himself treating her with the deference she demanded. He was not able to elicit any new information from her.

He didn't do much better with the bodyguard. Francese stuck to his story that the assailant was a complete stranger to him. He was finally prevailed upon to corroborate the doorman's description of a middle-aged man, dark, of medium height, and wearing a dark suit.

The maid, Vincenza Giannini, hadn't been in the apartment the night of the killing, but Joe talked to her anyway. She was in her fifties, with a strong, heavily lined, sallow face and stringy gray hair pulled tightly back into a bun. She spoke only broken English, and though Joe interrogated her in her own language, she remained reserved, even wary, with the characteristic mistrust of the peasant toward anyone official. She had been with the signorina four years; in fact, the signorina had brought her over from Muggia,

Italy. No, she knew nothing of the signorina's personal affairs. She had her own quarters elsewhere in the building and she retired to these early on the nights when a visitor was expected. Vincenza Giannini claimed not even to know the identity of the visitor.

Next Joe turned to the Lambroso murder. He interrogated the two teenagers who had been wounded during the shooting in front of the movie house. The two boys had sustained only minor injuries and were now enjoying their prominence. They were excited by all the attention they were getting and would have been only too glad to add to their importance by offering information. Only they didn't know anything. They had seen Vito Lambroso go down. Before they could turn to see where the shots came from, they were themselves hit. Later they had learned that the shots came from a passing car, but they hadn't actually seen the car. They were so eager. The danger was that too much urging might cause them to fabricate, albeit unwittingly. Joe left them alone.

Meanwhile calls were coming in on the special unit line—more than a hundred of them, mostly from people who had been lined up waiting to get into the theater for the next showing and some who had been passing on the other side of the street. The only fact they agreed on was that the shots had come from a car and that it was big and black. Otherwise you could take your choice: The car was full, men in front and back; there were only two men in the car, in the front; there was only the driver, though how he could drive and shoot at the same time the particular witness couldn't say. Nobody got the license number. Each caller was personally interviewed by a member of Joe's team. There were no useful results.

Joe put out the word that he wanted information, but none of the usual snitches came forward. The underworld was oddly silent.

Joe put the team on the long, tedious investigation of the backgrounds of the three victims that he had promised to do on television. Then Muscles Koslav contacted him again. Not about the murders, but about a new heroin shipment. He didn't know when it was coming in or from where, only that it was expected. The word was that arrangements had been made and that it would be another big one.

Joe mulled it over. As neither the Italian authorities nor Interpol had come up with anything either on Abruzzi or on his fellow tourists, the case had not been assigned to anyone else and remained nominally his. Muscles' first tip had specifically named Carlo Abruzzi as the courier; this time the courier was unknown, but suppose the shipment was intended for Abruzzi? Having failed to deliver once, would he have the nerve to try again? Why not, when Washington seemed bent on giving him a second chance? Joe thought bitterly. He consulted his notebook for the group's schedule. They were at this moment savoring the delights of San Francisco. They would be back in New York in four days. If Abruzzi was involved, that's when the shipment would be coming in.

Dietrich would have to consult State before allowing Joe to resume surveillance of Abruzzi. Suppose permission was denied? Joe didn't see how it could be, but you never knew. He checked his notebook again —the group was scheduled to remain in New York two days before flying home to Italy. Suppose he sat on Muscles' tip till the group was actually back in New York. Then, with time so short, Dietrich might give the okay for the tail on his own responsibility. That would be putting the inspector on the spot. Joe couldn't do it.

He was having a sandwich at the usual luncheonette down the street from the station house in which both the Narco Squad and his special unit were based when the waitress approached his table and told him there was a telephone call for him. That wasn't unusual. The Elite was the regular precinct hangout, and anyway, he'd left word that was where he would be. Joe picked up the phone, expecting it to be the desk sergeant.

"Lieutenant Capretto?"

The voice was low, harsh, not anyone he knew.

"Lieutenant Joseph Capretto?"

"Right."

"It's worth ten thou if you lay off."

Joe was stunned. Since being on Narco, he'd been offered bribes before, plenty of times, but nothing on this scale. God! "Who is this?"

"Think about it, Lieutenant. I'll get back to you." The caller hung up.

Slowly Joe walked back to his table.

Lay off what? he asked himself. The heroin shipment or the murder investigation? He didn't know enough about either to warrant a bribe, much less one of that size. Too perturbed to finish eating, Joe picked up his bill, paid it, and walked out into the street.

It was unnaturally dark outside and unnaturally still. The darkness washed out colors; the stillness muffled ordinary noise. The two together meant that the predicted thunderstorm was about to break, and a thunderstorm at this time of year was itself unnatural. Everybody on the street scuttled to get where they were going. The usually crowded thoroughfare of discount stores was almost empty; the shoppers were already inside; even the shambling loiterers with nowhere to go were sheltering in doorways. Joe didn't notice. He walked slowly in the direction of the precinct house. A couple of the first fat drops splattered on the dirty sidewalk; a couple splashed on his head. He didn't feel them.

What the hell was the bribe for? he kept asking himself. By the time he reached the precinct, Joe was drenched, but he had convinced himself that as he had nothing on the murders, but did have new information about a second heroin shipment, the bribe had to refer to the heroin. The caller had not been Abruzzi; of that Joe was positive. Even though only a few words had been spoken, Joe was certain he would have recognized Abruzzi's voice. It could have been someone acting for him or someone acting for the group who expected to take delivery. Joe went in to the inspector.

"Ten thousand!" Behind the rimless, pince-nez glasses Otto Dietrich's pale eyes flashed. "You could try for a meet," he suggested. "Even if the principal didn't show, which probably he wouldn't, we could put a tail on the messenger. . . ."

"They're not going to fall for that, Inspector. If I tell them okay, they're going to stash the money in a locker somewhere and mail me the key. Or deposit it in some bank to my name. Either way we're not going to have a clue as to where it's coming from."

Dietrich sighed. "I could take you off the case."

"They'll offer the bribe to the next man, and the situation will be exactly the same." Neither one of them mentioned that the next man might be less inclined to refuse. It wasn't a subject anybody in the department liked to discuss. "I could pretend to accept. . . ."

"I don't want to be fishing you out of the river, Cap."

Joe hadn't made the offer with much enthusiasm. The mob liked to think of themselves as businessmen; they preferred not to go around killing police lieutenants, but if double-crossed. . . . He was just as glad Dietrich turned him down. "Then what, Inspector? Obviously they knew a lot about me. For starters, they knew I'd be at the Elite."

"Hell, everybody knows half the precinct eats there."

"All right. They probably also know I've been offered bribes before and turned them down."

"So that's why they made this a big one."

"They must also have an alternate plan if I refuse."

The two detectives exchanged somber glances.

"We'll just have to wait and see," Dietrich said.

"Maybe that's it. Maybe that's what they want," Joe suggested. "Maybe that's the whole idea. The bribe could be a diversion. While we're waiting for the second contact, marking time, the shipment comes in; Abruzzi picks it up, delivers it, then leaves with his group and goes back to Italy, and I'm still waiting for the phone to ring."

"Well. . . ." Dietrich knew what Joe was after, of course. "Okay, okay, I'll contact Washington right away."

"Thank you, sir." Urgency overcame discipline. "In the meantime, wouldn't it be in order for me to get in touch with San Francisco and ask them to check on Abruzzi? Just to kind of keep an eye on him?"

Dietrich grimaced.

"The shipment could be coming in from that end. While we're waiting to get the okay from State, it could all be over."

"Hell!" Dietrich muttered. "All right, go ahead and have San Francisco PD verify Abruzzi's whereabouts. But that's all."

It was enough. Joe sent a telex to SFPD, but instead of a telex back, he got a call. His premonition of disaster was instantly fulfilled when he answered the phone. Abruzzi was gone. According to the local man, Abruzzi had checked into the Mark Hopkins with the rest of the group. He had, however, informed the tour director not to look for him for the various scheduled tours and outings. He had friends in the city and would be spending time with them. The detective had checked Abruzzi's room. It was clean. He hadn't checked out, but had taken his stuff and gone. Did New York want them to put out an APB, and if so, on what charge?

Joe said no, never mind, thanks, and hung up.

It was possible that Abruzzi was actually visiting friends. In that case, he'd turn up for the group flight back to New York. That was why Joe was late getting home on that fifth night after Thanksgiving—he'd gone out to Kennedy to meet the flight and to see for himself whether or not Abruzzi was on it. He wasn't.

When he finally got home that night, Joe was disappointed to find the apartment dark. It wasn't all that

late; he'd been a lot later and found Norah waiting—
in bed maybe, even dozing, but with the lights on and
ready to wake and call out at the first sound he made.
Then he'd go to her, sit at the side of the bed, and
take her, warm and sweet from sleep, into his arms. So
his first reaction to the darkness was alarm and that
flared into fear, but both passed quickly. Every instinct, finely honed by years of association with violence, reassured him—the atmosphere was normal.
Norah was all right. She was just sleeping. Joe was
relieved, then he felt a slight pang—it was the first
time she hadn't waited up for him. He was being un-
reasonable, he told himself. They'd been married two
years now, time to start taking each other for granted.
He closed the door softly, put on the hall light, hung
up his coat. Though he was careful not to disturb her,
he still expected and hoped that Norah would wake
up. But she didn't.

Maybe it's just as well, he thought as he got into his
pajamas. If Norah did wake, she'd sense right away
that he was worried, more so than normal when a case
wasn't going well, and she'd get it out of him. Joe
wasn't ready to tell his wife about the bribe, because
he was no longer as sure as he had been that it concerned merely the incoming heroin. He got into bed
beside her, kissed her hair, then turned over on his
side and went to sleep.

5

BOTH Norah and Joe were so intent on behaving normally the next morning that neither was aware of the other's effort. They left the house together, and usually whoever was to have the use of the car for the day dropped the other off, but Norah was due in court to give evidence and when she suggested she could as easily take the subway, Joe didn't try very hard to dissuade her. Norah hurried down the street, and Joe got into his car—each relieved at having got through the morning without betraying himself.

According to the group itinerary, Carlo Abruzzi was in New York at the time of Johnny Allegro's murder but at Disney World in Florida when Lambroso was shot, and at the time of Nerone's murder he was in San Francisco. Or was he? The group was in those places certainly, but Joe was interested to know just how fully Abruzzi had participated in the scheduled activities in Florida or whether he had, as in San Francisco, gone off on his own. He headed downtown to talk to the tour director.

Robert Oliva was no novice to the tourist business, but experience had not brought assurance. To the contrary. The more groups Oliva escorted, the more he became aware of how much could go wrong. The more sensitive he became to the possible pitfalls, the more nervous in anticipating them. This trip had been the worst—*il colmo!* Commencing with the delayed departure from Rome, the police waiting in New York to take one of his people off, the search for smuggled heroin, the trip had been agony. But it was nearly over. In two days the group would be departing for home. His ordeal was nearly ended.

Oliva was having breakfast in the blessed refuge of his room when the desk called to say that Lieutenant Capretto was on his way up to see him. What now? *Santa Madre di Dio!* What further disaster was there left that had not already befallen them? By the time Joe knocked at his door, the harassed man had convinced himself that the police were not going to permit the departure. He couldn't stand that. It was too much. He would resign!

It took nearly all of Joe's considerable tact to soothe Robert Oliva and to assure him that there was no question of even delaying the departure.

Oliva calmed down. He wanted to cooperate, he told the lieutenant, but he couldn't be held responsible for the activities of individual members. . . .

Of course not. Certainly not. All he wanted was information, Joe explained.

Oliva's plaint continued. The group was too large, too large. He'd told them at the agency before starting. Forty should be the maximum; usually forty was the maximum. But seventy-seven people! It was unheard of. Did the lieutenant have any idea of the logistics involved in moving seventy-seven people around in a foreign country?

"At the least I should have had an assistant, at the very least. I don't see how you can expect me to remember just who turned up and who didn't for every individual activity on the trip, Lieutenant. You can't reasonably expect it!" he reiterated, his agitation swelling once again.

"You must make a head count each time you go out on sightseeing or nightclub tours or optional excursions. You'd keep a list, wouldn't you, particularly of the optional excursions because of the extra charges?"

"*Certo, certo,* yes, of course. The lists, every night, the lists and the accounts. Too much. Too much."

"Could we just take a look at those lists together?" Joe suggested.

Fortunately Oliva was better organized than his agitation indicated. It took awhile, but between them they were able to draw up a separate schedule of the activities in which Abruzzi had participated. There were enough gaps in it to make it possible for him to have returned to New York at each of the pertinent times. He could have killed Vito Lambroso and returned to Disney World. Nerone's murder occurred the day after the group arrived in San Francisco; Abruzzi had plenty of time to make that flight.

Joe considered Carlo Abruzzi. The alleged drug courier was no young punk, but a man of years and substance. Not handsome but with plenty of . . . Joe searched for the right word and came up with the Spanish *machismo*. He was reminded of the late opera star Ezio Pinza, who in singing "Some Enchanted Evening" to Mary Martin had restored hope to every man over fifty. Also, Joe recalled how well Abruzzi had handled himself when he was taken off the plane on arrival, with just the right balance of indignation at being searched and tolerance toward the *tenente* (Joe), who was only doing his job. Grudgingly the *tenente* had to admit the man had style and, it now appeared, brains too. The drug market being nearly dry, he comes with a shipment large enough to give him virtual control. The Nerone organization hears about it and decides to stop it. They leak the information. Abruzzi loses the shipment and pays them off. Why not?

Sending for copies of Abruzzi's passport picture would take time; meanwhile Joe drew up a description of the missing man and supervised an indentikit drawing. Then he went to the inspector, and Dietrich gave him the go-ahead.

The drawing and description were circulated, and for the two days prior to the Italian tourists' departure a close watch was kept over all airports, particularly those in the New York area. Every passenger leaving the country was scrutinized. Everyone entering was thoroughly checked. Baggage inspection took hours. The backup was horrendous; the complaints were vociferous. Doggedly the customs officials continued their meticulous inspection. The second shipment of heroin was not found; neither was Carlo Abruzzi.

Joe waited to be contacted about the bribe. No call came. He decided the intensified security at the airports was considered his answer. He sighed; he'd been sighing a lot lately.

The Italians assembled for the flight back home.

There was little reason to hope Abruzzi would show up at Kennedy to rejoin the group, but just the same, Joe, his team, and an additional complement of plainclothesmen and Port Authority police covered the terminal and watched the departure gate. Oliva was frantic. Once again he called the consulate to ensure departure. With the consular officer, Aldo Donato, at his side, Joe checked every member of the party against the entry manifest.

The plane took off with one missing.

So now Abruzzi was in the country illegally. What should have been a routine alert by Immigration became a manhunt. What bothered Joe was that he and the team wouldn't be chasing Abruzzi, that he wouldn't have connected the man to the murders but for the bribe offer. He had the uneasy feeling that he was being manipulated.

Norah put the Janus business firmly out of her mind. She had made her decision. It was the right one—she was not meant to adopt. Thanksgiving past, she got ready for Christmas. Now that she was married there was a lot more to do, more presents to buy, more packages to wrap, more festivities to attend. First the whole family would go to midnight Mass at St. Pat's —they had already applied for their eighteen tickets. It was Elisabetta's turn to cook the Christmas dinner. Norah had offered, but was told it was done in strict rotation: Elisabetta was number four, so there were three more sisters before it would come around to

Norah. Anyhow, both she and Joe would be working a regular tour on Christmas day.

Norah particularly enjoyed shopping for the children in the Capretto family and for her brother's children. They were of various ages, but this year she found herself lingering in the infants' section of the stores. She spent more time and more thought selecting just the right cuddly bunnies and bears and floppy rag dolls than ever before.

The week before Christmas, on her day off, her father called and asked her to stop by.

"Dad, I've still got so much shopping to do," she protested.

"It's important or I wouldn't ask."

"There's nothing wrong, is there?"

"No, no," he hastened to reassure her. "Everything's fine, wonderful, in fact. Actually, there's somebody else coming over. Somebody I want you to meet."

"Oh? Who?"

"Around two o'clock. Can you come over around two?"

Right in the middle of the day! Norah sighed. "Okay, Dad. Sure. I'll see you at two."

Now what was he up to? Norah wondered. He'd sounded happy and excited, so whatever it was, it was good. One of her brothers in town for the holidays? No, he would have told her that right out. He'd said he wanted her to meet someone. In the old days, before she was married, Patrick Mulcahaney had had a disconcerting habit of turning up impossible boyfriends for her, but he'd hardly be doing that now. All during her morning's shopping, pushing through the crowded stores, Norah wondered. Who in the world did he want her to meet?

There was a bright glow in Patrick Mulcahaney's eyes as he let his daughter into the apartment. Norah noticed there was also a slight twitch in his welcoming smile and his hands were cold. He was nervous. Suddenly that made Norah nervous too.

"What's it all about, Dad?"

He led her into the living room. "I want you to meet Mark."

Mark was a little boy, a sturdy toddler of about three or three and a half. He had light brown, straight hair, an unruly shock of which fell forward, nearly hiding large brown eyes. He was dressed in a neat white shirt and long pants that were the bottom half of a snowsuit. He was standing in the middle of the living room regarding Norah gravely, shy but at the same time self-possessed.

"Mark, this is Norah."

The child walked toward her and held out his hand.

Norah felt all her strength drain away. There was a loud humming in her ears that almost caused her to lose balance. Her cheeks burned; her whole body burned. She wanted to turn on her father and vent on him all the accumulated frustrations and disappointments of the past weeks. But she couldn't ignore the child's outstretched hand. She took it. It was warm and incredibly small and fragile. She held it gently.

"Hello, Mark." Then quickly she let it go.

"Mark and I spend our Saturdays together," Mulcahaney explained, watching Norah carefully. "We thought, today being so nice and bright, that we'd go over to the zoo. We thought maybe you'd like to come with us."

"No." Norah was afraid that if she so much as looked at her father, she'd burst into tears, so she kept her eyes on the boy and saw that he flinched at her tone and turned to Mulcahaney instinctively for his protection. "I'm sorry," Norah amended hastily. "I'd like to come with you, Mark, but I'm very busy this afternoon."

The boy nodded.

Used to disappointments, Norah thought instantly. "Where do you live, Mark?" She wanted to gloss over the rejection.

"The Children's Institute of Manhattan."

The way he recited it, precisely as he must have

been taught just in case he should ever get lost, touched Norah, dissipating her anger. "Oh, Dad, you shouldn't have done this," she murmured softly.

"Why not, sweetheart? Why not?"

The tears would not be held back any longer. Norah shook her head and ran for the kitchen, pulling the swinging door shut behind her. Alone, she sobbed.

Her father followed almost immediately. He was shocked. Norah hadn't cried like this since her mother's death. He kept his voice low both to soothe her and to avoid alarming the child in the other room.

"I'm sorry, darlin'. I had no idea you'd take it like this. I never would have sprung Mark on you if I'd had any idea. . . . I would have prepared you first. I'm sorry, truly sorry, sweetheart."

"I don't understand what you're doing with this boy," she cried out. "Where did you get him?"

"I've joined a volunteer grandparents program. A lot of the foundling homes have it. You're assigned a particular child and you spend time with him, visit him, take him out, take him to your own home. The idea is for the child to have a personal relationship with an adult and to get a taste of life outside the institution."

"When did you start doing this? Why?"

"Why not?" He shrugged. "I've got time on my hands. There's not much politicking over at the district club in an off year. I can't be hanging out at Houlihan's all day, so . . . why not?" he repeated.

"Come on, Dad. . . ."

"All right, all right. I thought maybe adopting might be a solution to your . . . problem. I thought that the best way to get you to consider adopting was to—"

"I've been trying for weeks to find a baby! Weeks. I've been everywhere, seen everyone. I'd given up. I'd resigned myself, and now you show me this boy. . . . It's not fair."

Mulcahaney was stricken. He should have guessed, he told himself. No, he should have known that Norah would ponder what he'd said to her at the anniversary, party and that, being Norah, she would act. "You could have told me you were interested in adopting." He bristled. "Why didn't you tell me?"

Norah sniffed away the tears. "For the same reason you didn't tell me what you were up to, I suppose."

They looked at each other. Mulcahaney held out his arms and his daughter went into them. He held her. These moments of physical closeness were rare, but both cherished them.

"But then it's all right, sweetheart. Everything's okay. You can have Mark. You can have him as soon as you want."

Norah pulled away. "What's wrong with him?"

"Nothing's wrong with him."

"There has to be something wrong or he wouldn't be available. I know."

"He's three and a half years old; that's what's wrong with him. The women all want infants. He's too old." Mulcahaney answered bitterly.

Norah shook her head. "There has to be something else."

"No, I swear it, no." But his daughter's level look was too much. Mulcahaney took a deep breath. "His mother was an addict."

"So he was born addicted."

"Yes. And that puts people off. But it shouldn't make any difference to you—you know there's no medical basis for the fear that a baby born addicted has any special disposition toward addiction in later life."

Norah said nothing.

"Don't hold it against the boy."

"It's not that." Norah bit her lip.

"What, then? What?"

Norah was very still, then she said in a low voice, "I'm afraid they won't give him to me."

"Oh, my blessed girl!" Mulcahaney exclaimed. "Do you think I would have brought the boy to you if I hadn't make sure first that you could have him if you wanted him? Sweetheart, come on, dry your eyes.

Let's have a nice cup of tea. Then come to the zoo
with us, spend the afternoon, get to know Mark. Give
him a chance. Give yourself a chance."

"I want him, but you have to want him too," Norah
insisted.

Joe was unprepared for her intensity, for the flood
of maternal yearning. When Norah had suggested that
they wait a year before starting a family, he had readily agreed. That first year alone was important to
both of them. However, though he'd never admit it to
Norah, he was deeply disturbed that she hadn't conceived since going off the pill. That was why, without
saying anything to her, he'd gone for the checkup. He
did believe that his wife wanted children as much as
he did. If he misjudged her sincerity in this, then he
misjudged Norah herself, and Joe was very sure he did
not. Still, he considered himself the more eager; after
all, a child would change the outward tenor of his life
very little, but it would drastically disrupt Norah's.
Outwardly she appeared totally self-sufficient. On the
job she was eager and outgoing, but privately Norah
was cautious about committing herself.

During the two years of their marriage Norah had
become less guarded of her emotions, yet Joe was surprised at her decision to adopt. Was she doing it for
his sake? Looking at her tremulous face, Joe realized
that she was searching for her own fulfillment. He felt
a tremendous relief. Now he could pray to God with a
whole heart and no reservation that he might be able
to give her a child of their own. Meantime. . . .

"I want a son," Joe said.

Though the adoption was not yet final, Mark was
to be permitted to spend Christmas with his prospective parents. Norah thought that the tumult of the full
Capretto family celebration would be too much for
him, and Joe agreed. They excused themselves.

Signora Emilia received the news of the intended
adoption with dismay. No one in her family had ever

adopted a child; no one had ever needed to. She kept her feelings to herself, but she was deeply disappointed in Norah, though she had to admit grudgingly that the girl was showing good faith in trying to provide a family in the only way she could. So Signora Emilia argued that they should come to the family dinner and bring the child.

"So we can all meet him," she said. The words made a bad taste in her mouth.

Joe remained adamant. "Later, Mamma, when the papers are final, you can come here."

Now everything that Norah did in preparation for the holiday took on added significance. She would have liked to buy out the stores, but it was decided that Mark should have one gift from each of them—Joe, herself, her father, who was going to join them —more might overexcite him.

On Christmas morning they went to pick him up. Mark was waiting in the supervisor's office. He seemed very small in the big leather armchair, eyes bright with a mixture of eagerness and uncertainty. He clutched three gaily wrapped packages. Norah knew instantly that they were his gifts for them. She knew too that Miss Price, the caseworker, was responsible, that she had helped him either to buy them or make them, but just the same . . . just the same. . . .

The day did not go easily. Mark was well behaved, too much so. He seemed to be holding back as though, and Norah felt another twinge around her heart, as though he were afraid to let himself be happy. How long had he been at the institute? she wondered. How many times had he been looked over, considered, rejected? She wanted to take him into her arms, hug him, reassure him, but she was afraid to frighten him with too much love too suddenly. She kept her distance. Even Joe was at times overly hearty and at others overly casual.

They were both glad they'd decided to ask Norah's father over. As soon as Patrick Mulcahaney arrived, Mark's eyes brightened and his smile was real.

The gifts were exchanged. Norah had asked the salesgirl's advice as to what a three-year-old boy might like, then ended up following her own instinct. For herself she'd chosen a black and white, plushy, cuddly, stuffed dog. For Joe, a red fire engine that when wound up went scuttling around clanging its bell. Gravely Mark unwrapped the gifts. For a moment his eyes lit up, then he thanked them politely and set the toys carefully aside. Norah was deeply disappointed; she should have taken the salesgirl's advice and got a couple of those educational things she'd touted so highly. Her father had been smarter; he brought a game—a kind of miniature bowling alley—and while she cooked the Christmas turkey, she could hear him and Joe and the boy laughing delightedly.

The strain returned when it was time to take Mark back. Fumbling clumsily, Norah helped him into his snowsuit. When they were ready to leave, it was Joe who discovered the toys in the corner.

"Don't you want your presents, Mark?"

His brown eyes opened wide. He looked from Joe to her, then back again. "Can I take them with me?"

"Of course, they're yours."

Joe put the game back into its box and then into a shopping bag along with the fire engine, but Mark hugged the stuffed dog close. Norah's hopes soared.

The ride back to the institute was quiet but much less awkward than it had been on the way out. They turned Mark back to the matron, assuring him over and over again that they would see him very soon. Back outside, Norah and Joe looked at each other.

"What do you think?" Norah asked.

"I think he needs us. And we need him."

Like everyone else, Lieutenant and Mrs. Capretto had to submit to investigation into their fitness for parenthood. However, as the adoption was to be a private one, the social worker who called on them at their home was less disposed to carp over Norah's housekeeping and those who probed their economic and moral background less finicky than they might have been if the adoption were being handled through a public agency or if Joe had been in another line of work. The lawyer for the Children's Institute handled the paperwork. All Norah and Joe had to do was make a brief appearance in court—it couldn't have taken more than five minutes—and Mark was theirs. To Norah, after the disheartening rounds of the various agencies when she was trying to locate a child, the whole thing was a breeze.

Mark came to live with them on January 5. The sixth is the feast of the three kings, "little Christmas." Traditionally on the sixth the three kings come to the Christ Child bearing gifts, and in many countries, particularly the Latin ones, that is when presents are exchanged. So Norah thought of Mark as a gift for her and Joe. He came carrying a small suitcase packed with two sets of underclothes, two shirts, two pairs of socks; with what he was wearing, that made three of everything. He also had a robe, two pairs of pajamas, one pair of rompers, washcloth, toothbrush, comb. The toys she and Joe had given him at Christmas were the only toys he had.

Norah had moved the dining table out into the hall and fixed up the room with a child's bed, a chest of drawers, and a toy box that she vowed inwardly would soon be full. She'd arranged to take a week off so that Mark wouldn't have to go to the day-care center right at the start. But after the first flurry of settling him in, she didn't know what to do with him.

Unfortunately, with the search for Abruzzi in full swing, Joe couldn't take time off to be with them. Maybe if he had it would have been easier. As it was, the child continued obedient but passive. Norah took him shopping, to the zoo; she took him to the puppet show down in the Village just as her mother had taken her when she was a child. As long as they were engaged in some definite activity, everything was fine. Back home again, when they were alone, the awkwardness returned.

With Mark in bed and asleep, getting ready for bed themselves but with their door open so that they could hear him if he needed anything, Norah appealed to her husband. "I can't reach him. He sits wherever I put him; he plays with whatever toys I hand him, but he doesn't initiate anything."

"Maybe he senses the strain in you," Joe suggested. "Try to relax with him; try to be normal."

"I do; I am," she insisted.

"You're very cool, almost detached, with the boy."

"I don't want to force myself on him. I want him to come to me of his own free will, the way he does with Dad."

"Your father shows his love; you don't."

"Maybe I should ask for another week off?"

Joe considered. "No, I don't think so. The sooner he gets into the regular routine, the way things are going to be, the better. Maybe you're together too much."

Norah sighed. "I just wonder . . . have we done the right thing?"

Joe got into bed beside her. "We have. Believe it." He drew her close, and they fell asleep in each other's arms.

The next Monday on her way to work, Norah dropped Mark off at the day-care center. She had carefully explained to him that he would be going there each day and that each night she would come and pick him up and take him home again. He looked forlorn when she handed him over, but he went with the sister without a word, without so much as a backward glance at Norah. As she watched the sturdy little figure march stoically off, Norah wondered if he'd believed what she'd told him or whether he thought he was being given away again.

She had the answer when she called for him that afternoon. When Mark spotted her across the big playroom, he stopped bouncing his ball and stood absolutely still, just staring at her. Then suddenly he dropped the ball, broke into a run, and came charging across the room to throw himself at her.

"Norah! Norah!" he cried and wrapped his arms around her legs and buried his face against her slacks and clung to her.

She crouched down and hugged him and kissed him and then hugged him some more. When they were both a little calmer, she went with Mark into the cloakroom and helped him into his outer pants and coat without any fumbling at all. Then she took her son home.

Norah could hardly wait to share her happiness with Joe. The phone rang. It would be him to say he was on his way. She decided she wouldn't tell him over the telephone. She would wait till he was home so she could describe in detail just how Mark had looked when he saw her, how he'd come running, how he'd clung to her.

"Hello?"

"Mrs. Capretto?"

"Yes. Who's this?"

"How's the boy? How's Mark?"

The voice was a man's, low, harsh, uncultured.

"Who is this?"

"I have a message for your husband."

"Who is this?" Norah kept insisting.

"Tell the lieutenant that the adoption won't stand up. Tell him if he wants to keep the kid, he should lay off."

Norah choked, swallowed, cleared her throat. "Whoever you are, mister, forget it," she replied coldly. "Mark is ours. The adoption is absolutely legal. We have the papers to prove it."

"Papers don't mean much, Mrs. Capretto. Think about it and be sure to give the lieutenant my message."

"You listen to me, mister. There's no way those papers could be fakes. No way."

But the caller had already hung up.

6

NORAH'S indignation had been instinctive; when she told the caller that the adoption was valid, she believed it. Afterward she began to wonder. She rushed to the strongbox and got out all the documents. They looked all right; they were all right, had to be —the institute had handled everything and the institute was okay. She'd checked it out first thing, naturally. It was duly licensed; it had a good reputation. Norah and Joe had appeared in surrogate court, and the judge had duly awarded Mark to them. Where was the fraud? Where was the flaw?

There was none. Norah's next thought was to thank God that she hadn't accepted the baby Dr. Janus had offered, that she had resisted that temptation. If she was so frightened now, how would she have felt knowing that the threat had a real basis? Nevertheless, she was shaken. She knew everything was all right, but she waited for Joe to come home and assure her.

But he didn't. The thing hit Joe too suddenly for him to be able to cover his shock.

There had been no follow-up to the bribe offer. He had waited, expecting he hardly knew what. He was careful in traffic, avoided dark alleys, and kept his anxiety from Norah—which was the hardest of all. Abruzzi had disappeared without a trace, and the weeks passed. Joe reasoned that by now the second heroin shipment must have come in, been picked up, and passed on. He'd just about convinced himself that he was off the hook, and now this!

"Joe?" Norah appealed to him. "It's only a bluff, isn't it?"

From the beginning Joe had sensed that the bribe was merely a feeler, an advance notice. Now he knew why the next move had been so long in coming: They had been investigating him, looking for a weakness, a point of vulnerability. And they'd found it.

"Joe?"

"We'll have to make sure."

Oh, God, Norah thought, blessed Lord! "How close are you to breaking the case?" she asked.

"About where I was the day I was appointed."

"You must be on the verge of something, something big. . . ."

"I wish to God I knew what it could be."

"Think, sweetheart, think."

"*Santa Maria Vergine!* I am thinking. That Abruzzi character has vanished. If I hadn't seen him myself and talked to him myself, I'd be willing to believe he never existed." Joe's frustration exploded.

"Abruzzi . . ." Norah repeated. "I assumed the call referred to the Nerone killings. Could the two be connected? Have you thought of that?"

"I have. I even had copies of Abruzzi's passport photo run off; that's how desperate I am. I showed them to Miss Martinelli and the bodyguard and the doorman of her building. Nothing. The team's been running around with the photo showing it to the witnesses in the Lambroso shooting. Nothing there either."

"But that's it!" Norah cried out. "Don't you see, love? Abruzzi can't know you haven't got an ID from any of these people. He figures you've made him on the murder rap."

Joe frowned. "It could be."

"Sure. It has to be. He figures you've made him on all counts and he has to stop you."

"Except that I can't find him."

Norah had no answer to that. They both fell silent.

"The man on the phone—did he have an accent?" Joe asked.

"He said so little, but . . . I don't think so."

"Abruzzi has a very marked accent."

"Somebody could have made the call for him."

"Could be." The same man who had called and offered the bribe? He hadn't had an accent either. Joe looked squarely at his wife. "What do you want me to do? Should I ask to be relieved?"

"No, oh, no!" she cried out in dismay.

She hadn't thought it out, Joe told himself, and to make a fair judgment she should know all the facts. "This isn't the first try to get me off the case. I was offered a bribe back in November. At the time, Dietrich suggested replacing me. I wish to God I'd taken him up on it. If I had, this wouldn't have happened."

Norah put her arms around him and nestled her head against his shoulder. "How could you have imagined a thing like this? We didn't even have Mark then." Pity for him, for the strain he had been under, made her pretend a confidence she didn't really feel. "Anyhow, it's a bluff. We know the adoption is okay. Nobody can take Mark from us." Her eyes flashed. "They're trying to scare us, but we won't let them scare us. I say we ride it out."

"You're willing to take that chance?"

"The court accepted the documents. They have to be okay."

"Unless the flaw goes further back."

Norah turned pale. "To the mother? You think the mother wants him back?"

"She has six months to change her mind," Joe reminded her. "She has six months before the adoption becomes final." She looked so stricken that he added, "Maybe we should try to find out where the institute got Mark."

"This afternoon, when I went to pick him up at the day-care center, he came running to me. For the first time *he* came to *me*. He threw his arms around me and clung to me."

"So, *cara*, let's make sure about him, eliminate any possible doubt."

"You're right; of course, you're right." It wasn't

what Norah had been waiting to hear. She'd wanted Joe to tell her there was nothing to worry about. "I just don't see why they're doing this to us. What's the point? If you do retire from the case, somebody else will take your place. He'll have all the information you have. What does Abruzzi or the people behind him have to gain by getting rid of you?"

"That's the question," Joe said quietly. "They wouldn't go to all this trouble for nothing." He sighed. His first reaction to Norah's news, after the initial shock, had been relief—bad as it was, at least he was facing a known danger and could start to rally his defenses. His second reaction, almost simultaneous with the first, had been excitement—the case was opening up! Now that he was calmer, the full ramifications of the threat became evident. And they were staggering. He knew Norah hadn't thought of them yet, but she would sooner or later.

"Unless we make sure, one hundred percent, that Mark is ours, that the adoption cannot be overturned, we'll wonder about it for the rest of our lives. Every time the phone rings or a stranger comes to the door, we'll cringe. Do you want to live like that? Don't you think that after a while, when he's older, Mark will sense how we feel? Don't you think he's entitled to the security of a legal identity?"

Norah gasped.

Joe laid it on the line. "As long as we're not sure, as long as there's any doubt at all in our own minds, we're vulnerable. We may ride out this blackmail attempt, but there'll be others. Inevitably. They'd start out easy—ask one or the other of us to overlook a piece of evidence, later to suppress it; manipulate a lineup; go easy on an interrogation. You know the possibilities. Soon they'd own us. Both of us."

"But if we don't let ourselves be used. If we refuse. . . ."

"You're overlooking the biggest hold of all; *they* can inform on *us.*" Joe paused to let it sink in. "All it would take would be a phone call to Captain Felix or Inspector Dietrich suggesting that we're holding back or shading our reports in order to protect our adopted son and neither of us could ever be trusted again. We might as well quit the force now."

Norah took a deep breath. "All right. So we have to find out everything about Mark. We'll apply to the court for a look at his records."

"As the adoptive parents, the court will not allow us to see them."

"But under the circumstances. . . ."

"No. We're too deeply, too personally involved. It means too much to us. We have to turn the whole thing over to the Child Welfare League. Let them—"

"No!"

"They can be objective; we can't. A lawyer doesn't handle his own case; a doctor doesn't treat his own family."

"No."

"The Child Welfare people are experts. They know all the dodges, all the loopholes. We're beginners in this field; we'll flounder around, waste time."

"They'll take Mark away from us!" Norah cried.

"Of course they won't. Why should they?"

"If they find an illegality. . . ."

"We'll correct it—that's the idea, isn't it?" Though he spoke calmly, Norah's fears communicated themselves to Joe. "After all, we did act in good faith. Whatever may be wrong is not our fault. The court will certainly take that into consideration."

"Maybe. Maybe not. We could lose Mark. I won't take the chance. I won't do it, Joe." Tears welled up in Norah's blue eyes, but her chin was stubbornly set.

Joe knew the signs and what they meant, but just this once she was going to have to give in. "The worst that can happen is that they'll take Mark and keep him while the case is being adjudicated."

"And what's that going to do to him? Have you thought of that?" Norah demanded. "He's just beginning to feel secure; what will he think if we let him be taken away? He won't know the reason; he won't understand. Oh, God! Why did they have to choose this particular day, this particular moment?"

Joe wavered. In trying to resolve the dilemma he had been thinking only in terms of what it meant to Norah and to him. He had not considered the child. In the short time Mark had been with them he had become a part of their lives, but only a part. In Mark's life, he and Norah were everything. What would he think if he were taken away? How could he understand? Naturally he'd survive; he'd be fed and clothed and sheltered, and Joe was certain they'd get him back again—but how long before Mark felt safe once more, if ever? Danger, physical and moral, was a constant presence for them; they accepted it when they accepted the job, but Mark wasn't being given a choice. Norah was right: they couldn't inform the Child Welfare people till every other possibility had been exhausted.

"Okay," he said. "Miss Price has already told us as much about Mark's background as is permitted. We know his mother is an addict, that she didn't want to relinquish her son but was in no condition to care for him. So he was placed in a foster home while she tried to straighten herself out. Unfortunately she couldn't stay clean and so finally she had no choice but to give him up. Obviously we now have to know more. It could be that the mother changed her mind. I think it's more likely that someone got hold of her and prevailed on her to change her mind—as an addict she'd certainly be vulnerable to pressure. We also have to know something about the foster parents. It could be the threat is coming through them."

"I'll go back to the institute and talk to Miss Price. I'll explain the situation. I'm sure she'll cooperate."

"Good. Explain it to the captain too and ask him for some free time."

"Right."

"And *cara*. . . ." Joe hesitated.

Norah took a deep breath. "I know. You have to report the call."

He kissed her quickly, then turned away so that she wouldn't see how deeply disturbed he was. They should not have used the boy! The rage in him grew. Whoever was responsible, Abruzzi or the mob, was going to pay for that.

Captain James Felix's eyes were somber, his long lean face sympathetic as he listened to Norah. She had worked for him first as an undercover officer in a series of murders involving young widows. When she made detective, she had been assigned to his command and had been there ever since. He respected and admired her. What's more, he liked her. His association with Capretto went back over ten years. Joe had been his sergeant when Felix was a lieutenant.

"I have to go with you on this," Felix told Norah. "I think you should apply to the surrogate court for permission to examine the sealed records. I think it's the logical and direct way. I think the court will grant your request. But if you need added clout, just call on me. Call on me for any help you need."

While she waited for her request to be processed, Norah called on the head of the Children's Institute of Manhattan. Ida Malverne was a comfortable, open-faced woman accustomed to keeping calm in the face of emotional clients. It seemed to Norah as she told her story tersely that Mrs. Malverne was taking it very lightly.

"Ridiculous, Mrs. Capretto, I assure you. The boy is yours. You have nothing to worry about." She smiled blandly.

Her condescension riled Norah. "Have you ever had this kind of problem before, Mrs. Malverne? Have any of your adoptive parents been blackmailed?"

Mrs. Malverne drew herself up. Her matronly bosom overhung the desk and heaved with indignation. Her eyes fixed coldly on Norah.

"That is an ugly word, Mrs. Capretto. I reject it and your insinuation absolutely."

"I didn't intend to imply that you were personally involved. . . ."

"In all my years of social work, Mrs. Capretto, in all the hundreds of adoptions handled by this agency, you are the first one to come in here and question my good faith."

Now she'd antagonized the woman, Norah thought. She hadn't meant to. She was handling it badly, ineptly. She'd hit too hard, too soon. Maybe Joe was right and she was too personally involved to do the job. She must calm down, be cool, objective. "I'm sorry, Mrs. Malverne. I apologize. I had no intention of questioning your good faith, believe me. But it is possible that whoever turned Mark over to you did not have the legal right to do so."

Mrs. Malverne was not satisfied. "So now you're suggesting we were careless."

"No."

"That we were inept, then, that we don't know our business, that we let ourselves be hoodwinked."

Norah groaned inwardly. She acknowledged that she had been less than tactful, but she thought that the woman was overreacting. The question was how to soothe her and regain control of the interview.

"That's what it amounts to," Mrs. Malverne insisted.

"I'm sorry."

"Well. . . ." Norah's abjectness slowed the tirade but didn't stop it. "The answer is categorically—no: We were not careless; we did not fail in our responsibilities. We thoroughly investigate the people we deal with. Every child has been legally relinquished by his natural mother before we offer him for adoption. I suggest, Mrs. Capretto, that your problem stems not from our end but from yours, from the sensitiveness of your husband's occupation. And that is something

I cannot help you with. I can only tell you again that you have nothing to worry about—the boy is yours. If you get any more threats, and personally I don't think you will, just tell your caller to produce his evidence. I promise you he won't be able to."

Norah couldn't help but be impressed by her cool assurance, and under other circumstances it might have been enough. "May I see Mark's file?" she asked, but meekly, so as not to bring on another outburst.

Evidently she had struck the right note at last. Mrs. Malverne, having asserted her position, proclaimed her integrity, and thoroughly cowed Norah—she thought—now returned to her earlier condescending manner. "Now, Mrs. Capretto, you know better than that. You know that adoptive parents are not permitted information regarding a child's origins."

Norah was very careful to keep her tone conciliatory. "I don't think you realize how serious this is, what this threat means to us not only as Mark's parents but as police officers. We have to know about Mark. We have to be sure in our minds—" Norah forestalled the interruption. "Please, I've come to you unofficially, as Mark's mother, to ask your help."

"And I would like to help you, but I cannot open my files to you," Ida Malverne stated with finality.

Norah clenched her teeth. She'd apologized, she'd tried to mollify the woman. "I've applied for a court order to examine the records."

"Then why come to me?"

"To save time."

The head of the agency sat back. "I think you expect to be turned down."

"The juvenile authorities will certainly have access to Mark's file," Norah countered. "I could turn the whole matter over to them and ask them to make a thorough investigation of the institute at the same time. Naturally, I'd prefer not to do that—for Mark's sake."

That hit home.

A deep frown corrugated Ida Malverne's placid

brow; her heavily ringed fingers tapped nervously on
the desk blotter. "What you ask is highly irregular.
But I can see that you are deeply disturbed, so . . .
under the circumstances and just to put your mind at
rest, as you are, after all, a police officer. . . ." She
sighed, got up, and went around to the file cabinets
along the wall.

Mark's file was not there.

She picked through the folders in the drawer a
second time. Though she still couldn't find it, she
didn't appear at all upset. "Probably Miss Bunnell has
it," she said, returning to her desk, where she picked
up the phone. "Ah, Miss Bunnell . . . I'm looking for
the file on the Capretto adoption. Perhaps you have
it?" When she spoke again her voice had a slight edge.
"I am aware that you did not handle the case, Miss
Bunnell, but the file is not in central records; therefore it's probably still in your office. Will you take a
look, please? I'll hold." While she waited, Ida Malverne explained to Norah. "Miss Bunnell has been out
sick, so naturally she's not familiar with your case."

"It was Miss Price, Miss Janet Price, who handled
it."

"Yes, I know who handled your case, Mrs. Capretto.
Janet Price was replacing Miss Bunnell. Naturally
when Miss Bunnell returned. . . ." She broke off. "It's
not there? It has to be. Look again."

Norah knew Miss Bunnell wouldn't find it. The file
was gone. Up to now Norah had held to the hope that
the blackmail threat was a mere bluff. Now she knew
it was real, that they could lose Mark, and she felt a
terrible, cold emptiness.

"You're positive?" Mrs. Malverne demanded over the
phone. "You've looked everywhere? Now, now, Miss
Bunnell, there's no need to get flustered; nobody's
blaming you; nobody's saying it's your fault. . . ." She
listened a while longer to the protestations, then lost
patience. "Stop sniveling, Emmeline. I'll get back to
you later." She slammed down the receiver. It took a

few seconds for her to recover herself, but she managed quite successfully.

"It would appear that Miss Price took the file with her, by mistake, of course. There's no cause for concern. I will contact Miss Price. As soon as I have the file, I'll let you know."

It wasn't good enough for Norah. "How long was Miss Price with you?"

"I told you—during the period that Miss Bunnell was out sick, a little over a month."

"And how did you come to employ her?"

Ida Malverne answered confidently. "Miss Bunnell recommended her."

"I see. Was she qualified?"

"Certainly. Miss Bunnell would not have recommended her and I would not have taken her on otherwise. She is fully licensed."

"Isn't it odd for such a person to be willing to take a temporary job?"

"A few years ago it would have been, yes; there was a shortage of qualified people in the social field. Today there is an over-supply. So much so that some of the schools for social child-care workers are shutting down. Also, Miss Price had just recently arrived in New York and hadn't got herself situated. She took the job partly as a favor to Miss Bunnell."

"I see. Do you have Miss Price's address?"

"Certainly I have her address." Ida Malverne now regarded Norah with open hostility. "I really don't appreciate your attitude, Mrs. Capretto. We cooperated with you in every way so you could get your child as expeditiously as possible. Now you barge in here suggesting . . . well, at the least, that we were inexcusably careless."

Norah could see that the agency head was worried and that she was trying to justify herself.

"You intimate that I have been somehow irresponsible in selection of staff," Ida Malverne continued.

"You don't think it's odd that Miss Price, a temporary employee, took Mark's file with her?"

"I've explained that she must have done so accidentally. I've told you that I will contact her and that as soon as I do—"

"Why not give me her address and let me get in touch with her?"

"The file belongs in my records. I'll get it back."

"I don't think you can, Mrs. Malverne," Norah told her quietly. "You've been used."

Mrs. Malverne resisted for one more long moment, then abruptly she reached for a small metal box on top of the desk, fingered through it for a particular card, and copied what was written there. She handed the slip of paper to Norah.

Norah took it, folded it, and slipped it between the pages of her notebook. "Thank you. Now, I'll also need a list of your past adoptions going back . . . let's say a year. The names and addresses of the adoptive parents. . . ."

"I can't give you that! What do you need it for? It's got nothing to do with your case. It's out of the question."

"If Janet Price is behind the threat to us, she may have also copied names from your master files and may approach others. If she's innocent, then I promise you I won't use the list. You have my word, Mrs. Malverne."

"You don't understand. . . . I have to explain to you. . . . You see, from time to time I accepted . . . additional fees to expedite . . . where the need was great, on the part of the child as well as the parents . . . and only when the parents could afford it. Oh, Lord, it sounds terrible, but it isn't. Why shouldn't those who have the means pay a little more? We are government-funded in part, but only in part. We receive a certain sum per child per month, but we do not deny a child a permanent home just to hang onto that money. We do not farm a child out to a foster home just to retain the so-called administrative over-

head for that child either. But the money has to come
from somewhere."

Mrs. Malverne continued to plead her position. "You
have no idea what it all costs. Salaries for really qualified people, medical care for the children, mainte-
nance for the building. . . . Why, only last month the
service staff went on strike for higher pay! I had to
go in the kitchen and cook myself. We have to get the
money where we can. In each case the people were
more than willing to make an additional contribution.
That's what it was, a contribution."

"Were there any follow-up requests for money after
adoption?" Norah asked.

Ida Malverne groaned. "We have a yearly fund drive
and we circularize the people who have adopted
through us," she admitted.

"As long as the contributions are voluntary. . . ."

"They are, oh, yes, they are, I assure you, I swear to
you there's no pressure of any kind."

"Then you have nothing to worry about—on that
score. As for money being paid to expedite an adoption, you know that's illegal. Naturally each case
would have to be judged on its individual merits."

Ida Malverne covered her face with her hands.

Norah acknowledged that the pressures on the
agency head were great and she was willing to grant
that she hadn't acted for personal gain. "Of course, the
parents involved would have to bring charges. If they
don't, then no action can be taken against you. I'm
sure you know that."

"But if you tell them, if you urge them. . . ."

"I don't want to cause trouble or sorrow for anybody, Mrs. Malverne. All I want is whatever information you have on our son."

"I don't have any. There are so many children, so
many. I can't remember details about each one. I
would have to see the file."

"While I wouldn't want to distress your clients, I
would be bound to inform them that they are not
obligated to make any further contributions to your

fund drives." Norah applied more pressure. "In fact, I suggest that you make it inescapably clear in future circularizations that contributions are strictly voluntary."

"I don't know anything about your son!" Ida Malverne cried out, revealing the real reason and the fear behind the resistance and antagonism. "I don't know where he came from. Janet Price brought the boy in. She made all the arrangements. She handled all the details."

The address Ida Malverne had given Norah was legitimate. Janet Price lived there, but she wasn't there now. According to the doorman of the building, she was on vacation.

"When did she leave?" Norah asked.

"About a week ago."

Some doormen knew every detail of every tenant's private life; apparently this one just put in his time— he held the doors, carried the packages, and collected his tips. Too bad. "Can you be a little more specific? Try," Norah urged.

"Sorry, ma'am." Police officers don't tip. But deference on the job had become a habit.

"I suppose she had luggage."

"Yes, ma'am."

"So you had to get her a cab."

"Yes, ma'am." He wasn't impressed with the lady cop. He thought her dumb.

"Did you have much trouble getting a cab?"

"At that hour? Plenty."

"It was the rush hour? Morning or evening?"

"It was the theater hour, ma'am; around here that's the worst. I had to go down to the corner of York and stand in the soaking rain for near to ten minutes, it seemed like. I got wet through."

Resentment was better than apathy, Norah thought. "Wasn't it last Saturday we had that heavy, sleety rain? Later it turned to snow?"

A glimmer of surprise in his watery eyes was followed by grudging respect. "Yes, ma'am, that's when it was, all right. I remember now. I remember wondering whether Miss Price would get off. She didn't come back, so I guess she did."

Saturday morning she and Joe had brought Mark home. Saturday night Janet Price left on her vacation.

"So she was flying?"

The doorman shrugged. "She told the cabbie Kennedy."

So he wasn't all that disinterested. "Thinking back now, do you remember the kind of cab you finally flagged down?"

He really tried. "Sorry, ma'am," he said and meant it.

The rental office was on the premises and Norah went in. As soon as the dapper young agent realized that she wanted information, not an apartment, his subservient smile faded. Yes, he knew Miss Price, he admitted, anxious to be done with Norah. In fact, he was the one who had rented the apartment to her. Pride made him add it; and instantly he regretted it because it left him open to more questions. Fortunately all the lady officer wanted was a look at the lease, which he promptly supplied. It was for a furnished sublease, for a year with two months paid in advance —the first and the last—plus a deposit against possible damage to the furnishings. Standard, he assured the lady officer.

Would he mind if she took a look at the apartment? Norah asked.

Really, he had no right; he didn't know; he wasn't sure. . . . He hurried in to his boss, who after a few moments came out himself. He took a good look at Detective Mulcahaney's ID and an even closer look at Detective Mulcahaney herself before giving permission. But the agent was to accompany her.

"We can't permit anyone to enter the apartment unescorted. You understand?"

"It's for my protection as well as yours—yes," Norah acknowledged.

The boss nodded; he saw no irony in the remark.

The apartment Janet Price had subleased was small but luxurious, regulation modern. Norah was not interested in the decor; she went straight to the closets. Empty. The bureaus were empty too. No personal effects anywhere.

The young agent got the message fast. "She's gone! Cleared out!"

"It looks that way."

"I can't believe this! I can't believe it. She seemed like such a nice, reliable woman."

Yes, she did, Norah thought. She certainly did.

"But she signed a year's lease!" The agent couldn't contain himself. "I mean, we're stuck; it's the middle of the winter. Who moves in February?" His eyes narrowed; he forgot all about Norah. "I suppose we could raise the rent; that would make up some of the loss. . . ." His voice trailed off as he considered the options.

7

HEAVEN preserve me from self-centered fools! Norah thought and was instantly ashamed. The rental agent had reacted to the event as it affected him; why should he do otherwise? He had no idea why she wanted Janet Price. She was the fool. She should have known right away that something had to be wrong when a child like Mark, three and a half years old, white, healthy—never mind that bit about his being born addicted—was so providentially available. Joe had had no reason for suspicion, nor her father, but she had been the route; she had learned the hard way what was entailed in getting such a child.

She had simply been too eager, preconditioned in part by the near miss with the Janus baby. Joe wouldn't blame her; he'd understand. Nevertheless, the fact remained that through her fault Joe's whole career was now in jeopardy, for there was no doubt in Norah's mind that they had been set up, that Janet Price had been planted in the Children's Institute for the specific purpose of putting through their adoption of Mark.

Veering between anger and despair, Norah chose anger. She gave full vent to it. She stood on the corner of First Avenue and Fifty-seventh, fists dug into coat pockets, jaw set, shaking. A couple of taxis, seeing her standing there, slowed—it was midmorning and there were plenty of empties—but she didn't notice. Passersby looked at her curiously, but she wasn't aware of that either.

"Excuse me, miss."

An elderly woman walking an elderly dog peered at her anxiously. "Are you all right? Can I help you?"

The dog's rheumy eyes were as full of sympathy as his owner's. Norah managed a smile for both of them. "It's very kind of you, but I'm all right. Thank you. Thank you very much."

That bit of sympathy from a stranger made Norah pull herself together. She was behaving like a helpless female. She was far from helpless. She was a police officer with all her training and the resources of the department to call on. In fact, she decided, the time had come to ask Captain Felix to make good on his offer to expedite permission for a look at the sealed records.

Two days later Norah presented the judge's signed order to the clerk of the surrogate court and Mark's file was handed to her.

There was his birth certificate, stating date—March 11, 1971; place of birth—Hartford General Hospital, Hartford Connecticut; mother—Justine Ross, spinster; father—unknown. That, Norah had expected. What she had not expected and made her gasp aloud so that the clerk turned and shushed her sternly was a copy of a death certificate. According to that, Mark's mother was dead; she had died on November 28, just about three weeks before Norah's father had presented her to Mark.

The cause of death was not an OD; there was, in fact, no mention of drug complications; death was attributed to natural causes. There was no mention in the file of any foster home either. Mark had been claimed by his nearest surviving relative, and it was that relative who had officially surrendered him for adoption.

Her name was Janet Price.

Norah stared at the file. Just as Joe was running out of leads, the adoption opened up a new line of investigation. Janet Price would lead them to the killer. Setting up the adoption and then blackmailing the Caprettos would prove to be his fatal mistake Norah promised herself.

She returned the file and set out to look for the doctor who had signed the death certificate of Mark's natural mother.

She got the address easily enough from the AMA. It was in the Elmhurst section of Queens, a small, antiquated frame house on a rundown street, and as soon as she saw it, Norah knew the place was vacant; it had that abandoned look. The winter-eroded lawn was littered with leaves, trash, dog droppings. The windows were filthy. The mailbox hung by one rusted nail. The shingle was still on the door: Jasper Morris, MD. Norah tried the bell, though she didn't expect anyone to answer. She was right.

She canvassed the neighbors.

Old Doc Morris? Oh, he retired. No, not long ago. Christmas? No, make that Thanksgiving. Right, that's when it was, just before Thanksgiving. Should have retired years ago. Nobody went to him anymore. Drinking problem. Everybody knew. Sad. Used to be a real good doctor.

He had left no forwarding address. Nobody knew where he might have gone. Nobody cared. What void he might have left in the community had quickly closed over.

How about the house? Norah wanted to know. He wouldn't just abandon it. Surely he'd put it up for sale?

House didn't belong to him. Rented. Try Osborne Realty—over on Queens Boulevard.

According to Clarence Osborne, head and sole owner of the Realty company, Dr. Morris's decision to retire was sudden. Seems he unexpectedly came into money. Paid the balance of his lease and took off. No, Doc Morris left no forwarding address because he didn't know where he was going to settle. Said he was going to take a long trip, look around, see what part of the world suited him. Lucky guy! Clarence Osborne sighed. He wished he could just drop everything, get out of the rat race, find a nice warm place to do nothing in all day. But he didn't have any rich relatives.

When his relatives died, he'd probably have to pay the funeral expenses.

They were good at covering their tracks, Norah acknowledged as she headed back for Manhattan. But she wasn't discouraged. Maybe the woman who had recommended Janet Price as her replacement at the Children's Institute had done so in good faith. And maybe not.

Norah didn't go directly to the institute. She decided it would be better to talk to Emmeline Bunnell away from Mrs. Malverne's influence, alone at her home. That meant waiting till around six. In the meantime, Norah did her homework so that by the time she reached the converted brownstone on East fifty-first Street near the river, she knew the basic facts of Miss Bunnell's life. She was unmarried, forty-eight years old, and a fully qualified social worker with a BA in the social sciences, holding certificates from the New York Department of Education and also from the state. Behind her were twenty-six years of service in the social field. Her record appeared impeccable.

The downstairs door was open, so Norah walked straight up to the third floor and rang the doorbell of apartment C.

As everyone did these days, Emmeline Bunnell opened the door on the chain and peered through the slit. Having never met Norah, she couldn't recognize her, and as the ID named her Detective Mulcahaney, it took her a few moments to grasp the connection.

"May I come in, Miss Bunnell?"

She was a short, square woman with coarse gray hair chopped off in uneven layers and a face harshly lined. She wore black wool slacks with shine marks at the knees and a clean but frayed white shirt. She stood aside to let Norah pass, then carefully replaced the chain on the door.

The daybed against the far wall, the dining table in front of the bay window instantly marked it as a studio apartment. Stove, refrigerator, and sink were in a row along the wall opposite the daybed. There was a venetian blind that could be lowered to conceal the kitchen area. Norah wondered how long since Emmeline Bunnell had bothered to let it down. She slept and dressed and ate in this one room, and she'd been doing so for a very long time—everything was sadly shabby. There wasn't a piece of furniture that didn't need either reupholstering or refinishing. There were doilies on everything to hide the worst of the worn soiled spots. Yet it was not an unpleasant place: The plants saved it. Begonias and African violets in the window; philodendron, podocarpus in the dark corners; coleus and croton in between—all flourishing. The atmosphere was hot and extremely humid, geared to plants, not people, but to Norah, just in from the cold, it didn't seem uncomfortable. Suddenly she was startled by a frantic flapping of wings and saw a small bright green and yellow bird with a bright blue on wings and tail dart out from among the branches of a split-leaf palm and fly wildly around the room.

"It's all right, it's all right, Bonnie Boy." Emmeline Bunnell stood absolutely still in the center of the room and cooed to it. She patted her left shoulder encouragingly. "Come, Bonnie; come, Boy." But the bird swooped past her and into the open door of the bathroom.

"He's very shy with strangers. When I'm expecting visitors, I usually put him in his cage." She indicated a white, Gothic concoction half hidden in the vegetation.

It was, of course, an implied rebuke to Norah for having come without advance notice. "Is he a parakeet?"

"I prefer budgerigar," the social worker said. "The bird comes from Australia and that is the Australian name. Parakeet derives from the French *perroquet*, meaning small parrot, or some say the Italian *parrochetto*, meaning little parson—both are inappropriate."

"He's very beautiful."

"Thank you. He has a truly remarkable vocabulary, particularly in view of the fact that he was nearly a year old when I got him and started teaching him. It is considered extremely difficult for a bird over six months old to learn to speak." A slight flush of animation tinged her gray face and softened its bitter lines. "I wish you could hear him chatter, but as I said, he's very shy with strangers."

Probably wasn't used to visitors, Norah thought with pity for Emmeline Bunnell's evident loneliness. "I'm sorry if I frightened him."

"What can I do for you, Mrs. Capretto?"

"I want to talk to Janet Price. Mrs. Malverne gave me her address, but she's gone."

"Gone where?"

"I was hoping you could tell me that."

"I'm sorry."

"How well do you know Janet Price?"

The question couldn't have been unexpected, yet Miss Bunnell waited before answering. The tenderness she had evinced when talking about the bird was gone, leaving her features more bleak than ever. "Not well at all."

"Yet you recommended her as your replacement."

"She's qualified."

"May I sit down?" At Emmeline Bunnell's nod, Norah chose one of a pair of chairs beside the empty hearth, but the social worker remained standing as watchfully still as she had been in trying to calm Bonnie Boy. "How did you come to recommend Janet Price?" Norah asked.

The social worker stirred slightly and swallowed a couple of times. "Janet Price attended a series of lectures I gave two years ago in Miami at a symposium on the care of abandoned children. We got acquainted. When she came to New York recently, she looked me up and asked for my help in getting situated. As I hadn't been well and had been looking for an opportunity to take some time off, I suggested she fill in for me."

"I see. At the time of the symposium was Miss Price a resident of Miami?"

"Ah . . . I assumed so."

"Can you give me the date and place it was held?"

"It was July, '72, right after the holiday weekend. At the Fontainebleau Hotel."

Norah made a brief note. "I don't want to appear to pry, but you were absent from your job a considerable time. . . ."

"I have an ulcer."

"I'm sorry. And it was acting up?"

"Yes."

"You went into a hospital for treatment?"

"It wasn't necessary. All I needed was a good long rest without worry." As though expecting Norah to challenge that, she added, "I've lived with this ulcer long enough to know how to take care of it."

"But you have been under a doctor's care for the condition in the past? May I have your doctor's name?"

Mumbling something under her breath, the woman turned away.

"I didn't catch that, Miss Bunnell."

"Dr. Herbert Nicholson."

"Thank you." Norah gravely wrote that down. "So Miss Price's arrival in New York and her applying to you for help in getting work was just chance?"

"Yes."

"Suppose she hadn't shown up? Would you have taken the time off anyway?"

"I suppose I would have held on till Mrs. Malverne could find someone to fill in for me."

"You're very dedicated," Norah said and meant it.

"You have to be to stay in social work." She indicated the shabby, cluttered room with a faint trace of embarrassment. "There's no money in it."

Norah took another look around. The place was certainly in a sad state. Even the plants, which had at first glance seemed luxuriant, were now seen to be scraggly, in need of repotting and replacing. Maintaining plants didn't cost much, nor did the feeding of a small bird. The apartment was surely rent-controlled, and from the way she was dressed Miss Bunnell spent the minimum on herself. Yet, despite her deprecations, as a highly qualified social worker she had to draw a decent paycheck. Mrs. Malverne had specifically mentioned that salaries were up. So where did the money go? The hothouse atmosphere was becoming oppressive. Norah found herself sweating. Her thick sweater stuck to her; her feet swelled in the fleece-lined boots. Was Emmeline Bunnell a secret drinker? An addict? Norah could discern no signs of either. She was sure that Ida Malverne would have spotted anything like that and would not have kept her on. Besides, addiction, either to alcohol or drugs, left little time or love to waste—even on plants and a bird.

"A month seems a very long time to be out. You must have been really sick."

"Yes, I've already said so."

"How did you know you were well enough to go back to work? Obviously you felt better, but didn't you go to Dr. Nicholson for a checkup?"

"I've also told you that I've lived long enough with my ulcer to understand its symptoms better than any doctor."

"You said so, yes."

"All the doctors want to do is cut you up."

Norah let that pass. "It strikes me as odd that on the very day my husband and I took our adopted son home Miss Price left the institute and on the following Monday you returned."

"It just happened that way."

"And it just happened that Miss Price took Mark's file with her?"

"It probably got mixed in with her other papers when she was clearing out."

"And it just happened that on the day we took Mark home Miss Price cleared out of her apartment?" Norah persisted. "An apartment on which she'd taken a year's lease? She gave no notice and she left no forwarding address."

"I don't know anything about that."

"Wasn't she supposed to be relocating in New York?"

"That's what she told me."

"Why should she suddenly leave?"

"I don't know. I told you, I don't know." The stolid Miss Bunnell began to pick at a loose thread on the knee of her slacks.

"Did Miss Price discuss Mark's adoption with you?"

Evidently the social worker felt she was back on firmer ground, because she looked up. "No. Why should she?"

"Didn't she keep in touch with you? Didn't she call you from time to time for advice or information about cases pending when you left?"

"Why should she? She could go to Mrs. Malverne."

Norah was openly disbelieving. "You mean the entire month you were laid up she didn't contact you once? Not even to see how you were feeling?"

"I specifically asked her not to. The whole idea was for me to get emotional as well as physical rest. You can't imagine the emotional strain...."

"If you were that anxious not to be disturbed, why didn't you go away somewhere? Wouldn't that have been better? Surely, while you stayed here, Mrs. Malverne herself might have had the occasion to contact you."

Norah expected Emmeline Bunnell to protest that she couldn't afford to go away. Instead....

"Who'd take care of my plants? They'd die without me. And Bonnie Boy, what about him? He's used to flying free. He'd have to be caged. I couldn't do that to Bonnie Boy."

Norah got up, and there was no doubt that Emmeline Bunnell was glad that she was finally going.

"I'm sure that when Miss Price discovers that she has Mark's file she'll return it," she said as a means of speeding the detective on her way.

"I hope so." Norah handed her a card. "That's my phone number. If you hear from her, I'd appreciate your letting me know."

Without so much as glancing at it, the woman stuffed the card into her pants pocket—a pretty good indication that she didn't expect to hear from Jane Price. Or that she had no intention of notifying Norah. Norah let herself be ushered out. After the door closed behind her, she could hear the click of the lock and the rattle of the chain as it slid into place. Then she heard the social worker calling in a voice that was soft and tender, "Bonnie Boy . . . come out, Bonnie Boy. She's gone now. Don't be frightened. She's gone. Come to Emmie, love. Come to Emmie, sweetheart. . . ."

Dr. Herbert Nicholson was in his late sixties at the very least, a big man comfortably overweight. All that was left of his hair was a soft white fuzz through which the smooth pink of his pate glowed like an early sun through fair-weather clouds. His lab coat had ashes on the lapels; there were ashes on the old fashioned wool vest underneath. As he heaved himself out of his chair to greet her, the ashes scattered off him like water off a dog. His smile was warm, avuncular, and as he pumped her hand, he looked her over with the undisguised and delighted curiosity of a child.

"I've never met a lady police officer before."

His outer office was crowded, yet he waved Norah to a chair, offered cigarettes, lit up one himself, and settled back as though he had nothing else in the world to do but chat with her. "How can I help you Detective Mulcahaney?"

She liked him instantly. "I need some information about one of your patients."

"Hm." The hinges of the ancient leather chair squeaked ominously as he rocked back and forth. "You know that the information I may give you about a patient is very limited."

"The patient herself gave me your name, Doctor. She says that some time back you treated her for an ulcer. I just want to verify that you did, how long ago, and the seriousness of her condition."

Nicholson continued to rock; the hinges of the chair continued to protest. "Well, I don't see any impropriety in that." Cigarette dangling from a corner of his mouth, more ashes scattering around him, he got up and went to the files. "What's the patient's name?"

"Emmeline Bunnell."

He shook his head, indicating it struck no responsive chord. He opened the top drawer, found the card. "Ah . . . Emmeline Bunnell . . . yes, yes. I remember her now. Remarkable woman. Remarkable. I hope she's not in any trouble?"

"I can't say," Norah replied, then under his searching gaze admitted, "I don't know yet."

His look told her he appreciated the frankness. "Well, let's see what we have here." He lumbered back to the desk. Sat down. Pulled a pair of steelrimmed glasses out of the breast pocket of the lab coat, polished the lenses, hooked them over his ears, first on one side, then the other. He scowled at the card.

No wonder he scowled, Norah thought. She'd caught a glimpse of the card and the notations on it were chaotic—huge, erratic scrawls in every direction including across the corners, some circled, some underlined, in various colors of ink. Evidently it made sense to him.

"Ah, yes, here we are." He turned the card sideways. "Yes. September 8, 1971. Bleeding ulcer. Serious. I recommended surgery. She wouldn't hear of it. Refused absolutely." He looked up from the card to Norah. "I gave her medication, dietary advice, and the usual warning to slow down, avoid all nervous strain and emotional upset, but in her particular circumstance. . . ." He shrugged.

Norah waited, but evidently he didn't intend to say anymore. "Just what was her circumstance, Doctor?"

"I think, Detective Mulcahaney, we've reached the

point where to say any more would violate Miss Bunnell's confidence. I can only tell you that she consulted me"—he turned the card over—"a year later and that she was cured. The ulcer had healed. There was, in fact, very little scar tissue."

"She never had the operation?"

"No."

"That is remarkable. You did mention, Doctor, that you had advised Miss Bunnell to avoid all emotional and nervous stress. I would assume, then, that whatever had been bothering Miss Bunnell wasn't bothering her anymore."

Nicholson nodded.

"Would you be surprised to learn that her condition has returned? That the ulcer is acting up again?"

Nicholson pulled his lips in thoughtfully. With the same care with which he'd affixed them he now unhooked his spectacles and replaced them in the breast pocket of his lab coat. "Even after surgery, if the patient returns to his former habits, the condition will recur."

Norah leaned forward earnestly. "As far as I know, Doctor, Miss Bunnell has not done anything wrong. But she has been used, permitted herself to be used. Someone has a hold on her. I don't know what it is, but I'll find out sooner or later. Sooner would be better for both of us."

Nicholson resumed his thoughtful rocking to the accompaniment of the squeaking hinges. Finally he stopped, ground out his cigarette, but did not light another. "Emmeline Bunnell has a younger brother. Their parents died in a car crash when she was fifteen and he was . . . I think . . . nine. None of the relatives wanted to take the responsibility for raising them, so for the next several years they were passed back and forth. Naturally that made them cling to each other. Emmeline developed an obsessive sense of responsibility to the younger child. Unfortunately he continued to live off her after he grew up. He couldn't hold a job, he was constantly in debt, and he gambled. She had to pay his bills and his losses. It was destroying her. I told her that the next time he came to her for money she had to refuse. I told her she should stop treating him as though he were still a child and cut him loose. That kind of advice, Detective Mulcahaney, is easy to give but a hell of a lot harder to take."

"But she was able to do it?"

"Evidently. She told me so. She thanked me. She said that it was the best thing she had ever done for him as well as for herself. Knowing that he could no longer fall back on her had put him on his feet at last. Straightened him out. He got himself a job, moved out West, and was doing well. Naturally I was delighted—for both of them."

"Naturally," Norah agreed. "But a bit skeptical?"

Nicholson shrugged. "As I said, it wasn't an easy thing to do, but Emmeline Bunnell has remarkable willpower."

Except with regard to her brother. Norah thought. She got up and held out her hand. "One more thing, Dr. Nicholson, did Miss Bunnell mention her brother's name?"

Nicholson turned the card around a couple of times. "She called him Dolph. I assumed that's short for Adolph."

It was only midmorning, and Norah decided this time there was no need to wait till the end of the day to see Miss Bunnell at home. This time she could be interviewed at her office. The social worker would not be expecting a return visit so soon and would be taken off guard. Certainly Emmeline Bunnell was surprised when Norah walked in, but she showed very little reaction at the mention of her brother—as Dr. Nicholson had said, a remarkably self-possessed person.

"What do you want with my brother?"

Norah didn't answer.

"I haven't heard from Dolph in months." She decided her best chance was in being aggressive. "I'm outraged that Dr. Nicholson discussed my personal problems with you. What I told him was in strictest confidence, and he had no right—"

"He was only trying to help, Miss Bunnell, to take the pressure off you."

"I trusted him, I relied on his integrity."

"Please realize that this goes beyond a possibly illegal adoption," Norah explained earnestly. "My husband, Lieutenant Capretto, is investigating the murder of Giorgio Nerone. You must have read about it and the other two gangland killings. We have been told that unless my husband drops the case, we'll lose our son. So if pressure was brought on you through your brother to introduce Janet Price—"

"No!"

Norah didn't want to cause her pain, possibly to bring on an attack, but she couldn't stop. "Where is he, Miss Bunnell? Where is your brother? And please don't say you don't know. You can't expect me to believe that having raised him, been almost a mother to him, you would lose track of him completely. You must know where he is."

"He had nothing to do with Janet Price coming to the institute."

"Then there's no harm in telling me how to reach him, is there?"

"He's not involved."

The door opened and Ida Malverne appeared. "The last I heard, Adolph Bunnell was in Las Vegas."

Emmeline Bunnell stared at her superior. "Why did you have to tell her? Why?"

"I have to protect the institute."

"They'll kill him! Don't you understand? They'll kill him!" A spasm of pain turned the hard face into a grinning gargoyle mask. Emmeline Bunnell doubled up and clutched at her stomach, whimpering.

8

AS a KG (known gambler) Adoph Bunnell wasn't hard to trace. According to the telex report from the Vegas PD, Adolph Bunnell was alive and well and gambling again. He was known to the local police as a small-time gambler, compulsive—and a loser. He was into everybody in town; his credit shot, he'd been barred from just about every big casino and small back room. Till recently. Suddenly, about two months back, he'd resurfaced and started playing again. That meant not only that he'd found himself a stake but that his past debts had been cleared—somehow. Bunnell was pulled in for questioning, but all he would say was that his luck had changed. Familiar as he was with the various mob hierarchies, the local man could not discover how Bunnell had become solvent and gone back into the action. The Nerone faction did not operate in Vegas, but of course they had connections, any one of which would surely have been willing to put pressure on Bunnell as a courtesy. Pressure, Norah thought, was the name of the game—pressure on Adolph Bunnell to put pressure on his sister so that she would take sick leave and introduce Janet Price as her replacement, so that in turn pressure could be brought on Joe.

Questioned about Janet Price, Adolph Bunnell insisted he's never heard of her. It could even be true: He didn't have to know the name of the woman sent to his sister.

Joe took the new development to the inspector. Dietrich was not happy.

"I just don't get it," he complained morosely, staring

at the rain that splattered against his window. "Why are they so determined to get you off the case?"

"If I knew that, Inspector. . . ."

"Whoever takes over from you is going to have access to the same information and the same manpower."

They'd gone over that ground before—*ad nauseam*—one of Joe's handy Latin phrases, particularly apt in this instance. "Unless they have some way of knowing who the new head of the team would be and they think they have a better chance of controlling him," Joe suggested.

"Impossible! I don't know myself who would take over. It wouldn't be my decision. Probably the deputy commissioners would get together and make another special appointment. How could anybody anticipate the selection? No, no. You've got to be closer to a break than you realize."

"I've racked my brains, Inspector. I've gone over every shred of evidence a dozen times. I've read and reread every report."

"Do it again. It's there. It's got to be," Dietrich insisted. "They didn't go to all the trouble of setting up a fake adoption for nothing." Instantly Dietrich regretted having said that. He clamped his mouth shut and looked away.

Joe Capretto knew why. He himself had been looking for a way to frame his request, and Dietrich's own admission that the adoption had been rigged by the same people involved in the smuggling and the murders gave him the opening. But before he could speak, Dietrich was already trying to divert him.

"How about your snitch? Has Koslav heard anything?"

"Nothing. Nobody's talking."

Though it was midmorning it was so dark that the lights were on, but they did not dispel the gloom and depression shared by the two men. The only sound was that of the incessant, monotonous rain.

"Maybe I should withdraw, Inspector. Maybe in

view of my personal involvement it would look better if someone else. . . ." Joe let it trail off.

Dietrich was in no hurry to answer. He thought about it; he'd been thinking about it. It might be the best solution, after all. He removed the pince-nez glasses and rubbed the red crease across the bridge of his nose. In the resulting blurred vision he considered Joe Capretto. Could he be overlooking evidence, even subconsciously, in order to get help on his personal problem? No, not Cap. He was a good man, an honest cop, and having backed him for the special assignment, Dietrich didn't relish the idea of going back to the commissioners and telling them he might have been wrong. Especially if he hadn't been. But if he now told Joe to put the team on the investigation of the adoption, there was bound to be criticism, plenty of it; there would be those who'd say that he was letting Cap use his position for his private need.

Joe didn't want to give up the case, but he'd felt obligated to make the offer. The longer Dietrich pondered, the more certain Joe became that the inspector would take him up on it.

A large part of Otto Dietrich's talent lay in knowing when not to stick his neck out. Why not let the commissioners make the decision on this? But if he brought it to their attention at all, he'd be bound to make a strong presentation on Joe's behalf. If he succeeded in convincing them that the new line of investigation was valid, as Dietrich himself now believed it was, then they'd want to know why he'd bothered them with it.

"You're in charge, Joe. Follow whatever leads are available to you," Dietrich said and immediately broke out in a cold sweat.

"Yes, sir. Thank you." Joe sweated too, in relief.

"Okay, okay." Dietrich waved him off.

But Joe didn't leave. There was one more hurdle.

"Well, Lieutenant?" Dietrich asked testily.

"About my wife, Detective Mulcahaney. . . ."

"If you need more men, more equipment, or any

kind of damn thing, just ask and you've got it, but she's out. The commissioners particularly specified right at the start that your wife was not to—"

"I'm not going to be able to stop Norah, Inspector. I know my wife, and she's not going to be pulled off. You can flop her back into uniform, you can get her thrown off the force, but she's not going to stay out of this."

"What the hell, Lieutenant! You're her husband. You tell her she's out."

Joe shook his head. "I can't."

"All right, all right!" Dietrich shouted. "All right." He lowered his voice. "Let her work unofficially, not as a member of the team. And she's to get permission from her commanding. . . . Oh, what the hell, who're we kidding? Put her on. You might as well."

With the full team working on it, the cabbie who had picked up Janet Price at her apartment house was quickly located. His time sheet indicated he had indeed driven her to Kennedy Airport and dropped her at the Pan Am terminal. Her name did not appear on any of their passenger lists for that night or any succeeding days. Of course she could easily have gone from there to one of the other airlines. They were checked too—without result. Immigration had no record of her having left the country. She could have booked under an assumed name, which would mean a false passport too. Norah and Joe made up a description, and once again a police artist was called on to draw a portrait. Armed with copies, the team tried again. Nobody remembered her. It was possible that going to Kennedy had been a ruse; she could have got out of one taxi, waited, and hailed another to take her right back to New York. Using the identikit drawing, the cab companies were canvassed. Once again, negative. Janet Price had disappeared as completely as Carlo Abruzzi.

This was a week when she and Joe worked the night shift and her father would be picking Mark up from the day-care center. He would take him home, fix his dinner, put him to bed, and then wait till Norah or Joe, one or the other, got home. The odd time that unexpected work delayed her on the alternating week of her day shift, Norah knew she had only to call and Patrick Mulcahaney would be available. It was no imposition; he delighted in his baby-sitting job. He doted on Mark and the boy was crazy about him; it was a treat for both of them. Up to now, neither Mulcahaney nor Signora Emilia had been told about the threat to the adoption. Why cause them anxiety? Why spoil her father's pleasure in caring for Mark? For Mulcahaney would not only be distraught at the possibility of losing him, he'd blame himself for the predicament. Norah knew that no matter what she said, her father would hold himself responsible because the initial approach had been made through him. She would have done anything to spare him the pain and sorrow and self-reproach that were inevitable once he found out. But it could no longer be avoided. Joe agreed that he had to be told. In Patrick Mulcahaney lay their last hope of tracing Janet Price.

"Sweetheart! What a nice surprise," Patrick Mulcahaney exclaimed when he opened the door and saw his daughter.

He still lived in the old place, the apartment where Norah and the two boys had been born, where her mother died. It was big, cavernous, a seven-room labyrinth, but he resisted any suggestion of moving to something smaller, more comfortable, easier to take care of. Even the bait that he could be nearer to Norah and Joe failed. He clung to the old apartment not only for its memories but for the neighborhood. Mulcahaney's friends, his hangouts, his life were on the drive. There was still a sense of community up there, and he was very much a part of it. Still, it had to be a lonely life, and Norah worried about him. She had hoped that because of Mark he might finally be prevailed on to move. Now. . . .

His eyes were bright, his color ruddy—he'd just come in from his morning "constitutional," yet he seemed feeble, more so each time Norah saw him. How was she going to break the news? Her father loved Mark completely. What would the possibility of losing the child do to him? A new surge of anger welled up within her. She and Joe were fair game, but to use an old man and a boy. . . .

"How's Mark?" Mulcahaney asked. "How's he doing?"

"Much better. In fact, fine." Norah swept ahead of her father into the living room. The last time she'd been up was the afternoon her father had insisted she come and then had produced Mark. On that occasion she'd been too emotionally shocked by the meeting to notice the condition of the place; now nervous about how best to say what she'd come to say, she took a good look around.

Meanwhile Mulcahaney pursued the matter of Mark's adjustment. "I told you the boy just needed time. I've been thinking about it and I've decided that the reason Mark is so much easier with me and Joe is that he's never had a close relationship with men and so he's not afraid to make a commitment. But with a woman—well, he's had all kinds of women take care of him and then pass him on. I figure he's just afraid that you'll—"

"This place is a mess, Dad." Norah cut him off. "Honestly. When's the last time Mrs. Sullivan was in?"

It threw Mulcahaney off stride. "She was just here. . . . Tuesday, that's right; Tuesday as usual."

"Well, maybe she was here, but she sure didn't do much work." Norah marched into the center of the room and started picking up papers and magazines from the floor and the occasional tables. "These are a week old."

"They're the Sunday papers. I haven't read them yet. I told her not to throw them out."

Norah ran her fingertips over the top of the television set. "And did you tell her not to disturb the dust?

Honestly, Dad, you can't live like this! Mrs. Sullivan is just too old to do the job. Why don't you fire her and let me get somebody who will really—"

"What's the matter, sweetheart?"

"I know she needs the money, and you feel sorry for her and all that, but I can't be running over here on my day off to clean."

"Who asked you to come running over here to clean?"

"I'm afraid to even look at the bath or the kitchen!"

Nevertheless. Norah flounced on into the kitchen.

"You can look!" Mulcahaney shouted and followed. "Go ahead and look."

A stack of dishes still damp on the rack beside the sink indicated the breakfast things had only just been washed. But the counter top was still damp and so were the surfaces of the cabinets. "You're cleaning in here yourself!" she accused.

"Sure. I'm not a slob, you know, and I'm not helpless either."

"But you shouldn't be doing housework. You're paying good money to have it done."

"Norah." Firmly Mulcahaney cut her off. "Stop nattering and tell me what's wrong."

Even as a child Norah had been reticent about revealing her small hurts and disappointments; instead she would rage and fuss over something unrelated to the cause of her upset. Mulcahaney had understood and permitted it up to a point. But when he called her formally by her name and in that particular tone, she knew it was time to stop. So now their eyes met. Norah sighed and sat down at the kitchen table, and her father sat opposite her as they had done so often in the past.

"What's eatin' you, sweetheart?"

"There's some doubt that Mark is legally ours."

The fine, ruddy glow drained out of Patrick Mulcahaney's face. He gasped, and as he did so, the breath rushed out of him like air from a balloon. His entire frame seemed to cave in.

Norah was frightened. His color was terrible. She knew his heart was strong, very strong; if she hadn' known that. . . . She got up and rushed to the sink to get him a glass of water. "Here, Dad. . . ."

"I don't understand. . . . How can that be?"

Now that she'd started, there could be no turning back. Best tell it straight out. "We got an anonymous phone call warning us that the adoption isn't lega and that we could lose Mark."

Gradually he regained his breath, began to breathe regularly. "You've checked, of course."

"We don't think there's anything wrong with the adoption itself."

One more deep breath and Mulcahaney was able to sit up straight. He took the glass of water Norah had been holding for him and, though his hand trembled managed to drink it down without spilling it. " crank," he said, setting the empty glass on the table firmly. "A crank. You and Joe . . . you have to expec that kind of thing."

"The caller wants Joe to drop the case."

Mulcahaney knew what case; he'd seen his son-in law on television; he'd read about him in the papers He stared at Norah, then reached for her hand and gripped it. "Don't let him. Don't let him knuckle under. Once he does that. . . ."

"I know."

"Good." He gave her hand one more squeeze. "S what are you going to do?"

"We have to find out where Mark came from. How the social worker got hold of him. How he happened to be so providentially available to us. Naturally, w tried to contact Miss Price right away. She's disap peared."

"God!"

"How did you happen to go to the institute, Dad How did you happen to select that particular place You never told me."

Color returned to her father's face, the crimson anger. "Scum," he muttered.

"Dad...."

"Scum," he repeated and, letting her hand go, stared past Norah out the kitchen window at the winter bleak Jersey Palisades across the Hudson. He knew what she was after; it didn't have to be spelled out.

"I was taking my constitutional down by the river as usual . . . as usual . . . like I do every day of my life —same time, same place." He underscored it with the bitter realization that his rigid habits had been a factor in everything that had happened. "There was this nice young woman in the park with a boy . . . older than Mark, say, six or seven years old. It did occur to me to wonder why he wasn't in school, but I dismissed it. I thought it might be some kind of holiday that had slipped by me—one day is pretty much like another. . . ." He stopped abruptly; he didn't want Norah to think he was complaining or feeling sorry for himself either. "Anyhow, I didn't dwell on it; it was none of my business. The boy had a kite. It was shaped like a big silver bird, a beauty, but he couldn't get it up. The woman was trying to help him, but she wasn't much good. I went over and offered to show them how. I used to be pretty good with kites, if you remember."

They smiled at each other, sharing for just a moment the nostalgia of the time when Patrick Mulcahaney had taught his boys how to fly a kite, not the store-bought kind but painstakingly homemade. Norah had had no interest in the project till she saw the kites soar, then she'd asked to be taught too and built one that soared higher than the others.

Mulcahaney wrenched himself back to the present. "The boy was shy, but the mother was very glad to let me take over. Relieved," he added with the bitterness of hindsight. "Well, I helped Eddie—that was his name, Eddie. I helped Eddie get the kite up, and while he was flying it, his mother and I talked. She thanked me for my help and complimented me on how good I was with her son. She said obviously I had plenty of experience with children. She wanted

to know how many grandchildren I had. I told her I
didn't have any—yet—but that I was hoping."

"Oh, Dad. . . ."

"All right, all right! We know now that she was
leading me on, but at the time . . . it was just conversation." He couldn't help defending himself.

"What else did you tell her?"

"All I said was that you'd been married two years
and were hoping to get pregnant. I didn't say you
were worried or anything like that. I wouldn't."

Not that it would have mattered, Norah thought.
The woman had her own script to follow, whether
Patrick Mulcahaney fed her the cues or not. Her father being a friendly and outgoing man had just made
it easier for her. His favorite sport was talk. It was
the core of his existence. He spent every afternoon at
Houlihan's Bar nursing one beer through hours of
discussion—swapping stories, arguing any topic that
happened to come up with fierce tenacity and Irish
wit. He would have seized on the meeting as an unexpected bonus to his usually lonely morning. Probably they'd known that about him just as they'd known
when and where he walked.

"It's okay, Dad."

"I must have given it away because she asked me
right away if you had considered adopting." He
paused. "I suppose she would have asked me anyway."

"Yes."

"I told her I wanted to suggest it to you, but I
wasn't sure how you'd take it. Of course, I didn't
know that you were actually trying to adopt."

But Janet Price and whoever she was acting for
had known. Oh, yes, they'd known how she was going
from agency to agency, being interviewed, filling out
the useless forms, getting on lists. . . . Had they arranged for her to be steered to Janus? And when
she'd balked at the blatant illegality, had they then
conceived this second plan?

"I should have told you, Dad."

"I would have been that much more eager. You

know that, sweetheart. I'm a meddler. I always have been where you're concerned. I can't help myself. You'd think I would have learned my lesson."

He was referring to the days before Norah was married. Mulcahaney had brought home and introduced her to a young man, a stranger, who had turned out to be a psycho, a man who got his kicks from obscene telephone calls to young women.

"Nothing I try to do comes to any good."

"That's not true! You're not to blame yourself. They would have got to us some other way."

"But they did it through me. I can't forget that. Ever. And if you lose, Mark, poor lonely little guy. . . ."

"We're not going to lose him. We're going to fight every inch of the way. But you've got to help us."

"How?"

"Tell me the rest of it. Tell me exactly how this woman came to suggest the Children's Institute of Manhattan."

"Well, when I told Mrs. Hoyt that I had considered mentioning adoption to you, she became very excited—"

"She told you her name?"

"Certainly she told me her name." He flared with a return of his usual spirit. "You don't think I'd move on a thing like this unless I knew who I was talking to, do you? Mrs. Audrey Hoyt and she lives on Seventy-ninth Street."

Norah smiled because he was recovering. "I don't suppose she gave you the number?"

"No, and I didn't think to ask. But I could find her. I'm sure that—"

"I'll find her. That's my department. You just go on with the story."

"That's about it. She pointed out that adopting a baby these days was close to impossible, involved years of waiting, but that if you were willing to take an older child, she might be able to help. At first I balked, just as you did, but when she explained that it only meant a child over three years old, I was definitely interested. And when she told me that Eddie, her own boy, was adopted. . . . Well, he was such a fine, bright lad. She told me Eddie had been nearly three when she and her husband adopted him and it had worked out just beautifully. And there were advantages to adopting an older child—all the messy part—"

"I know, I know all that. Get to the point, Dad."

"I thought you wanted all the details?" he retorted. "All right. She said I should try the Children's Institute and ask for a Miss Janet Price. She said to mention her name."

"Why did you go yourself instead of telling me?"

"I wanted to look the place over first. I also wanted to make sure that there was a child available. A suitable child. I didn't want to get you all excited for nothing."

Each had been overly protective of the other. "You asked directly for Miss Price."

He nodded. "She couldn't have been more sympathetic. She told me about Mark. She said he'd just been turned over to the institute. She didn't try to push him on me. In fact, she suggested I spend time with him, take him out a couple of afternoons, get to know him. Once I did—"

"According to the records, his mother died and Miss Price is his nearest relative. She didn't want him."

"She told me he'd been living with a series of foster parents."

"No."

"That other business, about his having been born addicted, that wasn't necessarily true either?"

"Probably not. Just a way of explaining how he came to be available."

Her father sighed. "I'm glad of that anyway. But that Miss Price. . . ." He shook his head. "She seemed so nice, so . . . legitimate."

"She took us in too, don't forget, Joe and me. We never suspected she was anything but what she pretended to be."

"Maybe you would have if I'd told you the whole story."

"Look at it this way, Dad, whoever set this up did us a favor. They found us a son."

Her father's eyes filled; he blinked away the tears. "Thank you, sweetheart."

"Now tell me about this Audrey Hoyt. What did she look like?"

"Very good-looking woman, about thirty-five, big brown eyes, lovely smile," he replied briskly. "Tall, say, five-eight. It was a real cold morning, and she was all bundled up, had on one of those wooly fisherman's caps that pull down to the eyebrows, so I didn't see her hair, but I got the impression . . . her eyebrows were kind of reddish-blond so I put her down as a red-head. I think—I'm trying to remember whether she had freckles. I'm not sure. The boy was redheaded; maybe that's why I thought she was too, because I re-member mentioning that he looked enough like her to be her natural son."

"That's good, Dad. That's very helpful."

Her praise cheered Mulcahaney. "Say, why don't we just look her up in the phone book? You never know. . . ." Without waiting for an answer, Patrick Mulcahaney got up and padded out through the living room to the hall, where the phone was kept. Norah followed more slowly. He was already flipping the pages. "There's no Hoyt on Seventy-ninth, but there's an Ernest Hoyt on Seventy-sixth. I could have made a mistake about the street. Why don't I just go over there—"

"No. No, Dad, please." Norah didn't want her father involved any further. She had no idea how far these people might go, and she was afraid for him. But she couldn't tell him so. "If she spots you wandering around her neighborhood, asking questions, she's liable to get frightened and disappear. One thing we don't need on this case is any more disappearances."

9

THERE was no one by the name of Hoyt listed in the adoption files of the Children's Institute. Norah, working with David Link, went through the records. It was possible, in fact probable, that Audrey Hoyt was not the woman's real name; she was bound to have taken that much of a precaution. Anxious as she was to cooperate, Mrs. Ida Malverne couldn't be expected to identify her from among the hundreds of women who had passed through her office on the basis of Mulcahaney's description. Norah was inclined to think that Audrey Hoyt had never been a client of the institute at all, but they had to make sure.

The institute's adoption rate varied from one hundred and twenty-five to one hundred and forty children per year. If the boy with Mrs. Hoyt was presently seven years old and he'd been adopted at age three, they had to go back four years—six to be safe. That added up to seven hundred and ninety-five cases. Nonwhites and girl children could be immediately eliminated, quickly bringing the number down to a mere twenty-seven—a reaffirmation of the current baby drought. Of these, six adoptive couples were no longer living in New York, so their names were set aside to be investigated later if it should prove necessary. With the full team assigned, it was a matter of a day's work.

Though Patrick Mulcahaney's description hadn't helped Mrs. Malverne, the team found it useful. Many of the institute's clients on whom Joe's detectives called could be eliminated on sight if either the mother or son didn't fit the age bracket or coloring. From those who remained, every man on the team met with resistance. All spoke highly of the institute. They were eminently satisfied. There had been no repercussions from adoption; all vehemently denied any suggestion of blackmail as a result of it. Though each couple claimed that they had full legal rights to their child, they were instinctively defensive as though fearing that just the same, somehow, the child might be taken from them.

So they had to turn to the six who had left the city. Of these, one couple was in Hawaii and the other in Switzerland, where the husband was working for an American company. The others were traced, the local PD contacted and asked to find out if any of the women had been away from home on that day in December when Norah's father had met Audrey Hoyt in Riverside Park. While they waited for the reports to come in, Patrick Mulcahaney went to Norah's for dinner.

After Mark had been put to bed and they waited for the hockey game to come on TV, he turned casually to his daughter. "How's it coming? Have you found Mrs. Hoyt?"

"Not yet."

"Try this address." From his wallet Mulcahaney extracted a slip of paper and handed it to her.

There was a name and an address written there. "Who's Ernst Gundersen?"

"Eddie's father."

"How do you know?" Joe asked.

Mulcahaney only smiled.

"Come on. Dad, how did you find out?" Joe urged.

"I thought I told you to stay out of it," Norah scolded. "I thought I asked you not to go—"

"Near the mother," Mulcahaney finished for her. "And I promised. I didn't say anything about the boy."

"You found the boy!" Joe exclaimed.

Mulcahaney beamed.

And Norah smiled because it was exactly the kind of justification she would have made herself. She looked at the slip of paper. "Gundersen. I don't recall

that name on the institute list, do you, darling?" She
handed the paper to Joe.

"No."

"How did you happen to run across the boy, Dad?"

"I didn't happen to run across him," Mulcahaney
corrected; he would not be deprived of his triumph.
"I conducted a very scientific search."

"Come on, Dad. . . ."

But Joe was more respectful. The address on the paper, Sutton Place, was far enough away from where
Norah's father lived to preclude any accidental meeting. "How did you know where to look?"

"The boy has to go to school, doesn't he?"

"But how did you know which school?"

"Now, sweetheart, I've been around the two of you
long enough for the technique to rub off. It's only common sense, after all. I looked it up in the phone book."

"But there must be hundreds of—"

"Hundreds of public elementary schools, sure, but
not that many private schools."

"How could you know he goes to a private school?
Did his mother tell you?"

"If she had, I would have passed the information on
to you."

"Come on, Dad, don't drag it out."

But Mulcahaney was enjoying himself. "I noticed
how the boy was dressed. He had on a Windbreaker,
but he took it off because he was hot from running
with the kite. Underneath he wore a real natty outfit
—one of those green blazers with white edging and a
sort of maroon emblem over the pocket and navy
pants. I figured it had to be a school uniform."

"Great, Dad, just great. And you remembered the
name on the emblem."

"I wish it had been that easy. No, I went through
the Yellow Pages, nineteen of them to be exact, and I
made a list. Actually, when you eliminate the plumbing institutes, radio and TV schools, art, modeling,
karate, and judo academies, and belly-dancing stu-

dios, there aren't that many private schools for the elementary grades in the city of New York."

"And you visited them all?" Norah was impressed.

Her father was delighted. "Is that what you would have done?" he asked, then answered his own question. "I called them up one by one and inquired what kind of uniform their students wore. That way I narrowed it down to three possibilities."

"Dad, that's really terrific! So you went to the schools and spoke to the principals—"

"I didn't have to. All I had to do was wait outside the schoolyard. All the children were on view at recess. I looked them over."

Norah laughed gleefully and gave him a big hug. "I'm proud of you, Dad. But you shouldn't have done it. You shouldn't have stood around in the cold like that. You should have told us and let us—"

"Let you what?"

"Let us look for him, of course. Oh. . . ." Before either her father or Joe could point it out, Norah caught her own error. "We couldn't pick Eddie out. You're the only one who knows what he looks like."

"Now you've got it." Mulcahaney nodded with great satisfaction. "Once I did spot him, I waited till school was out to see who would come and pick him up."

"And . . ." Norah prompted impatiently. Her father was taking his time, savoring his success. Well, why not?

"It was her, all right, the same woman I'd talked to by the river."

"She didn't see you?"

"You warned me not to let her see me, didn't you? I wanted to follow them, but I decided not to take the chance. So I pointed Eddie out to one of the kids in the schoolyard. I got his name. The kid didn't know exactly where he lived, but he thought it was around Sutton Place. So then I looked in the phone book again. There are four Gundersens listed, and only one of them lives on Sutton Place."

"Marvelous, Dad, really."

"Good work, Dad." Joe added his congratulations. "You'd make a great detective."

"It's not so hard." Mulcahaney shrugged, but there was a twinkle in his faded blue eyes. Then he became serious. "I wanted to help. I had to. I felt responsible for your trouble. Our trouble."

"You shouldn't, Dad. I've told you—"

"And I was mad, real mad. Nobody makes a patsy out of Patrick Mulcahaney and gets away with it."

Joe assigned David Link to do the check on Ernst Gundersen. According to the information he compiled, Gundersen was an architect, head of his own firm, with offices on Madison Avenue. Prestigious. He was born in Sweden, brought to this country by his parents at the age of five, became a citizen through his father's naturalization. He had an unblemished reputation. The work done by his firm was mainly industrial, and as far as David could discover, neither he nor any of his clients had any kind of underworld associations.

With that out of the way, Norah and Joe were ready to call on Eddie's mother at the address provided by Pat Mulcahaney.

Though not one of the luxury palaces that dominate the Sutton Place area, the building was impressive enough, with a well-appointed lobby and a uniformed staff. They identified themselves, knowing the doorman would call and alert Mrs. Gundersen that they were on the way up. But if the encounter with Mulcahaney had been a chance one, then her knowing that police officers were calling on her would make no difference. If it had been contrived—and could there be any real doubt?—then she already had a cover story and surprise would count for little; anxiety, even the few minutes of it while they went up in the elevator, might be more effective.

Barely glancing at their ID's, Mrs. Gundersen ad-

mitted them. Her ready acceptance of who they were,
Norah thought, was a strong indication that she also
knew why they had come. She led them into a big
room, airy, almost blindingly bright. The light flooded
in from a wall of glass at the eastern end. The view
was the apartment's main feature—the Gundersens
must be paying plenty for it—so the drapes were
pulled back to show it. It certainly was impressive:
on the south the winding ribbon of the East River re-
flecting the winter sun; on the north the metal girders
of the Queensboro Bridge etched against a limpid
sky; between, Con Ed's tricolored stacks belching
black smoke over the tenements and factories huddled on the Long Island shore—the proud and the
tawdry, typically New York. Any shoddiness would
show up in that uncompromising light, but the room,
a modern monochrome of browns and beiges punc-
tuated by plenty of glass and steel, stood up well. Not
so Audrey Gundersen.

She was tall, with a full but still good figure. She did
have a spate of freckles across the bridge of her nose,
but they added piquancy to a fine complexion. Her
hair, as Patrick Mulcahaney had surmised, was a light
golden red. He had put her age at thirty-five, but the
hard light betrayed her. It showed up a tracery of
lines around her eyes and the shadows underneath as
well as a heaviness around the jowls that brought it
up to at least forty. She must once have been really
beautiful, strikingly so, Norah thought, could be still
if she took the trouble—in the softness of evening,
with full makeup. It was evident that this morning at
least Audrey Gundersen hadn't taken trouble at all.
She had on an old pair of slacks and a print shirt
worn tails out. Her hair was pulled severely back and
tied with a sleazy red ribbon that looked as though it
came off a Christmas package. She was wearing bedroom slippers, backless mules with soiled pompons
over the toes. She walked ahead of them to the center
of the room, then turned so that the light was behind

her. She didn't offer them chairs; she didn't say anything; she simply stood and waited for them to state their business.

Joe had intended to start with the Children's Institute and see where that led, but he discarded the plan. He could sense that this was not the first time Audrey Gundersen had faced the police; she would not easily give anything away. Therefore, she had to be jolted and jolted hard.

"It's about your son," he said. Just that, no more.

She waited. So did Joe. Finally she had to ask. "Eddie? What about him?"

Joe didn't answer. He wanted more than that from her. He didn't so much as glance at Norah—she was intuitive enough and they'd worked together often enough for her to know what he was up to. Keeping his eyes fixed on Audrey Gundersen, he could see uncertainty take hold.

"What about Eddie?" From uncertainty she passed to anxiety. "Is he all right? Nothing's happened to him, has it? He's in school, isn't he?"

"As far as I know he's in school and he's fine," Joe answered.

First there was relief, then anger. "Why did you imply something had happened to Eddie? Why did you do that? It was a terrible thing to do."

"I only said I wanted to talk to you about your son. You were the one who jumped to the conclusion that there was something wrong, Mrs. Gundersen. Why are you so afraid for Eddie?"

"It's only natural, isn't it? A couple of police officers show up at my door and ask about my son. What should I think?"

"Is it because Eddie's adopted that you're so fearful?"

"No, certainly not. Who told you he's adopted? What business is it of yours?"

She was fighting back, but the initial resistance had been broken. Joe nodded toward Norah. "My wife's father told us that Eddie is adopted. Patrick Mulcahaney. You remember him, don't you, Mrs. Gundersen? He's the elderly gentleman you met in Riverside Park down by the Hudson on the first of December. You were there with Eddie. Mr. Mulcahaney helped Eddie get his kite into the air. The two of you got to talking."

"No."

"No what. Mrs. Gundersen?"

"No to the whole thing. I never met any Patrick Mulcahaney. I never took Eddie down along the Hudson. Why should I? There's a fine playground right here two blocks up."

"Yes, we noticed. We wondered why you should go all that way and on a morning when, incidentally, he should have been in school. He wasn't in school on the first of December; we checked."

Mrs. Gundersen shrugged. "So I kept him home. He had a bad cold."

"You complimented Mr. Mulcahaney on his way with children and asked him if he had many grandchildren. He told you no, but that he was hoping. That was when you mentioned your Eddie is adopted. You suggested that if he was interested on his daughter's behalf, he should contact the Children's Institute of Manhattan. You even mentioned a particular social worker—Janet Price. You told him to use your name, Audrey Hoyt. That is your maiden name, isn't it?"

It was no guess; Norah had checked the marriage license.

That they had gone that far into her past jolted Audrey Hoyt Gundersen. "I don't think you heard me, Lieutenant. I said I never took Eddie over to that park and that I never met any Mr. Mulcahaney. It's the old man's word against mine."

"That old man is my father," Norah pointed out quietly.

The redhead was momentarily discomfited. "Well, I'm sorry, but your father is mistaken. Maybe he did meet some woman with a boy, but it wasn't me. You've got the wrong person."

"We're not investigating Eddie's adoption," Norah assured her. "You don't need to be afraid. We don't want to cause you any trouble. On the contrary, we—"

"You couldn't." Audrey Gundersen cut Norah off. "Eddie's not adopted. He's my own, natural son."

Norah and Joe looked at each other.

"Then why did you tell my father he was adopted?"

"God! What does it take to get through to you people? It wasn't me. You've made a mistake. You've come to the wrong place. You might as well accept it and go because I have nothing more to say to you."

Norah started to argue, but a glance from Joe stopped her.

"It is possible, I suppose," he acknowledged. "There is one way of clearing the whole thing up. Why don't we just ask Eddie?"

Audrey Gundersen's mouth fell open.

"I'm sure Eddie will remember a special outing with his mother, particularly on a day when he would normally have been in school. It must have been a very special treat for him. I'm sure he'll remember every little thing that happened that morning."

There was no defense against that and Mrs. Gundersen knew it. "You'd use a child—"

"Regretfully, Mrs. Gundersen."

"Nuts to your regrets!" she lashed out. "Regrets don't cost. Regrets don't mean a damn. Leave my son alone."

"We're not going to badger the boy. We're just going to ask him if you took him down to—"

"You people have no feelings, do you? No feelings at all."

Norah cut in. "My father went to the Children's Institute and to Janet Price. She showed him a boy named Mark. We adopted Mark, my husband and I. Now we've been warned that we'll lose him unless my husband drops a certain case he's working on."

"So it's tit for tat. Just because your boy is being used against you, you think it's okay to use the same tactics on me."

"How can we if Eddie is your natural son?"

Abruptly Audrey Gundersen sat down. "What do you want to know?"

Norah and Joe sat too, and Joe resumed the interrogation.

"Who told you to go to Riverside Park? Who told you when and where and who to look for?"

"Jan. Jan Price. She called me and asked me to do her a favor. She's an old friend. I owed her, so I did it."

"Just like that. Didn't it seem an odd kind of favor?"

The redhead shrugged. "I figured she had her reasons."

"You didn't ask what they were."

"If she'd wanted me to know, she would have told me."

They'd reached her second line of defense, Joe thought. How stubbornly would she cling to it before telling the truth? "How long have you known Janet Price?"

"Years. We used to work together."

"She must have done you a real big favor for her to feel that she could just call on you and you'd jump." No answer. "What did she do for you, Mrs. Gundersen? Did she get Eddie for you?"

"No. Damn you, leave Eddie out of this. I told you—"

"That he's your natural son, yes, I remember, but I don't believe it. I think he's adopted—illegally. I think that's the hold Janet Price has on you. I can check it, you know. I can examine the adoption records."

"Go ahead, go ahead and examine all you want. You'll find that Eddie's mine, all mine. You can't take him away from me. Nobody can, ever." She started to cry and was angry at herself for it and turned away to hide her tears.

Norah got up and went to her. She put out her hand, then decided it was best not to, that she wasn't ready yet for another woman's sympathy. "Why, Mrs. Gundersen? Why did you do what Janet Price wanted?"

"I didn't see anything wrong in it. Some poor girl died and left a kid nobody wanted and a nice couple was looking to adopt."

"If that's all there was to it, the boy could have been placed in the regular way," Norah pointed out.

"That was none of my business. Jan wanted me to do her a favor and that's all." She paused. Nobody said anything for a moment. "How could I know the kid was being planted to be used for blackmail later on?"

"Because Eddie was used to get you to do it. He was, wasn't he? Isn't that how Janet Price got you to go down to the park to start a conversation with my father and steer him, and through him us, to the institute—by threatening to tell what she knew about Eddie?"

Audrey Gundersen clenched her teeth so tightly that the nerves at her temples throbbed with the tension.

"Why should an old friend do that to you? Who made her do it? Who is Janet Price working for?"

"I don't know."

"Who did she use to work for?"

The name was mumbled, low. "Nerone."

So, Norah thought, so, and glanced at Joe. Up to now the link had been by inference; now it was fact. They were getting there.

"You too? You did say the two of you worked together," Norah reminded her. It was the one bit of information she'd volunteered, and as so often happened that extra bit betrayed her.

Audrey Gundersen sighed.

"Call girl?"

She nodded.

"Who ran the operation? I mean, who was in direct charge? Who was the madam?"

"Oh, no, it wasn't anything like that. We were dancers, Jan and me. We worked in the line at the Half Note; it was a club on Fifty-second Street. Between shows we mixed—sat with the customers, talked, had a couple of drinks. . . ."

"I know."

"We didn't have to." Audrey Gundersen hurried to defend herself and the job. "It was something to do, better than sitting in the dressing room two hours."

"Sure." Stripping off ten or fifteen years and twenty pounds from Miss Price, the social worker, removing her glasses and lightening her hair, Norah could visualize her as Jan Price, a late fifties version of a go-go girl.

"Sometimes one of the customers wanted to make a date for later," Audrey Gundersen continued to explain. "Or sometimes Mr. Brasso—he was the boss—wanted to fix up a friend. But it was always up to the girl; if she didn't feel like it, or if she went and it turned out she didn't take to the guy, well, that was okay. Mr. Brasso never said a word. He understood. He was okay."

"Charlie Brasso?" Joe asked.

"That's right."

The name didn't mean anything to Norah, so she expected Joe to take up the interrogation, but he seemed lost in thought. She went on. "Of course, your husband doesn't know anything about this."

"He knows. I told him. It was all over by the time Ernst and I met. I'd kicked the life. But I thought I ought to tell him."

"But if your husband knows about your past. . . ."

"I told Ernst about myself; I didn't tell him about Eddie. You see, Eddie is mine, but not by Ernst. I thought if he knew he might not want Eddie around. Eddie would be too much of a reminder of things we both wanted to forget. I was afraid that even if he accepted the boy, he couldn't really love him. So I pretended to adopt him."

"And Janet Price knew."

"Yes." Mrs. Gundersen was more anxious than ever to make Norah understand. "It's not a question of losing Eddie. My husband loves him; he'd never turn him out, but I don't think he could feel the same way toward him if he knew. Or toward me. We're so close, the three of us . . . so happy. . . ."

Following her earlier instinct, Norah reached out and put her hand gently on the woman's shoulder. "He won't find out from us, will he, Joe?"

But at the name of Brasso, Joe Capretto had stopped listening.

The name had gone off like a thunderclap inside his head. Charlie Brasso. Big Charlie. Joe hadn't thought about him for years.

10

BIG Charlie was dead. His body had been washed ashore along the Rockaways just about sixteen years ago. It was late September when an old man, a resident of one of the retirement homes along the strip, heading along the deserted beach to the jetty for a little fishing, had found him and called in. Joe, a rookie cop, working out of the One-oh-One, had, with his partner, taken the call—his first homicide. Even now he could recall every detail: the fine, mellow afternoon, light onshore breeze, calm water, tide high and just starting to go out, and the body an obscene, bloated, weed-encrusted hump on the clean sand. He remembered his own reaction—part revulsion at the sight, part pity that a human being should turn up like garbage on the shore, and curiosity, an overwhelming curiosity. From the first, Joe had deduced murder. Accidental drownings were rare at end of summer simply because few people went swimming; besides which, the ocean had been exceptionally calm, and anyhow the man was fully dressed. As for suicide, he couldn't see a suicide walking into the ocean with his topcoat on. Joe awaited the arrival of the detectives with great anticipation.

But if they shared the rookie's assessment, they kept it to themselves. Joe was bursting to offer his ideas, but he knew his place. Not till the assistant medical examiner arrived and announced that the victim had been shot did the detectives show any real interest. The search of the body revealed a gun, a wallet stuffed with money and papers that were illegible from long immersion, and a gold identification bracelet with the name engraved—Charles Brasso.

Brasso was a hood wanted for questioning in the recent shooting of a cop. In those days policemen were not used for target practice; a cop killing not only took priority over all other business, as it still does, of course, in those days apprehending the culprit was a crusade for the entire department. Therefore, the name on the bracelet stirred the blood of every officer in the small group on the beach.

Officially Joe had nothing more to do with the case, but he followed it avidly. There was plenty of talk about it at the precinct, naturally, and the papers played it up. He learned that the lab had restored the papers in the dead man's wallet and they confirmed his identity. The gun was test-fired, and the bullets placed under the comparison microscope revealed not only that Brasso had been shot with his own gun but that it was the same gun used to kill Officer Salenski. The case was considered closed.

It seemed to satisfy everyone that Officer Salenski's killer had been found, his murder avenged. The score was even. Nobody seemed to care who had evened it.

Except the rookie. It haunted Joe Capretto. With much trepidation, he went to talk to Frank Oakes, the detective who had carried the case.

Oakes was first annoyed, then patronizing. "We figure it was one of Brasso's own. We were after him. We were looking under too many stones, turning up too much slime trying to find him. He was an embarrassment to the mob, so they got rid of him."

Joe understood that simply tipping off the police about Brasso would have been risky; Brasso could retaliate by implicating others. Okay. But why dump him at sea? They must have known that it was possible the tide just might wash him up, as it had, in fact, done.

"You still don't get it, Capretto." Oakes was losing patience. "They wanted us to find him. They wanted us to know that they'd taken care of him."

"Sort of a *quid pro quo*," Joe mused, fond of his Latin even then.

"What? Yeah, you could say that."

"Then why not just dump him in an empty lot or an alley or prop him up on the steps of City Hall."

"Well, they didn't want it to look obvious, did they? Anyhow, Brasso had a house on the channel. That made it handy. They killed him using his own gun and dumped him off his own dock."

Joe wasn't satisfied. "But if they wanted him found, weren't they taking a big chance? I mean, how could they be sure the tide would wash him up? It would take an expert to figure when to drop him and how long before he floated to shore. Even an expert could be wrong. An unexpected storm, a shift in the wind, and the body could have been carried out to sea and never seen again."

"Who cares how they figured it? They figured it. It worked. That's it. As for who killed Brasso, we're still working on that, but the main thing is that Salenski's murderer has been taken care of. Right, Capretto?"

"Yes, sir. But—"

"So what's eating you?"

"I was interested. Since my partner and I took the call. . . ."

"If you're suggesting some kind of cover-up. . . ."

"Oh, no!" Joe was aghast.

"If you're trying to make points for yourself, you're going about it all wrong, fella."

"No, sir, I'm not trying to make points."

"Okay. So we got Salenski's killer. The lieutenant's satisfied. The captain's satisfied. Even the commissioner. . . ."

And he should be too, Joe told himself. He had one more question. It concerned the murder weapon. Ballistics had proved that the bullets from it had killed both Brasso and the police officer. Hoods carried illegal weapons, naturally, but lacking the registration, how could anyone be sure it was in fact Brasso's gun?

Just because it was found on him didn't make it his. Joe hadn't come to challenge or to quibble, just to get information and to learn.

He reminded himself that he was a rookie with little experience and that Oakes was a veteran detective. Yet he knew that in Oakes' place he wouldn't have been satisfied. Maybe he was misjudging the older man; maybe Oakes wasn't satisfied either but couldn't say so. He had no choice but to respect the detective's position.

Joe came out of his trance and returned to the present.

"Were you working for Brasso at the Half Note when he was killed?" he asked Audrey Gundersen.

"No, I'd quit about a month before. I'd got myself a job in a Broadway show, *Girls and Gobs*. I was in the chorus, but it wasn't the usual type of chorus job. Every girl was an individual character. I had lines. *Girls and Gobs*," she repeated. "Maybe you saw it?"

"Sorry. I remember reading about it. How about your friend, Jan? Was she still working at the Half Note then?"

"I guess so."

"Don't tell me you didn't get in touch with her and talk it over? It was a big case. You must have been interested."

"I thanked my lucky stars I'd got out in time. I didn't want to know anything."

Joe remembered the Half Note Club very well; he'd even taken the odd date there. It had been popular, had a big girlie show, and a really good Dixieland band. It was long since gone, of course, torn down along with most of the other clubs, large and small, legitimate and not so legitimate, that had made the Fifty-second Street block between Fifth and Sixth Avenues famous as "Swing Street." According to what Audrey Gundersen was now saying, the Half Note had belonged to the Nerone mob and was fronted by Brasso.

"That show you were in, *Girls and Gobs*—it didn't have much of a run, did it?"

"No, and it was a shame. It was a terrific show. Everybody that saw it loved it. It had a marvelous score. Nobody could figure why it didn't do better." The memory of her time in the limelight exhilarated the redhead. She was happy to talk about it. "We got great notices, the girls in the line, I mean. The critics particularly mentioned us. Like I told you, we were more like a group than a chorus line. We wore individual costumes and we were even listed individually in the program."

"So I guess you had no trouble getting into another show when that closed."

The girlish glow faded. "We closed at a bad time. All the new shows had already been cast, and most of them were in rehearsal."

"So you went back to the Half Note."

"It was better than Macy's basement."

"I guess you were lucky at that—getting your old job back, what with the new management and all."

"Oh, it was the same management. Mr. Brasso's partner, Mr. Allegro, took over. He was very nice to me. They didn't need any dancers, but he put me on as 'swing girl'; you know, to fill in if anybody took sick or wanted a night off."

Johnny Allegro! The aging Nerone soldier who had been shot and dumped off the East River pier. The first in the trio of mob murders. The happy warrior who couldn't do anything right, but whose ineptness was never punished, who was given busywork that amounted to being pensioned off. Could it be that once, far back, he had done something right? Had Johnny killed his partner, Big Charlie? No, Joe thought at his best, Johnny wouldn't have been up to anything like that. But he could have known who did it.

A thrill of excitement passed through Joe. Probably no one else would have made the connection or, if he had, dismissed it as irrelevant. Except himself. That was why they didn't want him on the case. That was why they were going to such extraordinary lengths to get him off it. Not because he had been on the stretch of deserted beach sixteen years ago when Brasso's body was washed up—there had been plenty of others there too—but because Joe Capretto, a rookie with curiosity, had asked questions no one else had asked and those questions had gone unanswered, and now Lieutenant Capretto could ask those same questions again. And would.

The relief was tremendous. Not till this moment had Joe realized how heavily the worry of not knowing why they wanted him off the case had weighed on him. He took a slow, deep breath, held it, then as slowly let it out again. He relaxed.

Norah saw it, knew he had something, but had no idea what. She too had been piqued by the mention of Johnny Allegro, but not knowing anything about the Brasso case, she waited for Joe to explore the matter, expecting to piece it together as they went along. Again he surprised her by dropping it.

"Where is Jan Price now?" Joe asked.

"I don't know," Mrs. Gundersen replied. "I talked to her that once on the telephone. I haven't heard from her since. I swear it."

"Have you any idea at all where she found Mark, the boy she put up for us to adopt?"

"No, Lieutenant. I swear I don't know anything at all about that part of it. She gave me instructions and I followed them. I went down to that park along the river with Eddie and there was the old man she'd described to me. So I got into a conversation with him and I steered him to the institute. And that's it. You've got to believe me."

"I do, Mrs. Gundersen. I believe that Eddie is your natural son and that the adoption was rigged. I have to ask you how it was done. It wouldn't have been all that easy to arrange. You'd have to relinquish Eddie temporarily. You wouldn't do that unless you were one hundred percent sure of getting him back. You must have had complete confidence in the person or persons involved."

The ex-call girl, ex-chorus girl didn't answer.

"Don't make me ask your husband."

She gasped. "You promised!" she accused. She turned to Norah. "You promised," she pleaded.

"In the understanding that you would cooperate," Norah replied.

"I am cooperating. I am. I just don't see that Eddie's adoption enters—"

"Somehow I don't think you would have risked turning Eddie over to a regular adoption agency even for a short while." Joe watched her carefully. "Who took care of Eddie while the adoption was being arranged? Your friend, Janet Price?"

She nodded.

"You had to have a lawyer. Not just any lawyer. How did you locate him?"

"Jan made all the arrangements."

"And what was his name? Come on, Mrs. Gundersen, I don't even need to go to your husband for that; it's a matter of record. I'm asking you to save us a little time. We're not going to tell him who put us on to him. It's not Eddie we want to talk to him about."

That finally convinced Audrey Gundersen. "Louis Heggerat," she murmured. "He used to have offices on Forty-second Street. I don't know if he's still there."

"We'll find him," Joe assured her. "Thank you." He got up, indicating to Norah that they could go.

But she hung back. "I don't mean to intrude, Mrs. Gundersen, but . . . why don't you tell your husband? Tell him the whole thing. Otherwise . . . has it occurred to you that this might not be a one-shot favor? Next time the favor might be a little bigger and a little harder to do and one you might not be able to justify —even to yourself."

Joe was excited. The link between Janet Price, the Nerone mob, and the old Brasso case opened up a whole new line of inquiry. It wouldn't be easy going back sixteen years, but he couldn't wait to get started.

"Where we made our mistake was in going against our first gut judgment," he told Norah as they left the Sutton Place apartment house and headed down York Avenue toward their old maroon Mustang.

"You're always saying there is no such thing," Norah teased, encouraged by his optimism, though she didn't understand the reason for it.

"No, ma'am. What I'm always saying is—don't label a hunch a fact. I never said ignore it."

"Okay. So what are we talking about?"

"Miss Price, naturally. Sweetheart, look—as soon as we found out that the adoption was rigged, we figured her for a phony."

"But she is! Mrs. Gundersen just got through telling us—"

"That the two of them worked in a Nerone-backed nightclub, that's all. Let's go back to when we first met the lady. Neither one of us, you or me, suspected she was anything but a *bona fide* social worker, right? She certainly knew what she was doing. We had long and intensive sessions with her and we never doubted her. Granted we were both under considerable emotional strain, still, and I'm not being conceited, if she had faltered or made a false move, one of us would have picked it up. She knew the ropes."

"She's not licensed. We found that out."

"Not in New York," Joe corrected. "She could be licensed in another state—Florida; according to your Miss Bunnell, she just moved from there. The credentials she submitted to Mrs. Malverne were faked, but she couldn't fake the work. Ida Malverne was satisfied, and she's no fool."

"She could have worked as a case aid," Norah mused aloud. "They don't have to be licensed."

"Right. We know that approximately four years ago Janet Price arranged an adoption for her own buddy, Audrey Gundersen. Maybe that was the first time, but I'll lay any odds you want that it wasn't the last. The

main thing, *cara mia,* is that now we know why we're
being blackmailed." Then he realized that of course
Norah didn't know. Quickly he outlined the Brasso
case. "I'll work from that end, you keep on the adoption, and we'll meet in the middle," he concluded with
satisfaction. But Norah didn't appear to share his
optimism. "You do see that it's interlocked, don't you?"

"Yes."

"So?"

"So every witness who could tell us anything is
missing—Carlo Abruzzi, Janet Price, an unknown
killer in a sixteen-year-old murder."

She was usually so quick, so perceptive; Joe was
surprised that Norah didn't immediately proceed to the
next logical assumption. Then his elation died and a
heavy sadness came over him. She saw it, all right; she
was ahead of him, too far ahead. They were on the
verge of finding out where Mark came from and she
was afraid to know. But she had to face it; they both
did.

"Janet Price worked with Louis Heggerat then;
she could still be working with him."

"And for the Nerones," Norah added, looking at her
husband with real horror in her eyes.

They had reached the car, but neither made any
move to get in. Joe took her hand in his. "They set us
up and they used Janet Price to do it. We have no
reason to assume that they also provided Mark."

11

LOUIS HEGGERAT had a history of operating on the shady side of the law. In fact, just after Eddie Gundersen's adoption he had been put under temporary suspension from the Association of the Bar of the City of New York for "converting to his own use" monies entrusted to him as guardian for an elderly man designated as "incompetent." Before that he had served time in the Federal Correction Institution at Danbury, Connecticut, for perjury in a stolen securities case.

According to the last available government figures, the ratio of agency to private or independent adoptions nationally was slightly over three to one. The New York State figures for '71–'72 were only a little higher. But then the baby drought was just beginning. Coinciding with the generalized use of the pill, it grew, gathering momentum with the liberalization of the abortion laws and the tolerant attitude toward unwed mothers. Eddie had been adopted in 1971. He had cost Mr. and Mrs. Ernst Gundersen $5,000 in legal fees to Louis Heggerat. Norah knew from her own experience that the fees since then had skyrocketed, like everything else, and were still rising. She had heard of babies going for $25,000. Heggerat might not have been in the baby racket at the time of the Gundersen adoption, but he was shrewd enough and venal enough to realize he had stumbled on a good thing.

So far there was no indication that the mob was involved in the burgeoning baby racket. But when there was a hunger—any kind of hunger—they moved in. They moved in and pandered to it. During

Prohibition it was alcohol. When that became legal, they switched to drugs. That was slowing down. Were they now selling babies? It made Norah sick to think about it. On the surface it appeared that the volume of business was too small for them, but that was balanced by the willing victims eager to pay and to keep their mouths shut. She should know—hadn't she very nearly been one of those willing victims herself?

She put those thoughts firmly out of her mind. For her immediate purpose it didn't matter whether the mob had moved in on Louis Heggerat as a silent partner or not. All she wanted from the lawyer was a lead on Janet Price.

Representing herself as interested in adopting a baby, a role she certainly had the experience to play, Norah called for an appointment. She had no fear that Audrey Gundersen might have warned Heggerat. Joe's promise to keep her out of it was what had finally prevailed on Eddie's mother to divulge the lawyer's name. By calling she'd be admitting she was responsible for putting the police on him. Had Heggerat asked for a reference, Norah intended simply to say it was a mutual friend, suggesting that the name was better not mentioned over the telephone. But Heggerat did not seem at all surprised to get a call from a stranger. He was genially accommodating, and the date was set for five the following afternoon at his home, because, as he explained, he was in the process of moving his office. Norah knew he had no office anymore; presumably he didn't need one.

Heggerat himself answered the door. He was a man in his late fifties or early sixties. Tall and dignified, with a full head of silver-gray hair and matching goatee and a florid complexion that with a comfortably rounded paunch indicated good living. He greeted his new client expansively, taking both Norah's hands in his and giving them a warm and reassuring squeeze. He looked straight into her eyes, a look that was intended to express sympathy but that was shrewdly assessing the measure of her desire.

Norah was glad that she had dressed carefully, wearing her new coat and the red fox hat Joe had given her for Christmas. As Heggerat helped her off with the coat and went to hang it in the closet, she knew he'd look at the label, which was Bonwit's, but he wasn't to know it came from their discount department, the Finale Room, bought at the post-Christmas closeout sale.

Smiling unctuously, Heggerat ushered her into a pleasant, well-furnished living room and placed a chair for her beside his desk. He offered a cigarette from an expensive Jensen's silver box, which Norah refused. Then, taking a standard-sized file card from a desk drawer, he prepared to jot down the relevant statistics. He apologized for the absence of his secretary by saying that she was supervising the office move.

Norah nodded, but she was sure that no other person was ever present at these interviews, no embarrassing witness who might later be subpoenaed if the prospective client changed her mind, balked at the price, and brought a complaint. The lawyer was a two-time loser; he'd evidently learned something about avoiding pitfalls. Norah had got in by posing as a client; she had no intention of playing out the charade. There was no point to it. Now that she was there, settled, and Heggerat poised to probe her, she opened her handbag and held out her ID wallet with shield.

He covered his shock well. The smile disappeared but only for an instant and then it was back, somewhat forced and a little too broad, revealing yellowed wolfish teeth. "Well, now, Mrs. . . . uh. . . ." He leaned forward to take a closer look at the ID. "Detective Mulcahaney. That wasn't exactly fair, was it? Entrapment. Could we call it that?" he asked blandly.

"Have I trapped you, Mr. Heggerat? How and into what?" Norah responded just as blandly. "As I understand it, entrapment implies causing someone to com mit an offense he would not otherwise have committed."

"Well, well, *touché*. You know your law." He leaned back, his good humor apparently restored. "But you did misrepresent yourself, you know, Detective Mulcahaney, and it wasn't necessary. Not at all, I'm always glad to cooperate with the police. What's the problem? How can I help you?"

"We've had a complaint against you. One of your clients claims that your fee for handling the adoption of her son was illegally high."

The smile remained fixed for a long moment, then the lawyer threw his head back and began to laugh. He took his time laughing and plenty of time to frame an answer. Then he leaned forward across the desk. "Now, now, Detective Mulcahaney, that's really not good enough. You were smart getting in here, so you're smart enough to know it's not good enough. If there really were a complaint, you'd be citing specifics. You'd also warn me of my rights. Or are you about to do that?" He chortled some more.

"Maybe I should." Norah got the card out of her handbag and began to read. "You have the right to remain silent. You have the right—"

"Please." Heggerat held up his hand. "May I tell you how I know there hasn't been a complaint? First, because I haven't done anything illegal, anything that might warrant a complaint. In granting you an appointment I have already admitted being a so-called baby lawyer. I do find babies for couples who want them; I do handle adoptions, and my fees are high. But nobody is forced to come to me, and nobody is forced to pay what I ask."

"That may be so—"

"It is so, and you know it very well. My fees are high, but they are completely justified. I have very high expenses. They include all medical costs for mother and child. Nowadays even a short stay in a hospital is astronomically expensive. For the average person his major financial asset is good health or a comprehensive hospitalization and medical plan," he digressed. "Therefore, if there should happen to be any complication connected with the birth either for mother or child—"

"And there often is, I suppose."

"Quite often." He ignored the irony. "The mother is usually indigent, which means she's also in poor health and needs, is entitled to, money to get back on her feet, to recover physically and emotionally. That's certainly fair, wouldn't you say?"

"I haven't come to discuss ethics."

He held up one finger. "Bear with me. The prospective parents are only too willing to pay for these things and for my efforts in locating a child for them—which I may tell you is not the easiest thing in the world. But you probably know that too. I have to maintain an extensive network of contacts. You wouldn't believe the research involved. I have agents on college campuses, among prostitutes, among housewives who occasionally find pregnancy embarrassing."

Despite herself, Norah was fascinated by the dissertation. She let him continue.

"Even the modern, enlightened young woman of today can get careless, carried away, forget to take precautions. The youngsters are shy about applying to a physician for the pill or other contraceptive device, afraid their parents might find out. They take a chance and they get caught. Some are frightened about undergoing abortion. Some can't afford it or have religious scruples. Some have the baby as a form of self-castigation. And still the supply is scarce. On the other hand, there are countless barren women who are emotionally and temperamentally suited for motherhood, but biologically denied." He stopped, evidently expecting a comment. "You agree?"

"Certainly."

"Good. When such a woman finally has a baby placed in her arms, at no matter what cost, when she is at last fulfilled, finds meaning in her life, joy, a family—is she likely to complain how she got the child? Never. On the contrary, she becomes atavistically fierce in protecting her possession of the child and therefore protective of the source. So that's why I know you have no actual complaint against me, Detective Mulcahaney, or ever will have."

Norah was silent.

Heggerat continued. "Furthermore, in the extremely unlikely event that there should be such a complaint, it would cause me only mild inconvenience. Even if proved, New York State classifies it as a Class A misdemeanor—a thousand-dollar fine and a year in jail—at most."

"For each offense," Norah pointed out.

"For each proven offense," the lawyer corrected. "And I believe we've already covered the very slim possibility of any being proven. Actually, Detective Mulcahaney, what's really so terribly wrong about bringing together two women—one to whom her baby is an encumbrance and the other who yearns for the child? It's a service and one for which I'm entitled to a fee."

"What's wrong, Mr. Heggerat, is that satisfying the need is predicated on the ability to pay. That's what makes it illegal."

"That is our free-enterprise system, Detective Mulcahaney, the law of supply and demand. As long as that operates. . . ." He shrugged. "Let me ask you a question. Do you have children?"

Norah hesitated. "No."

"But you want them?"

She nodded, wondering what he was leading up to.

"You look to me like the kind of woman who should have them. You're still young and I'm sure you will have. If not, come see me again."

Norah gasped.

"Oh, yes, I'll accept you as a client even though you're a police officer. I'll find you a baby and I'll charge you to the limit of your ability to pay. That's how sure I am of my position; that's how much I trust the maternal instinct," he finished smugly.

His arrogance was almost convincing. "All right, Mr. Heggerat, now I'll level with you. I told you that I was investigating a complaint and I am—on my own behalf. You see, I *am* Mrs. Capretto. My husband and I have already adopted a boy. It turns out that there may be something wrong with the adoption."

For once Heggerat was at a loss. "Why come to me?"

"Because you know the woman who handled the adoption for us; in fact, you and she worked together. Janet Price." Would he deny it? Norah thought he was too smart to bother.

"Ah . . . but no more, Detective Mulcahaney, no more." He sighed heavily. "That Jan, she would do it, place a baby on her own, I mean. Time after time. A greedy woman. I warned her, but she couldn't resist. Finally I had to fire her. I had no choice."

He wasn't going to get off that easily. "When did you fire her?"

"Hm . . . six months ago."

He couldn't know when they'd adopted Mark, so he was giving himself leeway.

"What can I say to you, Detective Mulcahaney? I'm sorry, sincerely sorry for your trouble, but I don't know anything about your case. If there's some technical difficulty about the adoption, I'll try to help, as a courtesy because Jan used to work for me, but you cannot hold me responsible."

"I don't intend to hold me responsible. I just want to find Janet Price."

"I wish I could help you, but I have no idea what's happened to her."

Norah paused for the effect, then let him have it. "We're being blackmailed over the boy, Mr. Heggerat." Then she added the clincher. "My husband is also a police officer—Lieutenant Capretto."

That shook him; that wiped away the fake geniality and charm. "Blackmailed," he repeated and shook his head. "I'm distressed to hear it." There was no doubt he meant it too. "I assure you that I have nothing whatsoever to do with it, that I know nothing about it." As before, he fell back for his defense on brutal frankness. "I never blackmail a client. Some do, I don't. Never. It's dumb. Risky. Unnecessary. As I told you, my fees are high; I charge as much as the traffic will bear, so there isn't enough left over to make blackmail worthwhile."

"I believe you," Norah replied. "But we're not being asked for money. What they want is for my husband, Lieutenant Capretto, to drop a certain case."

Heggerat turned pale. "Insanity!" he croaked. "Sheer insanity." He slumped in his chair.

Norah had to believe that he didn't know about the threat. If he guessed its source, he was too frightened to reveal it. "So I ask you again, Mr. Heggerat, where is Janet Price?"

He shook his head.

"You must have an address for her?"

"She's never in one place very long. She moves around, or used to when she worked for me. She was what I call a 'finder.' As I told you, I have agents all over the country looking for expectant mothers who might be likely to turn over their babies."

"Yes, on college campuses, among prostitutes and housewives. Just exactly what was Miss Price's beat?"

"No 'beat.' She just moved around."

"At random? I don't think so, Mr. Heggerat. I'm sure you're better organized than that. She must have had what salesmen call a 'territory.' Surely you can define Janet Price's territory."

Sweat broke out on the lawyer's face. Fat beads formed on his forehead and slithered down to hang like icicles on the tips of his shaggy, grizzled eyebrows. Some dripped into the deep groves on either side of his pinched nose and were trapped in the beard. His florid complexion turned to dirty gray, so that he had the forlorn look of one of the marble busts along the Central Park Mall after a snowstorm. He didn't answer. He didn't even take out a handkerchief to wipe his face because that would have admitted distress.

"Never mind," Norah went on. "I get the picture. Janet Price used to be in show business, of a sort. What more natural than that show business should be her territory? Young actresses, dancers, models—they're emotional, sexually liberated, and vulnerable. Motherhood would be a particular encumbrance in their careers. Beautiful girls, they'd produce exceptionally beautiful and marketable babies. Definitely a fertile and lucrative field and one in which Jan Price had plenty of expertise. She'd know just where to look and what approach to use. I imagine she was one of your most successful 'finders.'"

As she talked, Norah became more and more sure of herself. She had him. There were no loopholes left. Frightened as Louis Heggerat was to help, she intended to make him more frightened not to.

"Granted it's a big territory—New York, Hollywood, Vegas," she went on. "Miss Price has contacts, but so do the police. Also, there's a very active grapevine in the entertainment industry, as I'm sure you're aware. Everybody knows everybody else and they live on gossip. It will take a certain number of man-hours, but we will find her. And while we're looking, who knows what else may turn up? Old and forgotten crimes have a way of getting solved through a search like that. We may even turn up the people behind Janet Price."

She let it hang for a moment or two.

"Did I mention the particular case my husband is working on, Mr. Heggerat?"

"Please . . . I'm not interested. I don't want to know."

"The Nerone gang killings."

"Please. . . ." He cringed.

"I understand your situation, Mr. Heggerat, believe me. I just wonder how the DA is going to feel about you? When my husband solves the case, Miss Price will naturally be charged with complicity in the blackmail attempt at least, if not with being an accessory after the fact in the murders. I just wonder . . . would you be liable to the same charges? But you're a lawyer, so you'd know the risk better than I."

Heggerat shook himself. "I do have an old address," he admitted. "Jan Price used to keep a small apartment at the Belvedere on Central Park South. She wasn't in it much; it was a *pied à-terre*." Then in a last futile attempt to extricate himself he added, "I'm not sure she still has it."

12

IT was late, but Norah went straight over to the Belvedere. The address was prestigious, but the building itself was rundown, seedy. The lobby had once been handsome; now it was dirty, the carpet and furnishings soiled and worn. Half the light bulbs in the elaborate wall sconces were out—energy saving? Shivering in the damp chill of a lowered thermostat, Norah didn't think so; more likely the landlord was using the energy crisis as an excuse to save on his electric bill. The doorman, small, dark, unshaven, and unkempt, was what the Belvedere deserved. He was lethargically chewing gum and quite willing to let her walk by and save himself the trouble of asking her business.

Norah approached him. "Miss Janet Price?"

"Eight E." He shifted the wad from one side of his mouth to the other.

"Thank you."

He let her nearly reach the elevator at the back before calling. "She's out. Left maybe half an hour ago."

"Oh? Have you any idea when she'll be back?"

"If I was you, I wouldn't wait." He clicked his teeth on the gum.

"Oh?"

"She was wearing her glad rags." Trying to be "hip," he had dated himself. "She won't be back till the bars close."

Norah frowned. Had Heggerat called and warned his erstwhile associate that a police officer was on the way? If he had, Janet Price evidently wasn't concerned enough to change her plans for a night out.

Maybe Heggerat hadn't been able to reach her? Anyhow, there was nothing to be done till morning.

"How late are you on?"

"I go off at eight P.M. If you want to leave a message, I can pass it on to the night man, but she ain't going to be in no condition to read it."

He stood so close and was chewing so energetically that Norah could look right into his mouth at his white-coated tongue and stained teeth and see the heavy salivation. Somehow she managed not to wince. "Then I won't bother."

All she wanted was to make sure that nobody was going to tell Janet Price she'd been around.

The place seemed even more depressing when Norah returned the next morning. The lobby doors were wide open, dissipating what little heat there was. As there was no sign of any doorman this time, she went straight up. The hallway was narrow, walls gray, floors covered with chipped linoleum, the atmosphere close and reeking of last night's cooking. Garlic. Somebody sure liked garlic. Norah wrinkled her nose; she hated it. From inside 8E she could hear the faint sound of a radio tuned to a news station. So Janet Price was up. Norah rang the bell.

The radio voice stopped, making Norah think the radio had been turned off, but then she heard a time signal and the voice started again. She rang a second time. Still no answer and still the radio continued playing. She tried the door. The knob turned— Janet Price must have been in really bad shape when she got home last night. The building being run-down as it was, Norah wasn't surprised the door was not equipped with an automatic latch. She went inside.

The Belvedere, as its name implied, offered a fine view of Central Park—to the front apartments. This small, dingy box of a room looked out on an enclosed court: Janet Price might as well have been living in any tenement anywhere in the city. It appeared to be exactly what Heggerat had dubbed it—a convenience address, a place for mail, to keep clothes, to use as a tax deduction while Janet Price traveled and enjoyed better comforts elsewhere. Norah couldn't blame her for spending as little time as possible here.

The radio was still playing from behind a closed door—of the bedroom probably.

"Miss Price?" Norah called. "Miss Price?" She knocked on the door. "Hello? Anybody in there?" She opened it part way and looked inside.

Janet Price was home to stay. For a long moment Norah stared from the threshold at the social worker who had provided her and Joe with a son. She was much as Norah remembered—a short, dumpy woman with chestnut hair cut in bangs and china-blue eyes that had once been merry and now stared glassily at the cracked ceiling. In life she had been pert, doll-like; in death she looked broken, a plaything cast aside by a heedless child.

She was sprawled on the floor between the unmade bed and a cluttered vanity table. The chair that went with the vanity was overturned, a white girdle and half slip caught around one leg. Powder had spilled on the mirrored table surface; an open lipstick rolled just to the edge. Norah knelt beside the body.

Janet Price's plump face was puffy from the night's drinking probably. Apparently she had got up and started to dress—her half-open robe showed she was wearing bra and panty hose. From the bullet wound near her heart a blossom of blood had grown, staining the white bra and spreading down over the pale rolls of flesh to the elastic band of the panty hose. Norah touched one outflung hand. It was still warm.

The radio voice droned on portentously. Norah got off her knees, went to the bureau, and turned the radio off. For a moment she savored the silence. Then, using the bedside phone, she called the precinct and reported the homicide. After that she called the team office.

"David? This is Norah. Let me talk to Joe, please."

"He's not here," David Link told her. "He went to ACCB. You want me to get hold of him?"

That was Arrest and Conviction Central Bureau. Joe would be looking up the files on Charles Brasso. She could only hope that he'd be luckier than she, because as far as she could tell, they'd reached the end of the line on Janet Price. It wasn't like Norah to give up, but with the social worker's death the last link to Mark and his adoption had been cut. She had a terrible sense of defeat, a terrible intuition that Mark was already lost to them.

"Norah?" David repeated. "Do you want me to try to contact Joe?"

"Yes, okay. Tell him I've found Janet Price and she's dead."

"God!"

Norah gave the address. There was nothing more for either of them to say.

Depressed, nearly hopeless, it was out of sheer habit that Norah took another look around the crime scene, automatically attempting to reconstruct the events leading up to the murder. Had the killer spent the night with Janet Price? Had a quarrel developed the next morning? No. A woman puts a robe on getting out of the bath or out of bed. If she's dressing, she puts on a complete set of underwear—bra, hose, panties, girdle, slip, and then perhaps a robe over that. But Janet Price had got only as far as panty hose and bra; the girdle and slip were still on the chair. It looked as though she'd been interrupted; as though the doorbell had rung while she was dressing and she'd just thrown the robe on to go and answer. Before pursuing that line, Norah went back to the living room to check the front door. Yes, there was a chain on it. Surely Janet Price, like everyone else, would keep the chain on till she saw who it was. It appeared that she had willingly admitted her killer.

Now Norah returned to the bedroom. The position of the vanity chair interested her. It had fallen on its side in the same direction as the body, indicating Janet Price had been sitting in it when she was shot, slumped forward, overturning it as she fell. There must have been a considerable degree of intimacy between her and the visitor for her not only to admit him but to permit him to accompany her into the bedroom while she continued dressing.

Why had the radio been left on? If they were going to talk, wouldn't it be natural for Janet Price to turn it off? Unless the killer himself had turned it on to cover the sound of the shot? Not all killers came prepared with silencers. So he walked around to the far side of the bed to the bureau and switched the radio on— loud. Surprised, Jan Price turned in the chair, and he shot her. The ME would figure the trajectory of the bullet, and Norah was sure her reconstruction would be confirmed.

She sighed aloud. She didn't think Louis Heggerat had done it. The lawyer would hardly have given the address to Norah if he intended to kill his erstwhile associate. She had feared he might call Jan Price and warn her. Had he warned her bosses instead?

The dancer turned social worker had a long association with the underworld; she was an established and trusted employee, therefore it had not occurred to Norah that she might be in danger. Norah had long since learned not to hold herself responsible when one crime spawned another; just the same she wished she had waited for Janet Price to get home last night— no matter how late.

Assuming the social worker had been killed to keep from talking, it followed that there was nothing left in the apartment that might reveal the identity of who was behind her and the adoption. There might be records of other adoptions, though, either in association with Heggerat or, as the lawyer had indicated, transactions she had handled on her own, records of expectant mothers with whom she had been in touch. Norah decided to give the place a quick toss on her own. Deftly, careful not to smudge any possible latents, she went through the drawers and closets. From the jumble it was hard to tell whether someone had already searched or whether Janet Price just hadn't been very neat. Either way, Norah found nothing.

She went back into the gloomy living room. Soon the radio patrol officers would be arriving. Then the division homicide detectives, lab men, the ME and his people, the DA's men, the entire retinue that her call to the precinct had alerted. For the time being there was nothing more she could do but wait. In a way it was a relief. Unfortunately it also gave her time to think.

Lieutenant Joseph Capretto, head of the special unit instituted by the police commissioner, had full access to the Brasso file as Officer Joe Capretto had not had—from the initial patrol officer's report, his own, to that of the detective carrying the case, Frank Oakes, as well as the lab, autopsy, and ballistics information. Rereading what he had written sixteen years before brought a wave of embarrassment, like coming across an old high school essay: It seemed stilted, almost naïve. Nowadays patrolmen and detectives use printed sheets, just checking the item that best fits the circumstance and description of the victim; quicker and more efficient, certainly, but devoid of any hint of the officer's personal reaction.

Joe was particularly interested in the lab report relating to the fingerprints obtained from the body. Charles Brasso had been a "floater," in the water a considerable time, so the papillary ridges had been destroyed; nevertheless, the entire papillary pattern was found on the inner surface of the skin and photographed. At the time, developing the fingerprints had seemed an academic labor. They could not be compared, for the gun found on the body was clean —gun stocks do not take prints, and the barrel was wiped. Yet Joe had a strong feeling that the lab's thoroughness might prove to have been very much worthwhile.

The autopsy report stated that there was a high ratio of alcohol in Brasso's blood. It also listed a severely damaged liver, suggesting that he had been a heavy drinker over a long period. What really heated Joe's blood and caused his heart to pump faster was in the morgue report. Brasso had come over from Naples alone. In lieu of any close relative the official identification of the body had been made by his partner Johnny Allegro. Allegro also claimed the body when it was released for burial.

By the time David called to give Joe Norah's message he had returned the file and left.

He went to meet his informant, Stanley "Muscles" Koslav. Koslav had once been a fighter, a lightweight, one of a stable owned and controlled by underworld big shots. Even in his prime Muscles had been merely fodder for the preliminaries and sparring partner for contenders. The time of his prime coincided with that of Brasso and Allegro. Muscles had been the one who tipped Joe to Abruzzi and the two heroin shipments. Joe did not consider it a coincidence.

They met in a luncheonette on Third Avenue where hopefully neither the police lieutenant nor the informer was known. Koslav had a clown's face—skin flour white; flabby lips turned up in a perpetual grin; bulbous nose; dark, button eyes and heavy eyebrows like horizontal parentheses; even his black hair curled upward at the edges. The clown's paint and putty were Koslav's real flesh. Because of the real life mask it was hard to read him, yet Joe could tell he was more nervous than usual at a meet. He didn't want to talk about Brasso. He claimed he couldn't remember that far back. The truth was, as Joe well knew, that Muscles often forgot what had happened yesterday or the day before, but of the times of his meager glory he had almost total recall.

"I swear to God I don't know nuthin', Lieutenant."

"Well, you know Brasso fronted the Half Note Club over on Fifty-second Street."

"Sure, sure. Everybody knows that."

"You probably used to go in there yourself plenty of times."

"Well, yeah, a few times maybe. . . . I suppose. I didn't go to the night spots much, Lieutenant. I was fightin' then; I kept good training." Koslav continued to fidget and cast anxious looks over his shoulder. "I'd like to help ya, Lieutenant, but I don't know nuthin'. I'll keep my ears open and if—"

"What's bugging you, Muscles?"

"Nuthin', nuthin', Lieutenant, I swear to God." He stopped turning around and gave Joe his best, most earnest expression. "You know how it was for me in those days. I was young, ambitious, all I cared about was fightin'. I minded my own business, kept my nose clean, done what I was told."

"That's what you're doing now, right, Muscles?"

"The lid's on, Lieutenant," Muscles protested. "Like I told you on the phone, nobody's talkin', but nobody. I wouldn't even take the chance to ask around. Too risky. I don't know why."

"Who told you to tip us about Abruzzi and the heroin, Muscles?"

One of the unspoken rules of the game was that the informant never revealed his source, and the officer never asked. The grin remained fixed, but the fleshy lips around it quivered. "Gee, Lieutenant, you shouldn't ought to ask." Koslav was in deep distress. "You know I can't tell you."

"Okay, okay, forget it." The ex-fighter had given as much of the answer as Joe had expected and wanted —that the information had not been chance talk picked up in a bar or gym or around a gambling table. It had been purposely leaked, as he had suspected.

But Koslav was still upset. In his precarious life, treading a delicate balance between opposing forces, in constant danger from both, Muscles was constantly appeasing, experienced in offering just enough to prove his good faith to the one while staying out of trouble with the other. "All I know about Brasso, Lieutenant, is what everybody knows." Again he looked around, this time leaning out past the edge of the booth in which they sat to scrutinize the front of the luncheonette. Then he bent low across the table, getting as close to Joe as he could and whispered. "When Big Charlie came over from the old country, he moved right into the organization. He was ambitious, and he moved up fast. Some said too fast. He made a lot of the *capos* nervous, dig? They didn't like his style. So when he turned up dead, nobody was sorry. Get what I mean, Lieutenant?"

Joe nodded and reached for his wallet.

Muscles Koslav pulled back in alarm. "No, no! You don't owe me nuthin'. I don't want no payoff; I didn't earn it. I didn't tell you nuthin', nuthin' you couldn't find out from practically anybody. Right, Lieutenant, right?"

"Nothing I didn't already know, Muscles," Joe said soothingly.

The neighborhood of Joe's first posting hadn't changed much since he had patrolled it. There were a few more houses maybe, but they looked like all the others—small, unadorned boxes, each with its minuscle plot of land rigorously ordered. Every open bed was snugly blanketed for the winter under good salt hay, the rose canes cut back and hilled with rich soil. In the bare backyards Joe could see the wire mesh that protected the vegetable beds from rodents and the gnarled vines of the inevitable grape arbor. In summer there would be a table in the leafy shade of each arbor; the family would eat there and spend the long hot days and part of the nights there. The wine from those grapes was meanwhile quietly maturing in every cellar. The people here were predominantly Italian, of modest means, but they lived a good life. Someday, Joe thought, he and Norah might have a place like one of these.

The church too was as Joe remembered it—a modest white-frame structure built well off the ground because of the high water table. There was still plenty of open space all around. Joe climbed the steep steps to the front doors and stood for a moment looking out at the scrubby fields. The wind gusted, heavy with moisture. He sucked it in and tasted the sea. He went inside.

It was remarkable how the memories came back. Joe saw the interior of the church, not as it was now, gray and cold with the lights and heat turned prudently low, but as it had been—mellow with candles and incense, lavish with the funeral flowers, warmed by the body heat of the mourners. For a man without relatives or friends, the funeral of Charles Brasso had been well attended. Joe had been on patrol the morning of the service and he hadn't been able to resist looking in.

He took a few moments now to walk down the center aisle of the chill and empty chapel and kneel in front of the altar, cross himself, and say a prayer. When he was finished, he got up and looked for the small side door that usually connected with the parish house.

He found it, passed through, and followed a narrow corridor to the main foyer of the priest's residence. A squat woman seated at the switchboard back of the reception counter jumped as he came up.

"How did you get in?" she demanded, but didn't give him a chance to answer. "You're not supposed to come through the church. You're supposed to come around to the front and ring the bell and wait till I let you in. There's no point in keeping the front door locked if anybody can get in from behind!" she complained. "I keep telling Father that connecting door should be bolted as soon as morning Masses are over, but he forgets." The lay worker's sigh indicated the priest had his mind on higher things.

"I'm sorry," Joe apologized most contritely.

She looked him over and sniffed. "Well, you're a stranger so I don't suppose you knew any better." She heaved herself up, squeezed her bulk around the counter, and bustled down the passage. Joe heard the door he had just come through slam shut and the click of the bolt being turned.

"Anybody could walk in," the receptionist huffed on her way back. "We could all be robbed and killed. In my opinion the church should be locked when there aren't any services, but Father won't hear of it. You have no idea the characters that wander in—not to pray either, just to get out of the cold or to sleep off a drunk. Father insists they have a right to do that. Two weeks ago one of them hacked the chain off the poor box and walked out with it. You know what Father did? He said a Mass for 'the poor unfortunate'!" She raised the counter lid, squeezed through, then let it fall with a smart bang. "Well, what do you want?"

"I'd like to see the pastor, please."

It was typical of lay workers, Joe thought, that having put down her priest, she now became fiercely protective of him. "You'll have to wait. Father Meyerhoff is just going to have his lunch."

Typical of the church hierarchy too to put a Meyerhoff as shepherd over a flock of Italian sheep. "I'll try not to keep him too long," Joe promised. "But it is important. Police business," he added, showing his credentials.

"Oh." The receptionist stared first at the ID, then at Joe. "Why didn't you say so?" She sat down at her board, adjusted her headset, then stabbed one of the plugs into a hole. "I'm sorry to disturb you, Father." Her tone was syrupy. "There's a policeman out here to see you. I told him you were just going to sit down to—yes, Father. . . . Thank you, Father." She yanked the plug out. "First door on the right."

As the church suited its parish, so the pastor suited his church. The Reverend Father Paul Meyerhoff was big, raw-boned, ruddy-faced, graying. He wore old, baggy trousers, a much-laundered yellow and green plaid shirt whose open neck showed a snowy white singlet underneath. His pale eyes were tearing.

"I was just doing a little yard work," he explained.

"Sawing off some broken tree limbs, damage from last night's storm. Trees don't grow easily this near the shore; we have to take care of them."

It was evident that he had taken pleasure in the work, was exhilarated by the exertion and fresh air. Probably Father Meyerhoff, like his parishioners, also grew roses and vegetables. Probably he had a grape arbor and the juice of the grapes rested in the parish house basement. The bishop had known what he was doing, after all, when he assigned Meyerhoff.

"Mrs. Di Nardone says you're a policeman."

"Yes, Father. Lieutenant Capretto."

Father Meyerhoff indicated that he was not only impressed by Joe's rank but that he realized the matter must have unusual importance to bring him out.

"Sorry to disturb you just when you're going to eat."

"Ach!" the priest waved that aside. "The bell won't ring for another half hour at least. Mrs. Di Nardone wants to make a big executive out of me—everything by appointment. What's this about, Lieutenant? No serious trouble for one of my people, I hope?"

"No, Father. I'm looking for information regarding an old case. I don't really know that you can help me: It goes back sixteen years. I assume you have records and maybe you could put me in touch with whoever was the pastor at the time."

"Maybe I can help you. I wasn't pastor then, but I was here." He gestured to a chair.

Joe sat. "It's about Charles Brasso. He was one of your parishioners, I believe. He was buried from this church."

"Charles Brasso. . . ."

"He ran a nightclub in Manhattan, but he had a house out here on Reynolds Channel. He was drowned and washed ashore along the Rock-aways. . . ."

"Ach . . . that one. Yes, yes, I remember. Of course, I remember very well. Over in Long Beach they're more accustomed to such . . . tragedies, but here, in our modest parish. . . ." He let it trail off, opened a drawer and, rummaging, found a crumpled pack of cigarettes. Having offered a smoke and been refused, the pastor selected a bent cigarette, straightened it carefully, and lit up. "Just what do you want to know, Lieutenant?"

"Anything you can tell me about Brasso."

"That's not much, I'm afraid. As I said, I had just come here at the time, but so had he. He had just bought one of the big houses on the water. Caused quite a stir in the community, a lot of opposition too because of his . . . well, there's hardly any need for me to mince words with you, is there? People didn't want him here because of his underworld associations. They felt he should be on the other side of the bridge, along with the others like him." The priest sighed gently. "There was also considerable curiosity as to why a bachelor should want such a big place. Some of the resentment abated when we learned that he was planning to be married to his childhood sweetheart, that he was bringing her over from the old country. A lovely girl she was, a real Italian beauty. For her it was he'd bought the house, furnished it down to the last detail, even to the linens and the pots and pans."

That washed out the possibility that Janet Price might have been Brasso's girlfriend. "I didn't know that Charles Brasso was planning to be married," Joe said.

"The ceremony was to be performed in this very church. Normally, as you know, the wedding takes place in the bride's parish. But as the young woman was recently arrived, had no relations in this country and no official parish affiliation, Father O'Donohue readily agreed. It was doubly tragic, then, that within days of the intended wedding Charles Brasso should be buried from this same church."

"Where did the young lady stay before the wedding? I assume it wasn't in Brasso's house."

"Oh, no, no, certainly not. Mr. Brasso was punctilious about the proprieties. He put her up in a hotel in

New York—at his own expense; she had nothing. I understand he even paid for the bride's wedding gown and trousseau."

Up to now Brasso had been a piece in an old puzzle, a faceless hood, ruthlessly ambitious, who had killed and been in turn killed. The priest's story revealed a human being and an unexpectedly sentimental one at that. Big Charlie's love for his childhood sweetheart was at least indirectly responsible for his death, Joe thought, for it explained his determination to make money fast. The emotional climate—needs and passions frustrated or misdirected—spawned crimes; it could never be overlooked.

"What happened to the girl? What happened to the fiancée after Brasso's funeral?" Joe asked.

Father Meyerhoff hesitated. "I suppose she went back home. I assumed, we all assumed that she went back to Italy. She had nobody here, nor did Brasso. She hardly spoke the language. We took it for granted she would go back."

Joe could see that the pastor's uneasiness was growing. "It was natural that you should think so."

"But nobody took the trouble to find out. We were concerned about her welfare, naturally," Father Meyerhoff explained. "But the man, I don't recall his name, the one who made the funeral arrangements. . . ."

"Allegro? Johnny Allegro?"

"Yes, I think so. Mr. Allegro assured us that she'd be looked after. He said she'd receive whatever money was realized from Mr. Brasso's estate and if it wasn't enough, if she needed anything, it would be provided." He frowned. "I seem to remember he specifically mentioned the fare back to her hometown of . . . well, I can't remember that." He was offering, not information, but justification for not having taken greater interest in a lonely and bereft girl. "They'd already seen to it that she shouldn't be alone—Mr. Brasso's employers. They'd moved her out of the hotel and over to Long Beach to stay with the family of one of the *capos*. I'll admit to you, Lieutenant, that this troubled Father O'Donohue and myself. We didn't like her to be staying with such people, but what could we say? What could we do? And Mrs. Nerone was and is a good and pious woman."

"Nerone?" A quiver passed through Joe.

Father Meyerhoff nodded. "And when we saw how Mr. and Mrs. Nerone treated the girl, with such tenderness and concern, like their own daughter . . . well, we couldn't help but be struck. . . ."

He didn't finish. It wasn't necessary. Joe knew that both priests had been impressed by the consideration coming from the otherwise ruthless man.

"When was that? When did you observe her in the company of the Nerones?"

"At the funeral."

"She was able to attend?"

"Barely. She was in a bad state, very bad; Mr. and Mrs. Nerone just about supported her between them. Well, you can imagine . . . seeing the man she loved being buried from the very church in which she'd expected to be married."

Once again Joe mentally recreated that bright morning when he'd left the patrol car to enter the church, forcing the lens of memory to zoom in from the blur of golden light and stained glass windows to the faces of the mourners. No use. He could recall no particular person. When the cortege formed to carry the casket out, there had been two women in the group. They had passed by him. As was the custom among Italians, they wore deep mourning even to the long, thick black veils over their faces, so Joe wouldn't have got any kind of look at them even if he'd been interested, which at the time he hadn't been. One of them must have been Lucia Nerone and the other undoubtedly Brasso's fiancée.

"What was the girl's name, Father?"

The pastor shook his head. "I'm sorry."

"But you must have records. If the wedding date was set—"

"Of course, of course, the banns would have been

published and announced from the pulpit at the Sunday Masses. We did that back then." Putting aside his qualms of conscience, Father Meyerhoff got up to deal with the present. He gave Joe a wry smile as he indicated an ancient bank of filing cabinets. "We never throw anything away at St. Joseph's. Though it often takes awhile to find what we're looking for."

"Charles Brasso died in September, 1958."

"That should help." For a long moment Father Meyerhoff considered the array of drawers, then pounced on one, pulled it out, and fingered through the folders. "Well, what do you know? It's not usually this easy. Here we are—banns for the first week in September: between Frank Ruggiero of this parish, no; between James Santorini . . . ah! For the first time between Charles Brasso of this parish and Mariarosa Martinelli of Muggia, Italy." He looked up at Joe with satisfaction.

13

MARIAROSA MARTINELLI. Giorgio Nerone's mistress of many years. Sole witness to his murder and survivor of it.

On his way back to the city Joe was caught in airport traffic on the Van Wyck Expressway and had plenty of time to think it over.

Mariarosa Martinelli occupied a unique position in the underworld. Unlike most other kept women, she had not been call girl, actress, or model. She was the kind of good, Italian girl most *capi* looked for as a wife. In fact, the word was that Nerone had at one time come close to marrying her. He had been deterred partially by strong ties to his children, but mainly by the fact that at the time his wife's father was a bigger man in the organization than he and would have made him pay dearly for a divorce. So instead he set Mariarosa up as his official mistress, and his associates quickly learned that she was to be treated with respect.

Her position was maintained through the years. According to Joe's information, she had no part in any of Nerone's various rackets. Yet she lived off the proceeds. Nerone installed her in the penthouse on Park Avenue and then bought the building and turned it over to her. Joe had no doubt she received other incomes too. So, directly involved or not, she had made a moral accommodation.

Nerone had been killed in her bed. His blood had spattered on her nightgown, but otherwise she had escaped unscathed—except for the emotional shock, naturally. When the police arrived, she had been hysterical. She claimed that as soon as the killer entered the bedroom and leveled the gun, she shut her eyes and didn't open them again till the shooting was over and she found herself miraculously still alive.

In his interview with her Joe had not been able to get any more out of her. She had not deviated from the initial statement: She had never seen the killer before in her life, had no idea who he was, could not offer even the vaguest description. Joe had accepted that because he had to. Everything indicated that the three murders, of Allegro, Lambroso, and Nerone, were part of a gangland power struggle, and that being so, the killer would have nothing against Mariarosa Martinelli. Still, hadn't it been a terrible risk to leave behind an eyewitness to the actual shooting? How could he know that the woman would be so deeply shocked that she would remember nothing? Or so terrified that she refused to tell what she remembered? How could he be sure?

Murder is a secret crime, yet this killer had not only left a witness behind but had actually chosen the time and the place when a witness would inevitably be present. He had planned it that way.

From the start, the peculiar circumstances of Giorgio Nerone's murder had intrigued Joe and suggested an additional and more private motive.

"*Vendetta.*" He whispered the ominous word. "*Vendetta!*" he repeated aloud in the full Italian broadness, sinister resonance, and age-old implications of the word. Killing Nerone in his mistress' bed had been the final indignity, a breach of the underworld code. Now that Father Meyerhoff had revealed the origin of the affair between the naïve Italian girl and the gangland boss, Joe realized there had been a purpose. Death for Nerone and punishment for Mariarosa had been meted out at one and the same time.

Ergo, the killer and Nerone's mistress were not strangers; to the contrary, they knew each other too well. Joe refused to go beyond that, not yet, not till he confronted Mariarosa Martinelli once more.

Traffic was spacing out. He pressed on the accelerator and concentrated on getting back to the city as quickly as possible.

He went up to the penthouse in the private elevator and was admitted by the elderly Italian maid. She wore the regulation dowdy black dress and hose that the women in her village still wore and the women of the Italian community in New York who still abided by the old customs wore—Signora Capretto among them. Vincenza Giannini might have been a relative or friend except for the voluminous apron and her manner, which plainly said "servant." She was neither more nor less friendly toward the lieutenant than she had been the first time Joe had met her and interrogated her, and he made no further attempt to draw her out. She showed him into the living room and left him to wait.

Today the drapes were pulled back, revealing French doors and a spacious, well-landscaped terrace and admitting the winter sun. The fading rosy rays illumined polished parquet floors, Oriental carpets, tapestried chairs, somber paintings in bright gilt frames. It was refracted into rainbow colors by the prisms of a giant crystal chandelier. The room could have been in any Italian *palazzo*, probably had been recreated by an expert to satisfy an Italian peasant girl's vision of elegance.

"Lieutenant Capretto?"

He hadn't heard her come in. Turning at her voice and seeing her really well for the first time, Joe had to stifle an involuntary gasp. *Dio mio!* She was still one beautiful woman.

Why still? Joe asked himself. She wasn't that old. Say that at the time of her intended marriage she'd been eighteen; that would make her thirty-four now. Norah was thirty-two, but she looked ten years younger than Martinelli. Mariarosa had lived hard. Recent events had marked her too. Like the maid, she wore black, but with a difference—her gown was long, high-

necked, full-sleeved, unadorned, and it clung to her
every curve. It was dramatic but harsh. It made her
white skin sallow, emphasized the gray hollows under
her dark eyes. Though she was still in mourning, it
was evident that she had recovered her emotional
poise. She exuded the confidence, even arrogance, of
a woman who set a high price on her beauty and was
accustomed to have the price paid.

"I appreciate your seeing me, Miss Martinelli," Joe
said.

She nodded, sat down, and waved him to a chair.
Joe took it, finding it a lot more comfortable than it
looked. "I've just come from talking to the pastor of
St. Joseph's out in Inwood," he began, then paused.
There was no visible reaction. "I was inquiring into the
death of Charles Brasso. I was interested to learn that
you were engaged to Brasso and intended to marry
him."

"That was a long time ago." Her voice was low, not
particularly pleasant. She spoke correctly, as one who
had studied earnestly, but her accent was bad, clearly
an imitation of the people around Nerone. It was not
one of her assets.

"You were childhood sweethearts. You both came
for the same village."

"Yes."

"When Charles Brasso sent for you, you had no relatives or friends in this country. You had only your
fiancé."

"Why are you interested?"

"Routine, Miss Martinelli. You weren't questioned
at the time of Brasso's death. You didn't come forward
to claim his body."

"His friends spared me the ordeal."

"Of course. Was your fiancé a heavy drinker?"

She frowned slightly. "I would rather not talk about
him."

"I'm sorry to revive sad memories, but it's important."

She shrugged. "He took wine with meals."

Joe let it go. "Father Meyerhoff had the impression that you went back to Italy to your family after the funeral."

"I had intended to."

"But you changed your mind. Why, Miss Martinelli?"

"There was nothing for me there."

"And here?"

"Here there was Giorgio Nerone." She paused. Then she looked straight at Joe. "As you very well know."

"But you were in love with Brasso."

"He was dead."

"So you accepted Signora Nerone's hospitality and her husband's consolation."

"I'm not required to offer any explanation for what I did."

"Not to me, Miss Martinelli."

"I come from a very large and very poor family. You are Italian but born here?" She waited till he nodded, then went on. "So you cannot know the quality of existence in a place like Muggia." Her voice was uninflected. "By the time Carlo's debts were paid, the bills I had incurred settled, there wasn't much left to take home. I would have been one more mouth to feed. My family would not have been glad to have me back."

Joe had taken one trip abroad visiting his people in Grosseto, a small, comfortably affluent town near Rome, but he knew villages like Muggia—picturesque with their cobbled streets and charmingly crooked houses, but whose open sewers reeked, without electricity or plumbing, where water was still pumped from a village well. Muggia was in the north, near Venice, but industry had not embraced Muggia and the land was notoriously hard and infertile. He understood.

"Lucia Nerone is a good woman," Mariarosa continued. "She performed her conjugal duties; she gave

Giorgio children, but she couldn't satisfy him. That was not my fault. There had been others before me."

"When did you first meet Nerone?"

Again she asked. "Why do you want to know?"

Joe shrugged as though it had no real importance. "Just a hunch. Tell me, did you ever view your fiancé's body?"

"No."

"Not even at the funeral parlor when he was laid out?"

"The casket was closed. I wanted to see him, but they wouldn't let me. He had been in the water too long. They said it would be too terrible."

"Who said?"

"Everybody. Even the priest . . . but it was not Father Meyerhoff. It was. . . ."

"Father O'Donohue?"

"Perhaps."

"And did Giorgio Nerone also tell you not to look?"

"Yes, yes, since you insist." Her voice rose. "He also wished to protect me from such an experience. I don't see what that has to do with anything."

"So you had already met Nerone."

"I had met all of Carlo's friends and associates. Naturally."

Joe took a deep breath. "You were Brasso's girl. Nerone had a yen for you. He took you away from Brasso."

"That's a lie!" Her dark eyes blazed. "I didn't even look at Giorgio until after . . . when Carlo was dead, dead and buried."

"When you thought he was dead and buried," Joe corrected.

For a moment she just stared. A nerve under her right eye began to twitch, then her wide mouth jerked to one side; the twitching finally pulled her whole face out of alignment in a series of contortions so rapid they were superimposed one on the other like photographs of the same subject that didn't quite match. Gradually the spasms subsided, but they left the lovely face haggard. "You're crazy," she mumbled. "You're a crazy man."

"Who killed him, Miss Martinelli? Who killed Carlo Brasso?"

"Not Giorgio. Do you think I would have given myself to Carlo's killer? I would have gone on the streets first. I would have killed myself. I loved Carlo. *Dio mio!* Carlo was my life. I was so happy when he sent for me, so proud—"

"Who, then, Miss Martinelli?" Joe asked in that same quiet, patient way.

"You tell me, Mr. Policeman, you tell me. That's your business, isn't it? All these years and you still haven't found out," she taunted. She got up and slowly, carefully, as though she was afraid she might fall, Giorgio Nerone's mistress made her way to the bar and with shaking hands poured herself some sherry into a delicately stemmed glass.

Joe waited till she had taken a few sips and was at least partially composed.

"I don't believe that Carlo Brasso is dead."

"You are crazy," Mariarosa repeated as though by rote. "A crazy man. . . ."

"You told me that your fiancé took only wine with meals, no more. But according to the autopsy report, the dead man was a heavy drinker, with a badly damaged liver to show for it."

"That's all I ever saw him take. I don't know what he did when we weren't together. At the club, all those hours, he could have done a great deal of drinking then without my knowing."

"The dead man also had a fractured ankle, a childhood injury. It had been badly set, resulting in one leg being a fraction shorter than the other. Do you know anything about that?"

"Of course. Carlo walked with a limp, very slight, hardly noticeable unless you were looking for it."

"Ah. . . ."

"I remember when it happened. Poor Carletto. We

were playing among the ruins and he fell from a pinnacle. The stone crumpled under him. We had no doctor in Muggia, so naturally the bone had started to heal by the time he arrived from Venice. It had to be broken a second time."

Joe decided not to call her on it, not now. "I'll tell you how I think it was, Miss Martinelli; correct me if you wish. Carlo Brasso came here in 1956, leaving his family and you, his sweetheart, behind. He became connected with the Nerone organization. He was smart, ambitious, and he rose fast. Too fast." Unconsciously Joe now quoted Muscles Koslav. "He made the *capi* nervous; they didn't like his style. He was violent and impulsive at a time when the policy was to cool it, go legit. He made his own decisions and acted on them. He didn't take orders."

"He was gentle and kind."

"With you, certainly. But he had another side." Joe paused to decide how far he should go. After all, Mariarosa Martinelli had loved Charles Brasso with all the fierceness and singlemindedness and in all the glory of a young girl's first love. Whatever her subsequent actions, Joe believed that she had mourned him sincerely, if briefly.

Joe was compassionate; he didn't need to prove his own authority by harassing a witness; he took no pleasure in destroying a witness. Though this woman had lived off the profits of crime and the sorrow of others, had been the mistress of a gang boss and consorted with his criminal associates, it was not up to him to judge her, much less mete out punishment. There was enough of the innocent, nearly illiterate peasant girl in the crime boss' mistress for Joe to pity her.

According to the initial rationale of the Brasso case, his murder of Officer Salenski had made him an embarrassment to his associates and they got rid of him. The way Joe now figured it, when Brasso killed the cop, he realized he had gone too far. He knew that as a cop killer he was a heavy liability to the mob and that they would not hesitate to finger him to the police or to get rid of him themselves. Either way, he was finished. But Brasso didn't give up easy; he was resourceful, and he got the jump on both of his pursuers.

"I suggest, Miss Martinelli, that it was not Charles Brasso who was shot, dumped at sea, then washed up on the beach, but a substitute." He looked straight at her. "A substitute he himself provided."

"No," she replied coldly. "I will not believe that. Carlo would never do such a thing. I know he killed that policeman, but that was in a gun fight. It was an accident. He would never kill in cold blood . . . and an innocent man at that. Never."

Joe thought of Detective Oakes' patronizing explanation of how the tide shifted in the channel every six hours, how the body would be carried out and back, out and back, over a period of days till it was beyond the channel mouth and in the open Atlantic, where another shift of tide finally washed it up on the beach. Joe had objected then that though the tides might be predictable, the strength and direction of the undertow was not; that the undertow might have taken the body east or west too far for it ever to turn up again. He still thought so, but now he had an answer.

Brasso had found some poor drunken derelict—the condition of the liver—down on the Bowery or wherever, and put him out of his misery. He brought him home to the house on the water, dressed him in his own clothes, planted the murder gun on him, then anchored him in the water under his own dock for a few days. When the victim was in the right condition, he towed him—he had a boat—to open water and cast him loose where he was sure he would float to shore.

It covered everything: the victim being killed with the gun that was found on him, the way he was dressed, and the convenient way he was washed up, not too soon to be identifiable, but soon enough for

Brasso to beat the heat of both the mob and the police search.

Whether the mob bought it at the time or not, it got them off the hook. The Salenski case was closed, and Brasso was out of their hair for good. As far as Nerone personally was concerned, it gave him the chance to make a play for Brasso's girl.

"It must have been a tremendous shock to you, Miss Martinelli, to learn after all these years that the man you had loved and thought was dead was, in fact, alive. When did you find out? Or did he just appear that night in your bedroom suddenly, without any kind of advance preparation?"

She smiled scornfully. "If Carlo had been alive, I would have known it. If another man had been in that coffin, I would have sensed it. If Carlo had done what you say, if he had arranged for another man to be buried in his place, don't you think he would have made sure that I knew it? He wouldn't have put me through such agony. He wouldn't just have left me behind. He would never have abandoned me!" Mariarosa Martinelli got up abruptly and strode to the French doors of her terrace and stared out. "If I had known, if I had the slightest hope that he was still alive, I would have waited . . . as long as necessary."

Naturally that had occurred to Joe. "Perhaps he did leave word for you, Miss Martinelli. Perhaps he left a letter. But it was never delivered. Of course, he couldn't know that it was never delivered."

"Ah. . . ." It was half groan, half sigh.

"So he came back to avenge himself. He thought you had betrayed him. What else could he think? All those long years he believed that and planned his revenge. The longer he had to wait, the more exquisitely he refined his plan. Then finally the opportunity presented itself. He walked into your apartment and shot your lover in your bed. Maybe he intended to kill you too, but when the actual moment came, he couldn't. Was it because he still loved you?

Or were you able to convince Charles Brasso that you were innocent, that you never got his letter, that you didn't know he was still alive?"

She did the only thing left her—she put her hands up to her face and began to cry softly.

"*Mariarosa, per l'amor' di Dio, dica la verità.*"

But the appeal brought no response. He tried again. "Do you feel that Nerone got what he deserved? Maybe you feel Carlo Brasso had a right to his vengeance and so you're protecting him. But Mariarosa, he has killed other men. Allegro and Lambroso, what about them? And the derelict? Do you want him on your conscience? Mariarosa, where is Carlo Brasso?"

"In his grave."

Joe got up. "Okay, Miss Martinelli, if that's the way you want it, we'll have a look."

"What?" She dropped her hands from her face and stared. "What do you mean?"

"We'll exhume the body."

"No!"

It was a shriek, startling in its unexpectedness.

"Why should you do such a thing? Why? Please don't. Please leave him alone. Please. What do you expect to find after all these years?"

"The truth. You said that Brasso broke his ankle when he was a child. The autopsy on the body in the grave shows no such injury."

"But you said. . . . You tricked me!"

"I asked you if Brasso had suffered such an injury and you said that he had."

"I lied."

"Why?"

She swallowed. "So that you'd leave him alone. So that you'd let him rest in peace. *Vi prego, Tenente, lascialo stare.*"

"You leave me no choice, Miss Martinelli. I have to know. I can't afford to waste time chasing a ghost. I have to make sure."

Joe picked up his coat and started toward the hall.

"Lieutenant!" she called after him. "Carlo is alive. Everything happened just the way you said."

"Where is he now?"

"I don't know."

"Oh, Miss Martinelli. . . ."

"I swear I don't know. When Carlo walked out of here the night of the murder . . . that's the last I saw or heard of him. Now go away. Go away and leave me alone!" She ran out of the room and slammed the door shut behind her.

14

IF she did know where Charlie Brasso was, the first thing Mariarosa would do would be to contact him. As soon as he got out the door, she'd be on the phone to Brasso, and there was nothing Joe could do about that. He strolled thoughtfully to the corner and ducked behind the building from where he could watch the canopied entrance in case she came out. If she was telling the truth and really didn't know Brasso's whereabouts, then it would take her time to find out. Joe was sure she'd try. Meanwhile, he could set up a surveillance and be ready to follow her if there was a meet.

Joe could figure the motive for Allegro's execution. Johnny, the happy warrior, had claimed the substitute body and identified it as Brasso. That identification was a necessary part of Brasso's escape plan. With Allegro's identification the police and the mob both lost interest in Brasso and the heat was off. Allegro, as part of the plot, would logically have been the one to tell Mariarosa that her fiancé was alive, maybe even to tell her where she could go to join him. Evidently it had been more profitable to tell Nerone instead. Okay, that took care of Allegro, but what about Vito Lambroso? What did Big Charlie have against Nerone's second in command to gun him down in front of the movie house on Third Avenue?

Had Lambroso been a party to the deception of Mariarosa? Allegro, being of a lower caste, might not have had access to the big boss and had had to go through Lambroso with his information. But how could Brasso have known that? And why had Big Charlie waited so long for his revenge? It couldn't have taken him more than a few weeks to figure that his girl wasn't going to show up and that he'd been double-crossed. True, he couldn't come back on the next plane—he was wanted for muder. Still, sixteen years was one hell of a long time.

Joe glanced at his watch—ten minutes since he'd left the penthouse. He'd give her five more, then if she didn't come out, he'd go and find a telephone.

Suppose there was more to it than Nerone's stealing Brasso's girl? With the *capo* eliminated, Lambroso was next in the line of succession. With Lambroso out, the job was up for grabs. Suppose Brasso had waited so long because his revenge involved not only killing Nerone but taking over his organization. He had amassed his resources, bided his time, and chosen his moment. And he had chosen well. When the Nerone fortunes were at their lowest ebb, when the New York underworld was hurting from the new drug laws and the loss of their regular sources of supply, Charlie Brasso came back. He carried with him a supply of heroin large enough to put everybody back in business. Only Nerone found out and took steps to stop him. Information was leaked through Muscles Koslav to the police. The shipment was confiscated, but the courier got through. Carlo Abruzzi was Charlie Brasso.

The pieces fitted. The first shipment having been lost, Brasso sent for a second—evidently his sources were very good. What in hell had happened to it, though? Joe didn't think it had slipped in: There was no movement on the street, no buys of any size to indicate it. Maybe Brasso met too much resistance from the organization, decided to cut his losses, cancel the new order, and skip. That would certainly explain why there had been no further threats to him and Norah about Mark. But he couldn't believe that a man who had waited sixteen years for his chance, who had gone to the elaborate pains of setting up Mark's adoption to get Joe off the case, would give up easily.

Having decided Mariarosa would not be coming out, Joe briskly left the corner and headed for Lexington Avenue and a phone.

"David? Joe."

"Joe! Boy, am I glad to hear from you. I've been trying to—"

"Hold it. I've just left Miss Martinelli. You know her address?"

"Yeah, sure, but—"

"I'll be on the southeast corner of Park watching the entrance. I want you and whoever's available to get down here and relieve me. Make it fast."

"Sure. Only listen, Joe—"

"Tell me later." Joe hung up, left the booth, and raced back to his post.

Too bad he hadn't got a tap on Mariarosa's phone before the interrogation. Actually he hadn't had a valid reason for requesting it before and wouldn't have got it, so forget about it. He had what he'd been after—her identification of the killer. A pretty damn good day's work.

They still had to find Brasso-Abruzzi, but Joe was sure that they would—through Mariarosa. She would be kept under constant surveillance. That meant teams around the clock, each with a backup, and better have a standby team at the office ready to move in case of an emergency. While he was at it, why not put a guard on Mark? It wasn't the first time Joe had thought of doing that and rejected it. The threat was not to kidnap or harm the child; it was to deprive Norah and him of Mark's custody—a far more subtle threat and, as he had pointed out to Norah right at the beginning, one that could hang over them the rest of their lives. A guard would serve no purpose. That he should be considering it again at this moment indicated he had a bad case of the jitters. Joe paced to the corner. Where the hell was David? What was taking him so long?

He spotted the car a few minutes later, David driving and Roy Brennan sitting beside him. They were waiting to make the turn at the center island on Park Avenue. He signaled them toward the side street and the only empty space, in front of a fire hydrant. As he went to meet them, David rolled down the window.

Quickly Joe filled them in. As he explained, a new problem presented itself. Suppose Mariarosa did lead them to Brasso and then refused to identify him? They'd make him as Abruzzi, but what good would that do? If she changed her mind and denied he was the killer, all they could get him on was the immigration charge. Then Joe brightened. He was forgetting Janet Price. She could make him as Brasso; she'd worked for him, hadn't she? Mariarosa was in love with the man, but Janet Price wasn't. A little plea bargaining should work wonders with Miss Price.

"Norah call in?" Joe asked.

"Yeah, Joe, that's what I was trying to tell you on the phone," David began.

"So tell me now."

"She found Price . . ."

Joe grinned and slapped his hands together—once a case started to break, everything happened fast.

". . . Dead, Joe. Price is dead. Shot."

"Ah. . . . Time of death?"

"The ME hadn't got to the scene yet, but Norah thinks it happened sometime in the early morning."

So they were back to Mariarosa Martinelli. With Price eliminated, she was the sole witness against Brasso. He had trusted her loyalty and spared her once, but could he afford to do it a second time?

So now the surveillance had a double purpose: to follow Miss Martinelli if she should go to meet Charlie Brasso and to protect her in case he came looking for her.

The question was: Just how much did Big Charlie love his Mariarosa?

There must have been a quesiton in Mariarosa's mind too because twenty-four hours passed, then forty-eight, and Mariarosa Martinelli had not stirred out of her penthouse.

Meantime the reports on the murder of Janet Price were coming in and they were not helpful. The fingerprints lifted from her place belonged to the victim herself; no others had been found. As Norah had noted, the apartment door showed no signs of forcible entry. That, plus the position of the body and the estimated trajectory of the bullet, supported her reconstruction of the crime. Janet Price had admitted her killer, gone back to her bedroom, sat at her vanity table, and been shot. The division detectives agreed with Norah that it was hard to tell from the condition of the apartment whether or not it had been searched, but it was logical to assume that the killer would have made sure there was nothing incriminating around.

It was the ballistics report that was the shocker. The slugs removed from the bodies of the three gangsters all came from the same gun. The bullet removed from Janet Price's body didn't match.

Joe went down to the police test range himself and examined the findings. Not that he thought there might be an error, just that the report was so unexpected and disheartening he had to look into the comparison microscope himself. There was no doubt. The bullets were of the same caliber, but they could not have been fired by the same gun.

At the time of Abruzzi's disappearance the special team had been expanded to seventy men. After the initial flurry, when the routine moves had been made and there appeared nowhere to go, the men were returned to their regular commands and the team was reduced to a token force. At Joe's request it was beefed up once more to carry out the surveillance on Miss Martinelli. What was left of the original group gathered in the small office Inspector Dietrich had set aside in Narco headquarters and rationalized the use of two different guns.

The murder of Janet Price was not part of the original plan. It was an afterthought. Having finished with the three gangland enemies, Brasso-Abruzzi would certainly have got rid of the murder weapon. When it became apparent that he had to get rid of Price, he naturally had to acquire a second weapon. Possible.

Even logical. Everybody agreed. Nobody was convinced.

Suppose he gave out a contract on Price? Roy Brennan, like Norah and David Link, regularly a member of the Fifth H and A, suggested.

David shot it down. "The guy's a loner. He'd do it himself."

Norah agreed. "Anyhow, she wouldn't just let any stranger into the apartment, and not only into the apartment, into her bedroom. And she certainly wouldn't continue dressing in front of a stranger."

"We don't know she dressed in front of him," Roy, always exact, pointed out. "She had a robe on; she was decent. All she was probably doing was putting on her makeup."

"A woman would rather be seen naked than without her face on, Roy."

"Yeah, Roy. You don't need to be married to know that," David teased the confirmed bachelor, and everybody laughed.

"And there wasn't time to put out a contract," Joe commented. "Norah got the address from Heggerat late Tuesday; the woman was dead by eight the following morning."

"If I hadn't checked Heggerat's alibi myself. . . ." Sid Ryder, Joe's sergeant in Narco, shook his head dolefully.

"How could the killer have known Norah was on to Price unless Heggerat tipped him?" That was Ferdi Arenas, the youngest man on the team borrowed from plainclothes force and fresh out of the academy. "Couldn't we get him in here on more time?"

Ryder turned on him scornfully. "You expect him to admit it? Maybe to give us a name and address?"

Arenas flushed.

Joe intervened. "I agree with Sid that Heggerat isn't likely to change his story. But Ferdi's right, the tip-off had to come from him. So let's check him out once more, see if we can't turn up some—"

"The doorman!" Norah interrupted. "Sorry, Joe, but

it just came to me. The doorman at Janet Price's building. I talked to him the night before she was killed."

Everybody looked at Norah expectantly. "I didn't identify myself as a police officer or even give my name. I made sure not to. I didn't want Jan Price to know I'd been there."

"You wouldn't have to." David seized on the possibility eagerly. "If the doorman was being paid to keep an eye on Price, he'd report, and a description of you would be enough."

Joe nodded. "Okay. See what you can do with the doorman, David."

But the doorman played dumb; Heggerat held firm; and Mariarosa Martinelli remained in her penthouse apartment eighteen stories above Park Avenue. The order for the tap on her phone had been requested, granted, the tap installed, and so far it had not brought any results either. Seventy-two hours passed.

Norah was worried about Joe. He was putting in long, enervating hours waiting for some kind of movement from someone or somewhere. He was coming home exhausted and yet not sleeping. Joe was dedicated, but he was not your crusading TV detective operating at white heat, forgetting food, sleep, and family. He seldom was involved in a shoot-out or in physical violence. He considered police work a job, often boring, sometimes exciting, and often gratifying, but a job. Like a man with a trade—electrician, carpenter, dentist—he put the job aside after working hours. Not these days. It was because of Mark, of course. Before going to bed these nights, Joe would go into the boy's room and spend as much as half an hour just sitting and watching the sleeping child. It made Norah's heart ache.

As for herself, Norah was aware that she was undergoing a change. She had always been self-contained, had considered herself selective in choosing a friend, in giving her love. She was learning now to regard that less a virtue and more a failing. After all, it was easy to love when you were sure you were loved in return. Through Mark she was discovering that she could give love without expecting it back, simply because that love was needed. Her constraint and reticence dissolved. She no longer worried about what to do or say or how to keep Mark occupied. The hours they spent together slipped by, and Norah couldn't tell later just exactly how they had been filled, only that they had been happy and satisfying—for both of them.

She was sure now that she would be able to give Joe a son of their own. But no matter how many babies she and Joe might ultimately have, this boy, Mark, would always be special. She poured out her love unstintingly. And she could see that his trust in her increased as well as his dependence on her.

As her joy in Mark grew, so did her fear of losing him. The threat to the adoption had not been repeated, and that worried her almost more than if it had been. During the hours between the time she put Mark to bed and the time Joe came home she agonized over the possibilities. She drew up a list of the events of the case in sequence:

> the tip on the heroin shipment and Abruzzi's arrival
> the three murders
> Joe's appointment to head the special unit
> Abruzzi's disappearance
> the bribe offer
> her father's meeting Audrey Gundersen in the park
> the adoption
> the threat to the adoption

Having uncovered Janet Price's past association with Brasso-Abruzzi, it followed that he was behind the rigged adoption. But staring at her list, Norah had doubts. Abruzzi had disappeared before Audrey Gundersen even approached Norah's father. He was, in fact, gone before the bribe offer to Joe, totally and without a trace. By the time the adoption was finalized in January, the force of men organized to search for Abruzzi had been disbanded. The threat came nearly two weeks later.

A second flaw in their reasoning became apparent. How could Abruzzi-Brasso know that the lieutenant in charge of the Nerone murders was the same rookie who had asked penetrating questions about the body washed up on the Rockaway beach. Someone could have told him, of course. But who? Who was left from that time who knew or cared?

There were two left, Norah mused, and of these, one, Lucia Nerone, would hardly be likely to help her husband's killer. The other was Mariarosa Martinelli, and how would she have had that information? She had hardly been in a condition to notice Joe at that funeral, physically sick with grief and shock as she must have been. Joe had been in uniform at the time. . . . Startled by the appearance of a uniformed police officer, the bereaved girl might have been drawn to look at his face. But to remember it after sixteen years? Impossible.

Norah speculated about Mariarosa—about the girl she had been and the woman she had become, a woman who took what fate dealt and made her accommodation. When her childhood sweetheart walked into her bedroom and found her with Nerone, what was her reaction? Joy that he was alive or guilt and shame for what she had done? No matter how much she loved Brasso, after sixteen years of living with Georgio Nerone she must have had some feeling for him too. After that span of time the initial passion had been muted; still, for a nonmarital relationship to last, it must have had something pretty strong going for it. It would also be subject to certain stresses and strains, much like a marriage. Infidelities perhaps, on one side or the other. How could she find out? Mariarosa was a loner, without confidantes, but there had to be somebody. . . . The maid—what was her name? Vincenza . . . something or other. According to Joe, the maid was always dismissed early on the nights

Georgio Nerone was expected; in any case, the maid had her own quarters. Nevertheless, there were innumerable ways she would have been able to gauge the state of the relationship—by the frequency of the visits, gifts or absence of gifts, the amount of money circulating in the household, and above all, by her employer's moods, her elation or depression. The servants always knew what was going on.

Norah hardly expected Vincenza—whatever—to give the information willingly. She would be loyal and close-mouthed, chosen for those qualities. Still, a casual chat, informal. . . . If she could manage to run into the woman somewhere apparently by accident. At the market. . . .

Joe had gone back to the beginning and Charles Brasso. Norah went back to Mariarosa. She was the key. Innocent, naïve when she first came over, and . . . credulous? What exactly had the young girl been told about her fiancé's tragic death? Just that he drowned? Or that he had been shot first? The case had had plenty of publicity. Then Norah remembered that when Mariarosa came to this country, she spoke little or no English: She wouldn't have been able to read the newspaper accounts of her fiancé's alleged death; she would have had to depend on what his friends, specifically Giorgio Nerone, cared to tell her. But was she satisfied with that? Suppose she wanted to know more? The sight of a police officer at the funeral might just have spurred her to seek out that officer. Only she'd never got to Joe; that they knew for sure. She wouldn't have. Assuming that she'd had the initiative to go to the precinct, manage to make herself understood, and ask for the officer in charge of the case, she would have been directed to Detective Frank Oakes.

Norah got right to work tracing Oakes. It took only a couple of calls to find out that he'd retired from the force and was now running his own private detective agency. She got the number and though it was past eleven called anyway. His answering service wanted to take the message, but that wasn't good enough. On her insistence that the matter was urgent, the operator agreed to contact Oakes. Still not good enough. Norah pulled rank and finally got his home number.

As long as he thought she was a client, Frank Oakes accepted her apologies for disturbing him graciously, assured her he never turned in before one or two A.M. When he found out who she was and what she wanted, he was considerably less agreeable.

"It was one hell of a long time ago. You can hardly expect me to remember. . . ."

Norah was just as blunt. "You read the papers. You know the case has been reopened. You must have had some thoughts about it."

"Well, sure, in a general kind of way."

"All I want to know is whether Brasso's fiancé ever came to see you."

"You can't expect me to remember every witness in every case—"

"Just one, Mr. Oakes. A very beautiful, very young Italian girl who could barely speak English and who later became Giorgio Nerone's official mistress. Please don't ask me to believe that she doesn't stand out in your memory. All I want to know is what you told her. Of course, if you prefer the lieutenant to come to see you—"

"Okay, okay. You win. I didn't tell her anything. To start with, I could hardly understand what she wanted."

Norah had a sinking feeling at the pit of her stomach. "So you passed her on."

"Yeah, well . . . I figured he'd been the first on the scene anyhow. And he was so damned interested in the case—let him deal with her. Besides, he spoke the language. I mean, you see my point?"

Sure, Norah thought, he just couldn't be bothered. She wanted to hear him say it, though. "To whom did you send her?"

"Well, to your husband. To Joe Capretto."

There was nothing more to ask, nothing more Frank

Oakes could tell her, and Norah hung up. For a long time she remained seated beside the telephone, pencil in hand, though she hadn't needed to take any notes. For whatever reason, Mariarosa Martinelli had not followed through and contacted Joe, but she'd had his name, an Italian name, and she hadn't forgotten it.

It kept coming back to the same thing—what did it matter to Brasso-Abruzzi who was handling the case since he had already made good his disappearance? The answer was, it didn't. It could only matter to one person—Mariarosa herself.

For the first time in her professional life Norah Mulcahaney Capretto wasn't anxious to get the facts to support a theory. And for the first time she wasn't eager to share her ideas with Joe. In fact, she didn't even want him to suspect what she had in mind. Through the piling up of hard evidence, he was bound to crack the case; he was close, so close. Why not wait? Then if she was right, well . . . why put the burden of the dilemma on him ahead of time? If, God willing, she was wrong, why put it on him at all? The hours that had seemed to drag were now too brief. Norah wanted to slow everything down, to hold onto every precious moment.

She fled into the kitchen and busied herself. She put Sanka into the electric percolator and plugged it in. She made sandwiches. Joe's appetite hadn't been good lately, but maybe if he saw everything set out, he'd eat. Joe was always trying to lose weight, but lately he, like Norah, had lost too much: His nose was beginning to take on too much prominence in his dark face, and the skin around his jaw hung slack; he looked haggard. When the snack was ready, when she'd cleaned up, Norah went back to the living room and turned on the TV. But she couldn't pay attention. The problem would not be set aside. Praying wouldn't make it go away. She had to face it.

A little after midnight Norah heard her husband's

key in the lock and ran to greet him. His face was
pinched with weariness, but his eyes glittered. Something was up. She kissed him.

"You're frozen! It's got to be ten degrees out there,
and you're still wearing that thin topcoat. And how
about a hat? You must be the only man in New York
without a hat in this weather."

"Don't fuss, Norah."

"It's not going to help if you catch a cold. Look at
your ears; they're purple."

"I don't like hats. I hate hats."

She sighed, her exasperation only partly exagger-
ated, took his coat from him, and hung it up. "I've got
hot Sanka ready."

"I don't want—sure. I guess something hot would
go good. Thanks, honey."

They went into the kitchen. Joe slumped wearily
into a chair while Norah set the food she'd prepared
in front of him. He was about to say he didn't want
that either, but thought better of it. Norah sat with
him while he forced it down. She didn't ask any questions, but waited. After a few minutes he announced
bluntly, "We're going to force her out."

Of course, he referred to Mariarosa. "How?"

"I'm applying for an exhumation order."

15

"SURE we can get an exhumation order," Dietrich acknowledged, suppressing a belch and popping the second pair of Gelusil tablets into his mouth. "What's the point, though? Assuming you can prove it's not Brasso in there, what good is it going to do? How's it going to help find him?"

"I don't know," Joe admitted. "All I know is that Miss Martinelli doesn't want that grave opened. I put her through a tough interrogation, and she resisted every pressure till I mentioned exhumation. I just threw it out, frankly, because I didn't have anything else. But that was when she cracked. That was when she admitted that Brasso is alive and that he killed Nerone. Why should she suddenly reverse herself unless there's something there she doesn't want us to know about?"

Dietrich ground down on the tablets in his mouth. "You've queried Interpol and the Italians on Brasso?"

"Sure. We're getting to be regular pen pals."

"Are you going to inform Miss Martinelli about the exhumation?"

Joe took a deep breath. "I was going to, but I've changed my mind. I figure I'd better find out exactly what's in there first."

It was a bitterly cold morning. An ice storm the day before had devastated the city and environs. Radio announcers portentously intoned the list of disasters major and minor with equal relish. Power lines were down. Entire neighborhoods were without electricity or heat. Temperatures well below zero and, according to the long-range forecasts, liable to remain there for several days. Tides abnormally high. Driving hazardous. Travelers' warnings invoked.

The sky was blue and cloudless, the sun bright. The cemetery beautiful in its untracked white cover. The trees on the perimeter crystallized and shimmering in the sun's rays. As the wind passed through their branches, cracking the ice, a tinkling sound like chimes charmed the silence.

Getting out of the car, Norah slipped and nearly fell. What looked like snow was actually a frozen glaze. In the vista of open acres the tombstones stuck up out of the glittering ice like rotting teeth. Joe took her arm, steadied her, then carefully guided her out to where a group of men huddled waiting. He hadn't been enthusiastic about her coming, but she had insisted. Not that Norah had any desire or even intended to view the grisly contents, but she needed to know the results as quickly as possible.

As there was officially no suspect, the question of a medical witness for the defense did not arise. Usually a licensed funeral director would be in charge to disinter and deliver the body. In view of the long time lapse since burial, the entire matter was being handled by the police pathology department. As a favor to Lieutenant Capretto, the ME himself had come to the scene.

"You sure picked a great day for it, Cap," Asa Osterman growled as Joe and Norah came up. Despite his complaint, the gnomelike physician's eyes sparkled as he peered through the holes of a bright red ski mask, on top of which he wore his usual battered fedora. If that weren't enough, he had on enormous woodsmen's boots laced to the knee; since his feet were tiny, it must have taken several pairs of woolen socks to fill the empty space. In between feet and head, he wore an assortment of sweaters and mufflers that could only be described as thrift-shop rejects. Norah bit back a smile. But as the wind that had stirred the trees so melodiously stabbed through her,

Osterman appeared more sensible than ridiculous. She wished she had on a few extra layers herself.

The workmen had brought pickaxes to break the frozen ground and started swinging while the higher echelon of officials stamped their feet and flapped their arms to keep warm.

"Didn't expect you to turn up, Norah. No place for a woman," was Osterman's greeting. He turned to Joe. "You shouldn't have let her come. Not with her stomach."

Norah flushed. Her queasiness was well known. A couple of times she had been sick at the scene of a particularly messy homicide. Osterman had been present on each occasion. Actually he had been very considerate.

"Now that you're married to her, I don't suppose you have any control over her," the ME grunted.

Joe girnned. "She claims she's not going to look."

"Wanna bet? I know what she thinks; she thinks she can toughen herself up." Asa Osterman turned on Norah. "Let me tell you, my girl, you never get used to it. Even me, after thirty-five years, I still hold my breath before that first peek."

Having penetrated the freeze line, the diggers tossed the pickaxes aside and took up shovels. The work went faster. The officials stopped stamping their feet; small talk ceased. The top of the coffin appeared; earth was cleared from around it so that ropes could be passed underneath. By means of pulleys the box was hoisted high and swung to rest on the ground beside the gaping hole. The lid was wrenched open. Everyone held back for Asa Osterman.

"Huh . . ." he grunted and turned to Joe. "You didn't tell me this was going to be a double feature."

"What?" Joe, who had been sniffing at the faint and unexpected odor that should not have been present after the long years, jumped forward. The odor emanated from the grave's second occupant, lying on top of the bones of the first.

Everybody moved forward except Norah.

Joe knew the conditions that affect decomposition: amount of air, temperature, chemical composition of the surrounding soil. At optimum, assuming the body was not embalmed, it couldn't have been down there long. The face was still recognizable.

"Carlo Abruzzi," Joe murmured softly. Then aloud he asked, "How long has he been dead, Doc?"

"You know better than to ask this soon," Osterman scolded.

"A rough estimate, Doc, that's all I expect."

"You working on rough estimates these days, Lieutenant? I can't give it to you till I do the autopsy. There are just too many damn variables."

"A month? Two months? Come on, Doc," Joe urged. "Could he have been here since, say, Thanksgiving?"

"Maybe longer. I'm not saying it was longer, just that it could be."

Norah had caught Joe's whisper of the victim's name and she felt the strength ooze out of her. At the ME's reply, her legs began to tremble. It was what she had come to hear, all the while praying that she would not. There was no need to look, yet she was involuntarily drawn forward. She kept her eyes away from the face and looked at the rest of him. He was fully clothed and the body unmarked. So it wasn't as bad as she had feared, but bad enough. Doc was right—you didn't ever get used to violent death. She pushed by Assistant DA Dorn and the others and ran.

"Norah!" Joe called after her.

"Leave her alone; she'll be okay," Osterman assured him. "Well, come on, come on, what are we standing around here freezing our butts off for? Get 'em both to the wagon," he barked and his people jumped.

"Mind if I take a quick look for ID first?" Joe asked.

"You expect to find ID on him?"

"I don't know what to expect, Doc, but if somebody sometime didn't make a mistake, when would we ever solve a case?"

Osterman shrugged and waved a mittened hand. Be my guest, but make it fast."

Unfortunately whoever had put Abruzzi underground appeared to have been thorough. Wallet and documents were gone, and as far as he could tell from the cursory examination, all the labels had been cut out of the clothing. Joe, who was something of a sartorial expert, identified the suit fabric as British and the cut Italian. Such clothing could be bought in New York, of course.

"So, how about it, Cap?" Osterman prodded.

"I'm through, Doc. Thanks."

The men dispersed and headed back across the grounds to their cars. Joe found Norah shivering in the front seat of theirs. He looked at her anxiously. "You okay?"

She nodded.

"You don't look okay."

"I'm fine."

"Why didn't you turn on the heater?"

"I didn't think of it."

Joe gave her another long, hard look, then just shook his head and turned it on himself.

Neither spoke as they sped along the long line of cemeteries bordering that section of the Queens Expressway till they reached the entrance to the Midtown Tunnel. "Just drop me on the other side," Norah said. "I have to do some marketing."

"On Thirty-third?"

"I thought I'd go over to Ninth Avenue."

"Since when are you marketing on Ninth Avenue?" Joe wanted to know.

It was the area of Italian specialty food stores in the forties along Ninth that Norah was interested in. That was where Vincenza Giannini did her shopping. "Your mother's been after me and after me to go over there to get the really fresh produce. So I thought . . . today's as good a day as any. Unless you have a job for me?"

Joe shook his head. "We have to wait for the autopsy. I'll drive you over."

"I can hop the crosstown."

He stole a look at her. If she was thinking about marketing, she couldn't be very sick. So that was a relief. "I'll take you," he said firmly.

Even after the autopsy Doc Osterman couldn't do better than give Joe a six- to eight-week spread on the time of death; the soil temperature had fluctuated too much since the end of November, including a spell of mild weather in January. Abruzzi had been shot in the back four times. The bullets were shown to have been fired by the same gun that had been used to kill Janet Price.

The two men who had seen Nerone's killer were brought to the morgue to view the body. Neither Arnold Bush, the doorman at the Martinelli building, nor Bernie Francese, the bodyguard on duty outside the penthouse, could or would make a positive identification. Joe called Father Meyerhoff. With only a vague memory of his parishioner and having to make allowance for the passage of years, the best the pastor could do was to say it *could* be Brasso. Joe was reluctant to get Mariarosa herself to view the remains. A denial from her would be hard to overcome later.

At least they had fingerprints. As these were not on file with the FBI, Joe sent them off by radio photocopier to Italy and to Interpol. This time Interpol came through and promptly. They identified the prints as belonging to Carlo Brasso, arrested for drug smuggling in Marseilles, France, November 2, 1959.

Joe broke out into a cold sweat. Finally and at last! he thought.

He gathered the nucleus of his team for a briefing and discussion.

"Once they had the fingerprints, Interpol made him fast." He picked up the top sheaf from a stack of reports and handed it over to David, who was nearest. "That's Brasso's arrest record and mug shots."

David Link scanned it quickly. "Age forty-two, six feet one, one hundred sixty-five pounds, dark complexion, brown eyes, no identifying marks." Next he was handed a copy of Abruzzi's passport photo. "Same man," he concluded. "No question." He passed the material on to Brennan, and it was circulated around the room.

"No wonder the Italians couldn't make him," David commented. "He was in a French jail. Probably went straight to France. Figured the mob had too many connections in Italy."

Ryder had the papers. "They got him for fifteen years and he served the full sentence. They sure don't fool over there."

"So now we know why he waited so long to pay Nerone off." David grinned. "Once he got out, though. . . What was that release date?"

"July 12, 1974," Ryder answered.

"I suppose it took him that long to get hold of the heroin, the fake passport, and get himself affiliated with the tourist group. He shouldn't have rushed," David commented wryly.

Joe said nothing. Let them toss it around; let them put it together for themselves. In the process someone might come up with something new. That was the purpose of the meeting.

"At least we don't have to feel bad for not finding him." Ryder looked around the room.

There was a murmur of assent. Every man had taken it as a personal failure that they had not been able to get a single clue as to Abruzzi's whereabouts. Norah had not been a member of the unit then, but she certainly knew how they felt.

Only Roy Brennan showed no satisfaction on that score. He continued to scowl. "So Brasso killed Nerone and the other two. So who killed him? It looks to me like the organization didn't waste time putting out a contract. In that case, we're right back where we started."

Joe had to smile—Brennan was so predictably pessimistic. "It's not quite that bad. We have to ask ourselves who was left after all these years that could identify Brasso? Pretty hard to kill a man when you don't know what he looks like."

That didn't stop Roy for long. "How about Francese? He claims he was knocked out before he got a good look at the killer, but he was hit from the front, not the rear. He must have got a good enough look to recognize him and do the job."

Everybody liked it.

"Aren't we forgetting Janet Price?" Ferdi Arenas asked diffidently and colored when everybody looked at him. "What I mean is . . . it's the business about the gun one more time. According to ballistics, the same gun was used to kill Brasso and Miss Price."

"Right, Ferdi," Joe prompted the rookie.

Arenas swallowed. "There was a lot of time between . . . you know?"

"Two and a half months."

"Yes, sir." The flush deepened and the words came out in a rush. "Why would a professional hit man hold onto a hot piece that long?"

"Good point." Joe looked around to see if anyone had an answer.

Sergeant Ryder shrugged it off. "Maybe with the body buried, he figured the piece wasn't hot. Let's give Francese's place a toss. Maybe we'll find it."

"Get the warrant, and you and Ferdi take care of it." Joe looked around again, his glance lingering just an extra moment on Norah. "Any other ideas?"

"How about Miss Martinelli?" Brennan offered. "She sure knew what Brasso looked like. She could have fingered him."

Norah tensed and Joe noticed it, but before he could question her, David broke in.

"Oh, hell no! She was crazy in love with the guy. She couldn't do a thing like that!" He too turned to Norah. "Could she? You'd know better than us."

Norah hesitated. "I've never met Miss Martinelli. I don't know what she might or might not do."

"She sure didn't want that grave opened," Roy reminded everybody. "Why? Because she knew what we'd find. And if she knew he was in there, then she knew who put him there."

"That still doesn't mean she fingered him," David retorted, but he was less positive than he had been. She could know who did it. Maybe that's why she's stayed holed up in the penthouse all this time. We thought she was scared of Brasso, but it could be his killer she's scared of. With Price gone, maybe she figures she's next."

"How about it, Norah? What do you think?" Joe asked. "You haven't said much today."

"I haven't got anything to say."

"That's a change."

The men laughed, glad of a break.

"Maybe you could get her to talk," David suggested. "You know, woman to woman. Show her that telling what she knows is in her best interest. Offer her protection."

"How about it, Norah? You want to try?" Joe asked.

"Okay."

He frowned. The suggestion should have come from her instead of David. At least, once made, she should have responded eagerly. "Anything wrong?"

"No."

"If she refuses to talk, you'd better bring her in."

"Okay."

He stared at her. "That's it, then. David, you go with Norah."

"No. Alone, please, Joe. She's more likely to let her guard down if we're alone."

He paused for a fraction of a moment. "But with a backup, in case you have to bring her in. We wouldn't want anything to happen en route—to either one of you. God forbid somebody should try to gun her down while you're escorting her across the sidewalk to the car."

It was decided that David and Roy would wait downstairs in the lobby while Norah went to the penthouse. David thought they should all go in his car, but Norah wanted to take her own—she had a bundle to drop off at the Laundromat later, she said. The real reason was that she wanted to be alone. She couldn't bear the thought of company, even that of friends as close as the two detectives. For the two days since her talk with Vincenza Giannini and the subsequent trip to the private sanatorium in Connecticut, Norah had been in an agony of indecision. She had prayed for help. She had been on the verge of going to her father for advice, but of course that would have been wrong. If she were going to consult anyone, that person had to be Joe. Yet he was the one person she mustn't talk to.

At the first threat to the legality of Mark's adoption Joe's reaction had been to remove himself from the case. Dear God, how Norah wished now that she had let him do it! But she hadn't. Now again she had a choice, but she had to make it alone. In the hours of weighing, assessing, analyzing, Norah discovered that the possible loss of her job didn't matter as much as she had expected. Maybe because she was a woman, and her priorities, like those of the majority of women, were the age-old ones of home and family first. It was Joe she had to consider—and Mark. In the end it was the child's welfare that decided her. Being Norah, once the decision was made, she had acted. It was the hardest thing she had ever done in her life and now she was numb. She knew that the full reaction and the accompanying pain were yet to come. She tried not to think about that but to concentrate on the business ahead.

The evening rush hour had started; traffic was heavy; people gushed out of office buildings and stores, spilling from the sidewalks into the intersections, eager to get home. Norah drove mechanically, nursing her hurt. The light changed; she stepped on the gas. A car trying to beat the red hurtled from a side street. She slammed on the brakes, narrowly escaping a collision. For a moment everything stopped.

'hen horns blared; people yelled. Roy Brennan
mped out of his car and came around to her side
indow.

"You okay?"

"Sure."

She had been thrown forward, her right knee hit-
ng the steering column. It ached. She could feel the
welling, but there was no blood. She almost wished
he had been injured so that she'd have to go to the
ospital—it would have been a small price to pay for
temporary reprieve. "No, Roy, I'm fine, really. No
arm done. Let's get moving."

Beyond Sixty-sixth Street traffic eased and they
ade good time. They parked directly in front of Miss
Iartinelli's building, and when the doorman came out
) ask them to leave the entrance clear, they identified
emselves and Norah went up.

Undoubtedly the doorman had alerted Miss Marti-
elli that a Detective Mulcahaney was on the way,
r she was waiting in the vestibule, yet she addressed
Iorah as Mrs. Capretto.

"I've been expecting you, Mrs. Capretto."

At least there was to be no preliminary skirmishing,
Iorah thought. Despite her personal distress, a por-
on of her mind continued to function on a profession-
l level. She noted that Nerone's mistress appeared
omposed, that she was dressed in a tailored tweed
ants suit, that her gloves and purse were on the hall
onsole and a pair of suitcases, very elegant, stood in
he corner.

"I'm afraid you'll have to cancel your trip, Miss
Iartinelli."

"I'm prepared to make a full statement to you be-
ore going."

Norah shook her head. "That won't be sufficient."

"I read about the exhumation in the papers, Mrs.
Iapretto. I know that you found a second body in
he grave. I can tell you who he is."

"We already know. He's been identified as Charles
Irasso."

"Well, then, you don't need me. Your case is solved."

"We still don't know who killed Brasso and who buried him."

"I can't tell you that."

"I think you can. I think you know who killed him and Janet Price. They were both shot with the same gun."

The two women measured each other. Mariarosa's tongue flicked out, moistening her pale, dry lips. "I want to cooperate, Mrs. Capretto, but I have to look out for myself."

Evidently she was too anxious to get to the bargaining to bother denying she knew of Janet Price, Norah thought and felt the prickle of goose bumps all over her body. "I haven't come here to make a deal, Miss Martinelli. I can't do that."

Mariarosa frowned. "We can talk, can't we?" With a wave of the hand she led the way into the living room. "What we say doesn't need to go beyond these walls."

"No deal, Miss Martinelli."

"It's to your advantage as much as mine."

The words did not come easily, but Norah repeated them. "No deal."

"You're asking me to risk my life!" Miss Martinelli cried out.

So she wasn't going to be completely straight, after all. Okay, Norah thought. She wasn't the one in the hurry; she wasn't planning to run out; she could afford to play the game. "We'll give you full protection."

"You'll forgive me if I have more confidence in my own arrangements." Mariarosa Martinelli indicated the two suitcases in the hall.

"You'll be safe in jail."

That wiped the smile off. "You don't really mean that."

"Yes, I do."

"Your husband showed compassion. I expected at least as much from you. I should have known better."

"Yes, you should." Norah agreed quietly.

"You career women are all alike. You resent the really feminine woman. You pretend to sneer at sex. You claim we use sex as a commodity. Well, why not? The truth is you're jealous. You'd do the same if you could."

Norah didn't answer. The charge wasn't new; she was used to it.

"You think it's an easy life, all good times, parties, carousing?"

"No, I don't think that."

"You think I liked being completely dependent on a man? Everything I was, everything I had, depended on Giorgio Nerone. When he died, nobody knew me anymore. None of our so-called friends came to see me to offer condolences. Not one even bothered to pick up the telephone. They all went to her, to Lucia, to Signora Nerone. They buzzed around her, held her hand—the widow. I couldn't even show my face at the funeral. After sixteen years I'm nobody."

Norah seized the opening. "But while he lived, there were plenty who envied you and I'm sure were eager to change places with you."

"I suppose so."

"But he always came back to you."

Mariarosa pulled herself up. "He never left me."

"But there were other affairs."

"One-night stands. A man like Giorgio. . . . It's none of your business. It's got nothing to do with what we're discussing."

"On the contrary, Miss Martinelli, it has everything to do with it. When my husband, who as you noted is a compassionate man, explained to me the kind of girl you must have been when you first came here, I couldn't believe that you would be content as a kept woman." Norah used the pejorative term deliberately. "In fact, Nerone had initially promised to marry you, hadn't he? You must have been very disappointed that he didn't keep his word."

"He couldn't. The situation. . . ."

"But the situation changed," Norah insisted. "His

wife's father died and he became *capo* in his place, but still he didn't marry you. By that time he had another interest—a young dancer, Anita Andreyevna. You were afraid you might lose him completely."

"But I didn't."

"No. That was just about the time you brought Vincenza Giannini over from your home village. She's a distant cousin, I understand. Ostensibly she came to be your housekeeper, but actually you wanted someone near you whom you could trust, whose loyalty would be to you and not to Nerone."

"So?"

"You were very sick."

"Vincenza told you?"

"She told me that you had a nervous breakdown and that you checked into a private sanatorium just outside Greenwich, Connecticut. I went there and discovered that you stayed less than a week. Vincenza refused to discuss the details of your illness, but she saw no harm in talking about the past, about your childhood, about your family—your father, Marco Martinelli." Norah paused. "And your mother, Giustina. That would be Justine in English. Her maiden name was Rossi."

"So you know."

Norah sighed. "The birth certificate of my adopted son lists the mother's name as Justine Ross. His name is Mark. He was born at Hartford General at the time you were supposed to be at the sanatorium. It really is too much of a coincidence. According to the records, Justine Ross died last November, and shortly after, Mark was put up for adoption by the sole surviving relative—Janet Price."

Mariarosa Martinelli sighed. "Such things are not difficult to arrange when one has the money to pay. But I am sorry you've found out. Believe me, I hoped you'd never have to know."

"I'm sure."

"What I did wasn't all self-serving," she protested.

"I wouldn't have let you have my son if I didn't believe that you would love him and give him a good home."

Norah didn't reply.

"So what's eating you, Mrs. Capretto?" Suddenly Mariarosa lost patience. "What's your problem? You have the boy; that's all that should matter."

"I'm wondering why you gave him up in the first place."

"You're so smart, you should have figured that out. Giorgio wouldn't let me keep him. He claimed I'd let myself get pregnant on purpose so that he'd marry me. He was furious. He gave me a choice—him or the baby. What could I do?"

"You could have kept your baby!" Norah cried out; despite her training, when it came to Mark, Norah's control failed. "You were a rich woman; you already had your settlement. You didn't have to abandon your son. You could have kept him if you'd wanted to."

"All right, I didn't want to," Mariarosa snapped back. "You won't be satisfied till you hear me say it, will you? I never wanted the child. Giorgio was right; I did get pregnant in the hope of forcing him into marriage. When it didn't work. . . ." She shrugged. "Not every woman is willing to change her life-style and give up her emotional needs for the sake of motherhood."

Norah flinched. Mariarosa Martinelli couldn't know her own qualms of conscience, yet she'd hit close.

"And I didn't abandon my son. I turned him over to good people to raise and I paid them to do it."

"Why didn't you claim him when Nerone died? You could have. Instead you used him."

"And you got what you wanted, a son for yourself and your husband. Why should you complain?"

Norah wasn't ready to answer that, not now, at least. "At first I reasoned that you didn't claim Mark because of Charles Brasso. I thought that basically you still loved Brasso and were hoping to get together with him again. Having a son by Nerone around might be an obstacle."

"And that you would have forgiven? I didn't think you were so romantic, Mrs. Capretto. I was told that you were a practical, hard-nosed policewoman."

"Your information was correct."

"Good." She glanced at her watch. "So let's get down to it; we're wasting time." She took a deep breath. "I can tell you who killed Carlo Brasso and also Janet Price. In exchange, you let me catch my plane."

"If you're going to name Bernie Francese, we've already got a search warrant for his place," Norah countered, once again in control of herself. "Professional killers don't usually hold onto incriminating evidence, so if the gun is there, my guess is that it was planted."

Her antagonist was silent; she was waiting for Norah to reveal how much she had. As for Norah, there was no longer any reason to hold back.

"You killed Charles Brasso." She made the charge quietly. "Naturally you hadn't the physical strength to dispose of the body yourself. You had to have help. Francese. Was it your idea to put your fiancé in the grave that bore his name? I think so. Probably you considered it poetic justice, but it wasn't so smart, was it? As you say, money can pay for almost anything —except a murder charge. Faced with a murder charge, Francese will talk."

Slowly Mariarosa Martinelli got up and walked over to the glass doors that gave out on the spacious terrace. She stared beyond at the prestigious buildings around hers, at the elegant avenue below, the symbols of the position she had worked so hard to attain and keep. "I underestimated you, Mrs. Capretto," she admitted and turned. "Yes, I killed Carlo and I'm not sorry. I don't have one twinge of regret. If I could wish him back to life, I wouldn't. If he were standing here in front of me now, I'd do it again." She expected some comment from Norah, some indication of dismay; when there was none, she continued in the same dispassionate manner.

"Do you know why I killed him? Do you know what Carlo Brasso did to me? He sold me to Nerone. Yes. Your husband, Lieutenant Capretto, is a decent man —he thought that Carlo had surely left a letter so that I'd know his death was a fraud. Your husband assumed that Giorgio suppressed the letter. But there was no letter!" The blood had drained from her face; her dark eyes glittered. "Before Carlo I had not even kissed a man, but if he had come to me and told me that I could buy his life, I would have given myself to Nerone willingly."

As Norah still remained silent, she added, "And then I would have killed myself."

Melodramatic as it was, Norah was by now familiar enough with the Italian temperament to know it was completely sincere.

"Even so, in spite of what Carlo had done, I would have forgiven him. That night when he walked into my bedroom . . . the miracle of discovering that he was alive . . . the joy of it! I got out of bed. I threw myself on him. I wept. I covered his face with kisses. . . . He pushed me away and pulled the gun.

"I was still besotted enough to think that Carlo had come back because of me. I still believed that he had come, gun in hand, to claim me. Then they started to argue, he and Giorgio, but not over me. Carlo accused Giorgio of fingering him to the French police. Giorgio denied it. Carlo fired, hitting him in the shoulder, and still Giorgio denied it. He said he'd kept his part of the bargain; he'd helped Carlo get out of the country and that ended his responsibility. If Carlo was . . . *tanto cretino* . . . so dumb that as soon as he set up in business he got himself caught, well, tough. Carlo retorted that Johnny Allegro had already spilled everything. He'd taken care of Allegro and Lambroso and now it was Nerone's turn.

"By then I'd come out of the clouds. I knew that Carlo had no feeling for me anymore, that I was less than nothing to him, and I was frightened. For the moment he'd forgotten me, but afterward, after he killed Giorgio, he'd remember and what would he do? I stood there between them in my nightgown, and neither of them so much as looked at me. So I edged over to the night table where Giorgio kept a gun. I got it. Giorgio noticed. He hissed at me to shoot. I raised the gun. . . . Carlo watched me with such an expression . . . as though he didn't know me . . . as though I were a stranger. . . . I couldn't do it. I couldn't shoot."

The sweat was heavy on Mariarosa Martinelli's white, haggard face. "I don't know how long we stood there, the three of us, frozen like living statues—we used to play that game as children, Carlo and I. Then Giorgio opened his mouth; I suppose it was to tell me to go ahead, but before the words came out, Carlo killed him. He fired one shot, straight to the heart. Then without a single word to me, he started for the door. So then I fired and I kept firing till he fell.

"I don't remember things clearly after that. I don't know how long before I became aware that there was loud knocking at the front door and someone shouting. I thought it had to be the police, but then I recognized Bernie's voice and I let him in." Telling about it, Mariarosa Martinelli seemed to have fallen in that same dazed state.

"What did Francese do with the body?" Norah asked quietly; obviously there hadn't been time to get it out of the building.

"He took it to the floor below and locked it in one of the service closets."

And returned to his post, ready to put on his act for the police, Norah thought. Having also reminded the distraught woman to bolt the door behind him. As there had been no reason to think the killer was still in the building, there had been no search. So it had been good enough. Later, after the excitement was over and the police had left, in the predawn hours, Francese would have taken the body away to what should have been its final resting place. Norah sighed.

"Did you authorize the ten-thousand-dollar bribe offer to my husband?"

Mariarosa nodded.

"Francese made the call for you?"

"Yes."

"Sixteen years ago, right after your sweetheart's assumed death, you went to see Detective Frank Oakes for information. He referred you to Officer Capretto. You didn't follow up. Why?"

"Giorgio found out I was asking questions. By that time he and I . . . well, he didn't want me to pursue it."

That much Norah had surmised. "But when my husband came to interview you, you knew who he was."

"Yes, yes. As soon as it was announced that Lieutenant Joseph Capretto would be in charge of the investigation, I knew. It's not such a usual name, is it? I was so afraid he might recognize me. The first time he came here I had the curtains drawn; I wore dark glasses. He didn't recognize me. But there was always the possibility that he might later . . . anytime. . . ."

"So you had Francese offer the bribe, and when that was ignored, you took out other insurance."

That brought Mariarosa a measure of relief and with it the faintest of smiles. "That's all it was intended to be, Mrs. Capretto."

"And Francese handled that call for you too. Why didn't you just tell the officers how it happened? You could have claimed self-defense."

She shook her head. "I shot him in the back."

Of course. He had been on his way out. Thinking about Francese and the terrible, cold detachment with which he had delivered his message, Norah had momentarily forgotten. "Still, if you had explained the circumstances. . . ."

An uneven flush rose in Mariarosa Martinelli's face

—ugly, like a rash, destroying the alabaster beauty of her complexion. "I—I couldn't. I was ashamed."

Ashamed for them to know that Brasso had bartered her to another man, Norah thought. She could understand that, and if it had ended there. . . . "It's my duty to advise you of your rights. You have the right to remain silent. You have the right—"

"Just a minute. Hold it. You can't arrest me. If you arrest me, I'll claim my son. I'll take him away from you. I don't want to do it. I want you to have him, to keep him; I always have wanted that. But if you force me—"

"No court in the country is going to return a child to a woman who's committed murder."

"I'll deny everything. It'll be your word against mine. You can't prove a thing."

Would it be enough to tell her that their whole conversation had been taped? No, Mariarosa Martinelli would demand proof. The proof was in a pocket stitched over the lining of Norah's coat. If she revealed the recorder, would the woman jump her and try to take it away from her? Norah thought she could handle Miss Martinelli; still, it would be a gamble. She decided to take it. She opened her coat.

The woman didn't make a move. Her eyes were fixed on the little box. "You tricked me," she whispered.

"You told me your story freely, without coercion or any promise of a deal. I was very careful to tell you that I couldn't make a deal," Norah reminded her.

Mariarosa licked her lips. "You're not really going to arrest me, are you? I'm the child's mother. You love him. I know you do. Your husband loves him. How are you going to live with the knowledge that you turned your son's natural mother in for murder? Every time you look at him, you'll think of that."

"I know."

"And what about your husband? How will he be able to bear it? How will he feel toward the child if he knows who and what his parents were?" She stopped as though a new thought had occurred to her. "Is that it? Don't you want the boy anymore? Are you afraid that he comes from bad stock and that he'll turn out bad? He won't. My people are decent, hard working. . . ."

"It's not that."

"What, then? In God's name, what? Are you so hungry for justice that you don't realize who you're really punishing?"

"Mark."

Mariarosa was surprised at the policewoman's ready admission and encouraged by it. "Then be sensible, Mrs. Capretto," she pleaded. "For your son's sake It's so simple. You say your husband already suspects Francese. Leave it at that. Erase the tape. You can say the equipment was faulty; it didn't record."

"He won't buy that."

"From you he will."

"What happens when Francese starts talking?"

"Let him talk. Once the lieutenant finds the car Bernie used to transport the body . . . well, there are bound to be traces, aren't there? With all the sophisticated chemical tests. . . ."

"He used his own car?" Norah was surprised.

"There wasn't time to make other arrangements. And the murder gun isn't in his apartment. It's in a safe deposit box I rented in his name. There. Now you have it all. And if your conscience bothers you for framing an innocent man, forget it. Bernie Francese was one of Giorgio's busiest hit men. I can give you names and dates that will help your husband clear half a dozen cases from the books. What do you say, Mrs. Capretto?"

"May I ask you something?"

It was going to work—just as she'd planned it, Mariarosa Martinelli thought exultantly. She hadn't been wrong in her assessment of the policewoman after all. "Anything, anything you want," she replied eagerly.

"How did you happen to select Janet Price to handle the adoption?"

She shrugged. "I knew her from before. Giorgio sent her to me. He said she would find the baby a good, reliable Italian couple to take care of him. And she did. So it seemed logical to contact her. . . ." Too late she realized where Norah had led her.

"Was that one of Giorgio Nerone's sidelines? Black-market adoptions?"

"Giorgio never discussed business with me."

At least she had enough shame left to turn away when she said it.

Whatever slight sympathy Norah had felt for Mariarosa Martinelli was wiped out. She could feel only revulsion. She had done the right thing, Norah told herself; she could dispel those lingering doubts. All she wanted now was to get the rest of it over as quickly as possible.

"Was it the doorman of Miss Price's building who informed you I'd been there inquiring for her?"

Impatient to make her plane, the woman didn't notice the change of tone. "Yes, yes."

Janet Price had admitted her visitor to her apartment and into her bedroom and continued dressing because her visitor was a woman. "So you killed her too."

Mariarosa hesitated. "All right. Yes, I did. I had to: She was blackmailing me. So now you have that on your tape with the rest of it. I've told you everything. I've answered all your questions. So how about it, Mrs. Capretto? Are you going to let me catch my plane?"

"There are two other detectives in the lobby waiting for me to bring you down."

Mariarosa frowned over this new problem. "You wanted me to name the killer; go down and tell them I've done it. Tell them I'm cooperating fully. Send them to the bank for the murder gun. Tell them to seize Francese's car. My plane leaves in just under two hours. You can stall them that long, can't you? Come on, Mrs. Capretto . . . Norah . . . you've got nothing to lose and a son to gain." She waited anxiously. "If you're afraid I'll blackmail you later on, don't be. You'll never hear from me again. I swear it." Suddenly she smiled. "Anyhow, you've got the tape. It's a standoff."

Then she added the final fillip. "Whatever you may think of me, I do care what happens to the child. I want him to have a good home with decent parents who will love him and raise him to be a decent man. I want him to have his chance. I owe him that."

"Yes."

"Then we're agreed." She couldn't quite keep the triumph out of her voice. Turning quickly, she picked up her mink coat from the sofa and moved confidently toward the hall as she put it on.

Norah stood where she was. Emotionally drained, she seemed to have lost the ability to move; even her throat felt tight, constricted. "That's why I've turned Mark over to the Child Adoption Service of Children's Aid."

Mariarosa Martinelli stopped. "You did what?"

"I've relinquished Mark. This morning. I explained that there is a moral conflict and that we can't keep him. They'll find him another home. There won't be any trouble finding him another home. There are so many couples looking for a child like Mark, so many couples yearning. . . ." It wasn't easy to hold back the tears, but she did. "The adoption service will find him a home with people who don't know anything about him or you or about Joe and me. It's going to hurt him terribly; I know that. He's going to be upset, confused, but he's just a baby and he'll forget . . . quickly. Quickly, I pray."

"I don't believe it!" Mariarosa exploded in rage and frustration. "I don't believe you've actually done it. It's another trick."

"No, no trick, Miss Martinelli." Norah indicated the phone. "The adoption people won't give you any information, but you can call Sister Agnes at St. Vincent's Day Care Center. She knows. She'll tell you. . . . Unless you think a nun would lie."

"*Santa Madre di Dio!*" Mariarosa stared at Norah. "You really did it."

"I didn't want Mark ever to know about you."

A strangled sound came from deep down in Mariarosa's long, slim throat. The sinews of her neck bulged; her gorge rose and fell; her whole body convulsed as though she were trying to vomit, but it was words she finally spewed out. "You і : you're very smart, don't you? You think you've figured it all out and now you're going to take me in, parade me in front of everybody—the other detectives, reporters, show me off and make a big name for yourself."

"Believe me, Miss Martinelli, that's the last thing—"

"You think I'll just go with you quietly? Never. Never. I won't be made a public spectacle. I won't have everybody knowing, laughing."

"Nobody's going to laugh, Miss Martinelli. It won't be like that, I promise." With a tremendous effort of will, Norah forced herself to take a step forward.

In planning against all contingencies, the once naïve girl from Muggia thought she had figured every angle, and the policewoman who had come to arrest her thought she had too. They were both wrong.

"Keep away. Don't touch me," Mariarosa warned and backed toward the terrace doors.

Norah stopped instantly. "Why don't you call your lawyer and have him meet us at the precinct?" Norah suggested as calmly as she could. "He'll see to it that your rights are protected and reporters kept away. You're entitled to call your lawyer. Go ahead, please, do it now." Norah kept her eyes firmly on the woman in front of the terrace doors, but while she spoke, she opened her handbag and felt inside for her gun.

Mariarosa saw it and laughed derisively. "We both know that you're not going to use it." Quickly she turned, pushed the doors open, and before Norah could do anything to stop her, she was out on the terrace and standing close to the parapet.

A cold wind swept into the room from the open

doors. Norah shivered, then she lunged forward, but only to the threshold.

"Stop. Stop right there."

It had been a dark day, but though it was now well past five, thanks to the new year-round daylight saving time, there was still good visibility and would be for . . . another half hour at least. After that . . . Norah refused to think about the added problems that darkness would bring. The building was eighteen stories high with the penthouse at its very top. The fire department would bring ladders, of course, but that would take time, and what would happen while Norah went inside to call them? She took a quick look around: There was no kind of superstructure from which the woman could be reached, no adjoining building high enough or near enough either. The terrace itself was bounded by a waist-high brick wall with an iron railing about two feet tall embedded in the top. The woman now climbed the wall and threw one leg over the palings, straddling them. Her dark hair had come loose and the gusting February wind blew it across her eyes. Her mink coat had fallen open, and the wind was making it billow out behind her, dragging at her. Added to the danger that she might jump was the danger that she could, without intending it, fall.

"For the love of God, Miss Martinelli," Norah begged. "For the love of God, come down. You believe in Him; don't add this sin to the others."

"Don't kid me that you care about my soul; you don't care if I burn in hell. It's your own soul you're trying to save. If you arrest me, what happens afterward won't be your responsibility. I could get the death penalty and you can tell yourself you had nothing to do with it. But if I jump, that will be your fault—yours and nobody else's."

"There is no death penalty anymore, Miss Martinelli. It was abolished a long time ago. You won't die."

"So I'll spend the rest of my life in prison. Thanks a

lot. I've seen what prison does to people. I'd rather die." She half turned, carefully shifted her hands on the railing, then swung her leg over so that she was completely and precariously positioned on the outside of the wall.

"How do you know what your sentence would be?" Norah argued. "Give yourself a chance in court. That's what trials are for. That's why we have juries. Give yourself a chance to explain, to tell your side."

It seemed to Norah that the woman's hands tightened on the railing and that she was being very careful not to look down. She was listening. Thank God, at least she was listening.

"You'll be able to testify in your own behalf. You'll be able to describe what you felt when the man you loved and thought dead suddenly appeared in your bedroom. How you felt when you discovered that he'd betrayed you and then had to watch helplessly while he gunned down the only other man who had ever meant anything to you." It wasn't specious argument; any good lawyer, and Mariarosa Martinelli could hire the best, would appeal to the jury's sympathy. He'd get a distinguished psychiatrist to testify that the ordeal had unbalanced his client, caused a period of temporary insanity. He might even get her off. At the worst, Norah thought, she'd be placed in a mental institution from which in time she would probably be released. In trying to talk her down from the ledge, Norah almost convinced herself of the extenuating circumstances. Except that they didn't apply to the murder of Janet Price. There was no way that could be called anything but cold-blooded and premeditated.

As Ferdi Arenas had said—everybody kept forgetting poor Miss Price. Norah hoped the woman on the wall wouldn't remember her either, not yet.

The light was failing fast, much faster than she'd anticipated. Or was it time slipping away? From the terrace door Norah could see out past Park Avenue.

The streetlights were already on. Lights were also starting to appear in the windows of neighboring buildings. Was it already too dark for the woman poised and ready to jump to be spotted from below? Or had she already been seen? Was a crowd gathering at this very moment, necks craning upward? If so, David and Roy would have noticed and gone out to see what it was all about and would have sent for help. She wasn't sure whether or not that would be a good thing. God knew she wanted and needed help; at the same time she was afraid of it. Would screeching sirens, flashing lights, loudspeakers add to Miss Martinelli's confusion? Norah set aside all other thoughts but getting her down.

"You've still got a chance, Miss Martinelli. Don't throw it away. Don't throw your life away."

A fresh gust of wind swept across the open terrace. It made a small whirling maelstrom of dust and grime, and it also got under the mink coat again. The coat billowed and dragged at the armpits and pulled Mariarosa backward. She took one hand off the railing and clutched at the coat trying to gather it around her.

Norah ran to her. "Take my hand."

The wind died. The coat fell in place. "I don't need your help."

"Dear God, don't jump out of spite!" Norah cried out of frustration and instantly wished the words back. Then she saw Mariarosa's face contorted with fear and noted that both hands were back on the railing, that the knuckles were strained white from the desperation of the hold. Maybe she had unwittingly hit on the way to get the woman down off the wall. "Don't jump just to spite me," Norah repeated quietly and backed off a couple of steps.

"If you jump, I won't be around to see it," she called out across the intervening space. "I'm leaving. Right now. If you want to jump, go ahead. I won't be here. Nobody will be here to see you." Resolutely Norah turned her back and walked inside to the room that was now in darkness and made her way to the front hall.

It seemed all too short a distance.

"Wait! Come back. . . ." The voice was faint; it seemed very distant, but Norah heard.

She took the chain off the front door, unlocked it, and threw it open, making as much noise as possible. A rectangle of light from the outside vestibule reached the living room. It should be visible from the terrace.

"Please!" A shriek from the parapet. "Please! Come back. Help me!"

Norah ran. She grasped the trembling creature by the forearms.

"You can let go now, Mariarosa," she said. "Let go. I've got you. I won't let you fall."

Joe put his key in the door, turned the lock, and remembered to smile as he entered the apartment.

"Hi, love, I'm home," he called. "Sorry I'm late."

There was no answer. "Norah?" She wasn't in the living room. With the smile fixed, Joe went into the bedroom.

Norah, wearing robe and slippers, was sitting by the window staring out vacantly. He bent over and kissed her. She was still warmly scented from the bath.

"Hey, why aren't you dressed?"

"I'm not going."

The smile slipped, but he kept his annoyance out of his voice. "Why not?"

"I don't feel up to it."

"You can't back out now. Mamma is expecting us."

"I'm sorry. You go."

"Without you? Don't be silly. Come on, sweetheart. We've turned her down twice already; we can't just not show."

"So you go. You're the one she wants to see anyway. The two of you can talk about it all night. Bat it back and forth between you."

"That's nasty."

Norah was instantly contrite. "I'm sorry. Oh, God, I am sorry. I don't blame your mother for wanting to know all about it, but I just can't bear the thought of explaining all over again . . . justifying . . . I can't take it."

"You can't go on like this, either. You can't go on denying that Mark ever existed."

Norah flinched and turned back to the window. It was ten days since Mariarosa Martinelli had been take into custody. In that time Mark's name had not been spoken by either one of them.

"I loved him too, you know," Joe went on. "Losing him was just as hard on me. Remembering him hurts, but I don't want to forget. Mark gave us a lot of happiness while he was with us." He pulled the vanity stool over close to Norah and sat. "You're making yourself sick, *cara*."

She still wouldn't look at him. "I can't help it."

"Yes, you can. You made the only possible decision. I only wish that. . . ." He let it go. "You did what had to be done, and I know it was hard. But now you're behaving like . . . like. . . ."

"A woman?" she challenged.

"A female. A mid-Victorian female. You've indulged yourself long enough. It's time to snap out of it."

She turned at that, looked straight at him, but a moment later lowered her eyes. "I'm trying."

"No, you're not. You're keeping it all locked up inside, hugging your grief to yourself. For days I've been waiting for you to turn to me so we could share our loss—*our loss*, Norah. You won't let me share it. You won't let me comfort you. You give me no comfort."

She winced, but there was nothing she could say.

"If that's the way you want it then, okay, keep it to yourself. But no more long faces and sighs and no more moping around. If you want to pretend it never happened, that's what we'll do. So get your clothes on and let's go. I'll be in the car." Joe walked out.

They maintained a heavy silence all the way to Brooklyn. Joe parked, locked the car, and they walked the short distance to his mother's house. At the front door of the apartment building Norah couldn't hold it in any longer.

"I'm sorry, darling. I didn't mean to shut you out."

"Okay. Forget it."

"No, I don't want to forget it. I didn't realize what I was doing."

"I know; that's what bothers me. You've shut me out on this whole thing right from the start. You didn't tell me you wanted to adopt till you'd gone ahead and found a child. When you discovered who Mark's mother was, you didn't tell me that either. I was certainly entitled to the information if only because it concerned the case."

He had never spoken to her so coldly before. Norah had never seen his dark face so pale and so forbidding. She had not realized how deeply hurt he was . . . and disappointed. "I meant it for the best."

"I'm not questioning your intentions. When I first met you, I was impressed by your self-reliance; I thought it was admirable. I even found your determination to make your own decisions and act on them . . . endearing," Joe admitted wryly. "As far as the job was concerned, I figured you'd smarten up and learn to work as part of a team. In the private part of your life, of course you'd always been on your own, but you'd had an unusually lonely childhood with no friends of your own age and too many responsibilities too soon. I hoped, I expected, that marriage would make you feel that you were no longer alone. I hoped you'd learn to trust me and share your problems with me."

"You don't understand."

"No," he agreed, "I don't. But this isn't the time or place to discuss that." He held the door for her and there was no choice for Norah but to enter.

Patrick Mulcahaney had arrived before them and

he let them in. One look at their set faces and he fell back without a word. Signora Capretto came bustling out of the kitchen, and after one look she threw her arms around Norah with a tenderness she had never shown her daughter-in-law before.

"Now, Mamma, I want you to leave Norah alone," Joe warned. "We're here for a nice, cheerful, happy evening. No discussion, no argument, nothing. What's done is done, okay?"

"Is that a way to speak to your mother?"

"I just don't want you to hassle Norah."

"Hassle? What is hassle? What did I say? Did I say one word? One? Did I open my mouth? Norah, I ask you—did I open my mouth?"

"No, Mamma."

"Okay. So I'm sorry. I apologize"

"Don't apologize. You protect your wife; you have that much sense. Good. But you do not understand her."

Joe gaped at his mother. He shook his head in bewilderment. "That's the second time tonight I've been told that."

"So since you bring the matter up, I will speak what is in my heart."

"*Mamma, per l'amor' di Dio* . . . leave it alone."

"Emilia, I really don't think this is the time . . ." Patrick Mulcahaney began.

"It is exactly the time. We will speak of it now, once and for all, and that will be the end of it." Signora Capretto's pronouncement brooked no further argument. She gave Norah a slight push. "Sit, *cara*, sit." She indicated the couch and sat beside Norah. "Well?" She looked at the two men, and obediently they took chairs.

Signora Capretto addressed Norah. "I know that what you did was for the child's sake principally. If you had kept him, sooner or later somebody would tell him about his mother; somehow it would slip out. What would his reaction be not only to discover that she had committed murder but that you and Joe were responsible for her conviction? He might understand, but would he forgive? He would say to himself: If the two people I love most in this world could do such a thing, then who or what can I believe in? Who or what can I trust? You did not want him to be without the faith that every human being must have. Is that not so?"

Norah pressed her lips together and nodded. She had not expected Signora Emilia to be so perceptive.

"So you gave him up to save him from this double disillusion. Now you are afraid that you have made a mistake."

Joe jumped out of his chair. "What?"

"Sh . . . *taci.*" His mother waved him back. She took Norah's hand in hers. "You have had time to think and to consider this Mariarosa Martinelli and the terrible things she has done. You know that she comes from a poor land, rocky and unfertile, where the people struggle every day of their lives just to survive." The signora paused for a moment to let them all dwell on that point, for she was speaking to her son and to Patrick Mulcahaney as well as to Norah.

"So this Mariarosa left these hardships behind to come and marry her childhood sweetheart and also to live a different, easier life. When he died, or she thought he did—it is the same thing—her sorrow was undoubtedly real, yet she found another man quickly enough. She survived. Then when this other man, this Nerone, got tired of her, she conveniently produced a son in order to hold him. But Nerone did not want the boy. It seems strange to you that a man like this Nerone—an Italian, whatever else he may have been —should deny his own seed. You ask yourself: Is it possible the boy is not his?

"And the next question follows inevitably: Is it even possible the boy is not hers? She gave him up so easily when Nerone refused to acknowledge him. But she held onto her man. She survived. When Nerone died, though, she still did not claim her baby. How could a natural mother reject him a second time, take him away from the people he knew as his mother and father and hand him over to total strangers?"

Alarmed because he could see what was coming, Joe intervened. "Enough, Mamma. Stop."

"But the birth certificate," Patrick Mulcahaney protested. "The name, Justine Ross. . . ."

"There was a death certificate also," Signora Capretto reminded him. "If one is false, why not both?"

Mulcahaney groaned and cast a glance at Norah, whose head was bowed.

"*Basta, Mamma, basta!*" Joe implored, appalled. "You don't know what you're doing."

But Signora Capretto would not be deterred. "Since this Mariarosa wanted you to know that she was the boy's mother, since she ultimately intended to reveal herself as his mother, why should she kill the woman who had arranged the adoption? The one woman who could prove her claim?"

"Because she's not his mother. It was all a fraud," Norah murmured, not daring to look at Joe.

He was beyond words. He was sick with anguish for Norah. Helpless. What could he do? What could he say now or ever that would ease her guilt over this terrible, tragic. . . .

"I made a terrible mistake," Norah admitted, her head still bowed.

"No," Signora Capretto countered very firmly. "You did the right thing. You did the only thing there was to do. You could not prove the child was not hers, and as long as this Miss Martinelli could claim he was, you had no other choice. Not if you wanted to protect your husband."

"Me?" Joe exclaimed.

"*Eh tu, certo,*" Signora Capretto replied. "Sometimes, *figlio mio,* you are not so smart. You are hurt that Norah did not consult you in this important decision. It concerned you both and so you feel that you both should have shared in it. Do you think that your wife did not want your support and comfort? Do you think it was easy for her to bear the responsibility alone?"

"Well, no, of course not, but—"

"But she couldn't tell you. You loved the boy and you knew how much he meant to her. She was afraid you might decide to keep him."

"*Afraid* that I'd decide to keep him?"

"As long as you kept him, this woman could use the threat of revealing herself to him as a threat against you. You would be subject to constant demands from her and from others in the criminal world. You could not remain an effective police officer. So Norah did what she had to do—the only thing to save your career."

Joe stared at his wife. "I should have realized. I should have known. . . . Norah?" He went to her, knelt beside her, and tilted her chin gently up. "Ah, sweetheart, don't cry. . . ."

"Why not? Why shouldn't she cry?" Signora Capretto demanded. "What is so bad about a few tears? Let her cry. It will do her good." She glanced at Mulcahaney, whose eyes were filling. "And you too, Patrick, you loved the boy; there is no shame to show it. I will cry also. Though I was not permitted to see the child even once, I will cry because I have no memories of him to cherish."

"Now, Mamma, don't start."

"We will all cry together a little. Then we will have some cognac and after that we will eat, and we will all feel much better."

"Oh, Mamma!" Norah had to smile at Signora Emilia's offer of food as the unfailing panacea. "I couldn't eat a bite."

"Certainly you will eat. You will force youself. You are too thin, very pale." The signora's bright eyes narrowed as she scrutinized her daughter-in-law. A smile softened the harsh lines of her face. "*Figlia mia,* tell me, when is the last time you visited the doctor?"

"Mammal" Joe's eyes flashed a warning.

Signora Capretto threw up her hands. "I was just asking. I can ask, can't I?"

ABOUT THE AUTHOR

LILLIAN O'DONNELL is a former dancer and stage and television actress who turned to writing suspense novels after she married. Her novels, *Dial 577 R-A-P-E, The Phone Calls* and *Don't Wear Your Wedding Ring* have been book club selections and published in eight foreign countries. Ms. O'Donnell lives in Atlantic Beach, New York. *The Baby Merchants* and *Leisure Dying* are the latest in the Detective Norah Mulcahaney series.